C000137281

ACROSS

THE

PARALLEL

ACROSS THE PARALLEL

E-Book Available

www.daisapublishing.com

~

Other books by H.O. WARD

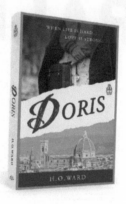

'DORIS'

5 STAR REVIEWS

"The storyline had me hooked and wanting to know more about Dorothy's story as each chapter ended. I was able to laugh, smile and cry in equal measure..."

A Historical War Romance published in 2020
by Daisa Publishing

ACROSS THE PARALLEL

A NOVEL BY

H. O. WARD

DAISA
PUBLISHING

Across the Parallel published in Great Britain in 2021

Written by H.O.WARD

Copyright © H.O.WARD 2021
H.O.WARD has asserted his right to be identified as the author of this Work in accordance with the Copyright, Designs and Patents Act 1988.

The editors have ensured a true reflection of the author's tone and voice has remained present throughout. All characters and places – other than the obvious historical places and people, are fictitious and any resemblance to real persons living or dead, is purely coincidental.

All rights reserved. No part of this publication may be reproduced, stored in a retrieval system, transmitted, or copied in any form or by any means, electronic, mechanical, photocopying, recording or otherwise, without the prior written permission of the publisher and copyright owner.

A CIP catalogue record for this book is available from the British Library.

Paperback ISBN 978-1-7399246-3-8

Book cover design by: Partnership Publishing
Book Cover Image and Internal Images ©Shutterstock 1625900530, 1690467907

Book typeset by:
PARTNERSHIP PUBLISHING
Lincolnshire
United Kingdom
www.partnershippublishing.co.uk

Printed in England

Partnership Publishing is committed to a sustainable future for our business, our readers and our planet. This book is made from paper certified by the Forestry Stewardship Council (FSC), an organisation dedicated to promoting responsible management of forest resources.

We operate a distinctive and ethical publishing philosophy in all areas of our business, from our global network of Authors to production and worldwide distribution.

DEDICATION

'Across the Parallel' is dedicated to the
understanding of the order of time, past present
future, the relevance of space, the vastness of the
universe and the mystery of consciousness.

~

The Present Parallel

In this present moment, this finite moment of time in which you are reading these words, you are experiencing life in the present parallel reading what is your future existence before it becomes the history of your experience.

You should now realise that your True Self, your Subconscious, that spiritual part of you which is part of this world, has lived through lifetime after lifetime, experience after experience, change after change, and still remains essentially you, with all your quirks, your gifts, and the lessons you have learned. It has travelled a path of eternity through many rebirths, with many more to come.

Once you turn this page, you will cross the parallel of universal time, a rebirth path to a new parallel of consciousness, the present, the moment of everlasting consciousness when all things exist, past, present, future.

-

That Path Is The Tao, And The Tao Is You.

Parallel One

'Tao'

The Way Of The Universe

Before The Beginning
There Was Wuji

Emptiness - Stillness
A Single Point Of Time Within The Universe

-

A Pivotal Action Of Taiji
Brought Imbalance And
The Dual Polls Of
Yin Yang
Came About To Restore
The Cosmic Balance

The Beginning And The End

-

The space-time moment of the Wuji umbrella shadows the tall grass growing between the cracks in the long concrete strip stretching across the emptiness of the still and quiet wasteland. Damp moss reaches out amongst the potholed tarmac winding between abandoned huts and derelict buildings, their dirty windows cracked and broken. Brown faded notices flap fleetingly on the noticeboard, a wooden office chair, tipped over against the wall lay behind a rusting steel desk, and the office door hangs lopsided on one hinge.

Like chanting monks, the eerie hum of a gentle Taiji breeze blew through the pane-less windows of the vacant and neglected control tower and stirred the energy of Chi. The way of Tao slowed his vibration, and space-time conscious quickened his thoughts.
His actions and movements functioned in slow motion while all around him accelerated and raced swiftly past. He slowly materialised, merged into the bright white light surrounding him and he crossed the parallel.

-

January
1943
Waltham

It was cold and crisp; bright sunlight was reflecting off a thin covering of snow and a north-easterly wind was blowing across the open expanse of the airfield at RAF Grimsby. George was standing in front of a group of rowdy aircrew laughing and joking outside a mess hut, sheltering from the wind.

Learning facts about each other, they discovered it was the Skip's birthday and a spontaneous chorus of happy birthday erupted.

George stood quietly, rubbing a sharp pain in his neck while his moment of déjà vu passed.

"Where am I, it feels like I've been here before?" George thought to himself.

"How old are you Skip?" called one of the crew members.

"I'm as old as my tongue and a little older than my teeth," replied George, to which impulsive jeers and laughter burst out from the jovial group.

George tried to recall his thoughts about his déjà vu moment. He could not remember what he thought, or where he had been, just that it seemed like he had been somewhere, and he had done all of this before.

George rocked his head from side to side, stretching his neck tendons to relieve the sharp pain in the back of his neck. He pulled himself together, shrugged off the feeling and joined in with the rowdy merriment.

It was early January 1943 and the RAF command had recently issued orders for the re-formation of 100 Squadron. George had been drafted to skipper one of the planes that was shortly to arrive and to assemble his new crew. They too had been drafted to the station as part of the build-up of the squadron. Runways had been upgraded to concrete structure the previous year, the first for North Lincolnshire air bases, and strong enough to accommodate the arrival of the squadrons new Lancaster Bombers.

"Right, which one of you noisy rabble is my engineer?" called George, loudly, in an attempt to apply some order to the cheery group. He stood waiting for a response, playing with his fingers behind his back.

"That would be me, Sir. Flight Sergeant Charles Dormer, Flight Engineer. Call me Charles or Charley; either will do fine, Sir."

"Where are you from Charley?"

"Ottawa Sir, Canada."

Ottawa, that's down the road from me, Toronto. Good to have you on board, we'll look to you to keep us going in the hard times Charles, and just make it Skip if you would."

"Yes Sir, sorry Skip."

"Welcome to the crew. Any other Canadians amongst us?" asked George.

"John Collins, Flight Sergeant, Hamilton, Lake Ontario, Sir, I'm a Gunner."

"Welcome John, you should feel at home here in Grimsby."

"Yes Sir, there's a Grimsby not far from Hamilton back home Sir."

"Any connection?" asked George.

"Not sure Sir, I only found out when my posting came through Skip."

"Any preference for gun position John?"

"Rear would be fine by me Sir. I'm a bit of a loner so it will suit me. Save anyone else having to do it Skip."

"Can I ask how old you are John; you look mighty young to be here?"

"I'm just eighteen Sir. Everyone says I look too young to be in the Royal Canada Air Force but don't let that fool you. I can give more than I get."

"That's just the spirit I need from a rear gunner. I'm sure you'll do your bit," concluded George. "Who's next?"

"Flying Officer William Wells, Wireless Operator. Everyone calls me 'W', though I'm not sure why!"

The group cheered and joked as they stamped their feet against the cold wind and pushed their hands deeper onto their coat pockets.

"Welcome 'W', good to have you with us," laughed George. "I'm sure you'll keep our spirits up. It's good to have a joker around. Next, no wait a minute, where are you from 'W', England?"

No Skip, Wrexham, Wales." The crew burst into spontaneous raucous laughter at 'W's witty reply.

George smiled, and then laughed with his crew. "Next?" he called above the laughter of the airmen.

"My name is James, I'm from New Zealand Skip, I'm a Pilot Officer, and I'm a Bomb Aimer and Front Gunner."

"A Kiwi, now we're getting seriously international," commented George. "What's your surname, James?"

"Just James, straight and simple Skipper."

"Come on, we all have surnames," requested George.

"It's Cook, Sir, but just keep it to James please, Sir."

"And you're our bomb aimer?"

"Yes Sir."

"Well, if you're as good as your forefather finding New Zealand across that ocean of water, you shouldn't have too much difficulty in finding our targets across the little bit of water we will be crossing. Captain James Cook eh, well, we'll keep it to James if that's what you prefer James," said George.

"No Sir, thank you, Sir," replied James.

"Who's Next?"

"Flying Officer Henry Lumley, m-master of n-navigation at your service, Sir."

"We're all friends here Henry, no need to be nervous, where are you from?"

"Oxford, England, Sir."

"Oh, our first English crew member, in fact, I think you're the only one who is English, Henry. Well, we need someone to guide us to where we're going, so who better than someone local," George commented. "Why master of navigation, what's that about, Henry?"

The crew gathered round, closed rank against the cold, and listened to what Henry was about to say.

"It's n-not nerves, Sir, slight impediment Sir. However, I regard myself as an excellent n-navigator, and I won't let you down, Sir."

"Sorry about that Henry, the impediment I mean, but so long as you get us to our sorties and back and not lost, that will do for me."

"We always have James Cook to find the way Skip," one of the crew added.

"Yeah, he was a master mariner and navigator," responded another.

"Alright crew, a bit of order. We've not met before have we Henry, you seem familiar?"

"N-no Sir, n-not to my knowledge Skipper."

"Right, last but not least, you are? And I don't want to hear anymore Sir! It's Skip or Skipper for everyone from now on, is that clear."

"John Adams, Flight Sergeant, Gunner, Sydney, from down-under, Skipper."

"Another famous individual, what a crew this is turning out to be. Do you know anything about your namesake, John?"

"No Skip, not really Skip. I didn't know I had one."

"John Adams was America's second president," George stated.

A raucous cheer of joviality, backslapping, and pretend bugle blowing erupted from the crew as George announced John's namesake.

John smiled awkwardly through a look of embarrassment, partly from his lack of knowledge, but mainly from the boisterous response of his spirited crewmates.

"I didn't know that Skip," John eventually replied.

"Well, you won't forget it now John, welcome to the crew Mr President. And it looks like you're left with the upper gun position. We don't have a down-under one on the Lancaster,

9

sorry, but you'll be able to see anything coming our way from up top."

"You can count on me Skip," replied Mr President.

"Right crew, we know who is who now, so how about getting out of this cold. I will go to The King's Head in the village this evening and stand everyone a drink. I hope you can all make it. In the meantime, I'll go and find out what's happening around here, we should be getting kitted out soon. See you all later," concluded George before heading off along the snow-covered pathway.

George made his way to the admin office, walking briskly along Cheapside, a narrow lane that ran towards the guardhouse and then round the airbase. It seemed strange that for a wartime operational RAF station there were almost no aircraft present at the Waltham based airfield, though it was clearly busy in preparation and anticipation for the arrival of the squadron's Lancaster Bombers.

Waltham Airbase had previously been known as Grimsby Municipal Airport before being taken over as an Air Ministry Flying Training School and then by the RAF as a bomber station, operational with Wellington bombers of 142 Squadron. In late December 1942, 142 Squadron relocated just a few miles across Lincolnshire and along the River Humber to RAF Kirmington, leaving Waltham to organize itself for the re-assembling 100 Squadron. The building of accommodation huts for an additional fifteen hundred personnel was in progress at several requisitioned sites between the airfield and Waltham village, a mile or so along Cheapside that ran adjacent to the airbase limit. Additional crew lockers and drying rooms with extension to the station's operational facilities and new fuel and bomb storage areas were all taking place.

Having gained the information he wanted, George headed for the NAAFI and something to eat before going to the village pub for drinks with his crew. It was dark as he passed through the station's entrance gate and guardhouse and began walking along Cheapside. To his left, he could just see the sails of Waltham Windmill protruding into the night sky. The windmill was also one of the communal sites for the WAAF, with access possible through the sick quarters here on Cheapside then over the field, or the long way round via Brigsley Road.

He next passed the Temperance Hall, to his right, occupied by the WVS and adapted as a canteen. The second accommodation site for WAAF's quickly followed on his left. On the corner junction with Brigsley Road and High Street, the village blacksmith was still busy, finishing off shoeing one of the local Shire horses. George turned right onto High Street; the road dipped and began to rise just before the pub doorway. It continued to rise, turning to the right, and reaching its pinnacle at All-Saints Parish Church. The rowdiness of the busy pub spilt out through the blacked-out windows of The King's Head as he approached the entrance to the public house.

George stepped inside the doorway and closed the door behind him before opening the blackout curtain. The bar was crowded, mainly aircrew with a scattering of locals around the fire and gathered at the far end of the bar. He spotted his crew in the corner between the fire and the blacked-out window.

"Evening Skipper," said Henry and Charles in unison as George approached.

"Evening everyone," replied George, unfastening his heavy blue overcoat, and shaking down the collar as he welcomed the warmth of the fire. "You boys all got drinks?"

"W's at the bar now Skip, I'll have him get you a drink, what will you have?" asked Henry.

"I'll have a beer, but it's me that's supposed to be buying, I invited you all here remember," commented George.

"It's your birthday Skip, so this one is on us... well, it's on 'W' to be technically correct but we're n-not counting," replied Henry. "He won't notice an additional one on the order."

"Have you all been here long?" inquired George.

"Still getting our first drinks," replied Charles. "Apart from Mr President, he's been here a while."

"Mr President?" queried George, not following Charles' reference.

"John Adams," said Henry. "Mr President. We have two John's in the crew so we decided Adams will be Mr President and Collins will be Collins."

"Oh yes, I'm with you all now. And do you all agree to this, what do you say, John?" replied George, looking at Adams.

"It's right by me Skip. Do I get other presidential privileges too?"

"Slow down there cobber, you didn't know you were a president until a few hours ago," quipped James.

"Yeah, well said there Captain Cook," added Henry.

"It's James please Henry, my name is James."

"So where is Collins?" asked George.

"He said he doesn't drink, and he wouldn't get in the pub as he looks too young," answered Charles. "I tried to persuade him to come and at least try."

"Well, he's not wrong about looking young, but we need a full house on these occasions if we're going to get through this as a team. We're all in this together. Charles, have a quiet one-to-one with him will you, one Canadian to another sort of thing," said George.

"He'd be alright in the pub not drinking, do you think?" added Mr President.

"He did say he was a bit of a l-loner," Henry commented.

"Not in this crew he's not," stated George, responding spontaneously, then quickly thinking about what he had so instinctively said and why he said it. Deep down he somehow intuitively knew Collins would turn up.

George's comments instantly struck home and caused a moment of silent reflection within the crew. Each man recognizing their Skipper's intention to this being a team, and not just being one member of the crew. It also gave them a warm feeling of belonging, of comrades, all in it together, as George put it.

Hey, here's 'W' with the drinks. About time I say," said Henry, breaking the silence. "A man could d-die of thirst around here."

The crew gathered around 'W' and focused their attention on whose drink was whose.

"That one's mine," said 'W'. "Yours is the darker one."

"It's not like Aussie beer," commented Mr President.

"That's 'cos it's not upside-down," replied 'W'.

"Ha, ha, very funny," said Mr President.

Conversation and banter continued between the crewmembers, laughing and joking between comments of who, what, and where. So engrossed they became, that no one noticed

Collins enter the bar. He pushed his way to the middle of the crew to stand in front of his Skipper and show his presence.

"Happy birthday Skip, hope I'm not too late," said Collins, putting out his arm to shake his Skipper's hand.

"No, not too late at all John," replied George with a relieved knowing smile, and shaking Collins' outstretched hand. "I'm just about to buy drinks for everyone, what will you have?"

"Hey Collins, glad you made it buddy," said Charles, also smiling at the arrival of Collins, and knowing there was no need for his team play chat.

George stood each member of the crew a drink, as he said he would and the team building merriment continued into the evening.

During a quiet moment, George suddenly had a premonition about singing and thought of the tune to 'Greensleeves'. He wondered why he would have such a thought and why it would come during a social occasion with his crew, as he could not make any sense of it. Eventually, he let the thought go as he stood up in front of his crew, placed his hands behind his back, and twiddled with his fingers as he began to speak to his crew.

"Can I have everyone's attention a minute," said George, loud enough for all his crew to hear. "Look it's nearly twenty-one-hundred, I have a good walk back to digs ahead of me and an early start in the morning. There's a short progress briefing for everyone tomorrow at zero-eight-hundred, so I'm going to push off and see you all in the morning. Thanks for coming. After what I've seen tonight, I'm sure we'll all get along just fine, and you made my birthday enjoyable too, so thank you all for that."

A rowdy response of good nights and happy birthday resounded from the jovial crew.

"I'll get my coat and walk some of the way with you, Skipper," said Henry. "I'm just down Cheapside a short distance. In one of the new wooden huts they've been building, much warmer than the old Nissan hut."

"Yes me too, in a new hut I mean," replied George, fastening the top button of his blue RAF overcoat and pulling his collar up around his ears. "You know, it gets much colder than this in Canada, but I'm telling you, this cold and dampness you have here, it gets right through to your bones."

George and Henry said more farewell's as they departed the crew, exited the bar, and proceeded left along High Street.

"I'm pleased Collins turned up, eventually. I thought there was going to be a problem with him saying he's a bit of a l-loner," Henry commented as they walked along with their shoulders hunched up against the cold wind.

"I don't think he is a loner."

"You don't?" startled Henry.

"No, he says he is, but I think he's an only child who hasn't had much social contact. I think he's just shy," stated George.

"You could be right there, Skip."

"I'll have a quiet chat with him, find out his background, but keep this to yourself, Henry. I don't want to embarrass the boy with the rest of the crew," stated George.

"W-will do Skip."

The two airmen turned left into Cheapside and felt the full force of the cold easterly wind blowing into their face. Their conversation ceased and they marched briskly into the wind and back to their respective accommodation hut and bed.

It had been a busy day and George lay reflecting on events, unable to sleep. He was happy with how his crew bonded together in a natural easy way, without any real hiccups, as if it was meant to be. He wondered why James was insistent about being called James and pleased that Collins eventually turned up. He smiled to himself as he thought about how he had enjoyed his birthday and how the crew responded to make it that little bit special.

"Henry, I like Henry, it's like I've known him for years," he said to himself.

George also thought about his déjà vu moment, trying to understand what had actually happened. Had he been somewhere, or just thought he had? It was just that one finite point in time when he thought he knew what was happening. He knew where he was but wondered where he had been, and it seemed to last a long time. It was as if time had stopped for just a moment, as if he had been absorbed by time itself, and he was in two places at the same time, standing still. Then it was gone in no time at all and he was not actually sure about what had happened, but it had left an impression on his mind.

Suddenly his thought about singing and the tune 'Greensleeves' returned, which he found confusing as he had no connection with singing and wondered why he would have such a thought, especially a folk tune.

What a day thought George, his mind flitting from one event to another and back again. George pondered a while on where his intuition came from to know that Collins would turn up and continued turning his thoughts about the day's moments and events over and over in his mind until he eventually fell to sleep.

Duck Skip

The next two days were busy, following the morning's progress briefing, the crews dispersed to training activities around the station. James practised the correct technique for dropping bombs from a Lancaster on a simulator, as well as joining Mr President and Collins in gunning practice.

Henry spent time familiarising himself in the navigation centre, where he would soon be spending time preparing his maps and flight charts directly before each sortie. Vital for night flying, Henry also attended night training where he could practise sextant shots of the stars through an astrodome fitted to the roof of the building.

Charles got his hands dirty in the maintenance and repair sheds familiarising himself with new equipment, he also joined 'W' in the wireless maintenance and training centre. All air and ground crew personnel received small arms pistol and machine gun training at the MG range, and it was at breakfast on the second morning that Henry and 'W' were being nominated to be responsible for the pigeon.

"Why should that be our responsibility?" responded 'W', laughing.

"Well, you're the communications men who should know where we are," stated Collins. "I just look at where we've been."

"Henry, you can attach the note giving our position," said Mr President. "You're the one with that information, so to me, it's logical that you should be responsible."

"Yeah, you do it, Henry, I don't like pigeons," quipped 'W'.

"Look, it has to be done. Every plane has to take a pigeon on sorties, just in case," stated Charles. "All you have to do is collect one before we take off."

"Y-you do it then Charles. We haven't even got a plane yet, and we're arguing about who's going to look after the bloody p-pigeon," laughed Henry.

"Alright, I'll do it," responded Charles.

"Good on ya, mate," said Mr President. "I'll buy you a beer for that."

"I'll hold you to that as well," responded Charles, pointing his finger at Mr President.

"Yeah, good on ya mate," added James.

"Alright, change of subject, seeing as we've just about murdered the pigeon," announced Charles. "Planes start arriving tomorrow, apparently."

"How do you know that?" asked Henry, suddenly paying attention.

"It's all the buzz with the ground crew boys," Charles replied. "Erk's from 101 and 103 squadrons, with experience on Lancs, have been transferring over these last couple of days. Have you not noticed this place is swamped with people right now, something's got to be happening?"

"I'll ask the Skipper," said Henry. "He'll know about p-plane arrivals."

"Where is Skip anyway? I haven't seen him since the other night in the bar," queried Collins.

"He was on a flight trainer yesterday, learning to fly I think," said 'W'. "He popped into the wireless office. Said he was passing, see how I was doing."

"The same thing for me, said he was across the road in the w-watch office and called in the maps room to see how I was getting on," added Henry.

"Hey, I think he's a good guy. He's done alright by us all so far, I like him, he's different to other Skippers. I think we can be a good crew together, even with a Kiwi in it," commented Mr President, laughing and looking at James.
"Yeah, well we'll soon find out when we're in one of these new planes we're getting, can't wait to get in one," replied James.

"Anyway, how did you score yesterday in the gun turret, Mr President?"

"I got two, how about you?"

"Haha, three," said James. "Did you get the one that came down from the right corner?"

"No, I missed that one, didn't see it until the last minute."

"I got it," smiled Collins.

"Really, it was hard to see at first, the film was a bit faded I thought. How many did you score?" asked James.

"Three," replied Collins.

"There you go Mr President, we got three each, to your two, not bad for a young gun and a Kiwi," said James.

"You win that one James, but let's see who wins the real thing," challenged Mr President.

"Right, you're on, look out Germany, here come the bomb boys," said James, excitedly.

"Let's just wait and see, shall we. We haven't got a p-plane yet," said Henry.

"But we will soon," smiled James.

"Well, I reckon we'll find out at tomorrow morning's briefing," concluded Charles. "In the meantime, I'm reporting for training, 0-nine-hundred boys. See you guy's later."

At the following morning's briefing, it was announced that planes for 100 Squadron would start arriving that day, as anticipated, and that allocation to each relevant pilot would be notified on their planes arrival day. George called his crew together and informed them to carry on with their ground training as instructed until he has news of the arrival of their plane.

"Sixteen squadron planes plus two reserves are expected, so it could take a day or two before we get ours. Just be patient, one of them has our name on," George informed the crew.

"Talking of names, what should we call it Skip?" 'W' asked.

"Hmm, I've not thought of that, been too busy I guess," replied George. "Any ideas, anyone?"

"How about 'duck skip?" said James.

"Duck skip," laughed Mr President. "What sort of name is that?"

The rest of the crew equally responded with jeering and laughter.

"No, I mean duck," replied James.

"Where do you get d-duck from?" added Henry.

"It's like a warning name, telling Jerry to duck, we're coming to drop our bombs," explained James.

"Any other suggestions?" asked George as the crew responded with boos and comments of amusement at their dislike of James' suggestion.

"What about Mable?" suggested Collins.

"I heard some other crew saying they were going to use M-Mable," said Henry.

"Well, let's just think about it until our plane arrives," suggested George. "Give you all something to think about while you're training. Come on, jump to it, we can't sit around here all-day chatting."

Just one more day of ground training followed before George called his crew together again after the morning briefing. It was a typical January, cold and blustery day for RAF Grimsby.

"Well, this is it boys, today's the day. A bit windy, but our Lancaster should arrive around noon." George announced. "Once she has landed ground crew will taxi her to number thirty-two dispersal pan. The Erk's will be swarming all over her, checking her over and there's paperwork and such, but we can check her out for ourselves too, unofficially mind and if we're quick."

"Hooray for that, m-maybe James will calm down now he'll have a plane to play with," commented Henry.

"Yeah, I can't wait to get in it, where's pan thirty-two, Skip?" asked James.

"On the right just along the taxi track from the technical block, and be patient James, you'll soon have had enough of being in it," replied George.

"That's by the Bomb Dump isn't it Skip?" queried Collins.

"No, that's been moved to the other side of the station," answered Charles.

"Well I'm pleased about that," replied Collins. "I wouldn't want to be near that if it went up."

"Right, back to training stations gentlemen, and I'll see you all at the dispersal pan later," said George.

It was twelve-fifteen when George stood on the balcony of the Watch Office Control Tower, mixing with other officers, his squadron leader, senior WAAF officers, and the station wing commander. All attention was in the direction of the approaching aircraft.

George leant against the railing, his hands behind his back, slowly twiddling his fingers, the cold wind blustering and flapping his trouser legs. He put his hand up to hold his cap on and shield his eyes from the gusting cold wind as he looked out over the airbase for the approaching Lancaster.

He could just hear the deep drone of Merlin engines above the wind blowing in his ears. His thought about singing and the tune 'Greensleeves' popped into his head as he spotted the plane coming in over the bare flat fields from the southwest, aligned with runway 18/36, and flying sideways into the strong north-easterly wind. The plane got bigger, lower and louder, and still flying sideways as it approached the edge of the runway and about to touchdown. At the last moment, the plane twitched and turned, aligned its large wheels parallel with the runway, and landed smoothly onto two thousand yards of hard concrete strip. George smiled; he was impressed and had forgotten about his singing thought.

"There you are Flight Lieutenant Finch," said his squadron leader, turning to look at George. "I believe that one is yours, take good care of her."

"Thank you, Sir, I will," replied George, as he left the balcony and headed for the dispersal pan to inspect his new plane.

Frances

George hitched a lift on a service vehicle heading towards the dispersal pan. He stopped to pick up Henry along the way. Henry jumped onto the runner board of the Crossley QA Tender and held onto the door pillar as the truck continued along the taxi track.

The plane was coming to rest as George and Henry arrived at the dispersal pan. George got out of the truck and watched. The draft from the four Merlin driven propellers nearly blew him over as the plane swung round into its rest position on the pan. When the Lancaster Bomber stopped, it was facing George head-on, like a dog sitting in front of its master, its nose pointing upwards, as if looking and waiting for the next command.

One by one, the engines cut with a belch of black exhaust smoke and its large black, three-bladed propeller stopped turning. The new paintwork gleamed like a pedigree's coat, the underside's mat black cloak, invisible in the night sky, its camouflage-patterned topside of brown and green, simulating the rolling fields of Lincolnshire.

Momentarily George stood there looking in awe of the plane's magnificence. He felt proud he was to be its pilot.

"W-what do you think?" said Henry.

"What can you say," replied George, suddenly distracted as the main hatch dropped open from the Lancaster's underbelly.

George and Henry walked under the plane's huge wing and felt the heat from the two silent engines radiating warmth into the cold easterly wind. George ran his hand across the top of the warm landing gear tyre, wanting to get a first touch of the plane.

He joined Henry and stood by the open hatch. A stepladder swung down followed by a kit bag hitting the floor. Legs began descending the ladder followed by an attaché case and a body's torso. Finally, the head of a young dark-haired girl emerged from the hatch.

"Morning Sir," said the girl, in her ATA uniform. "Sorry I'm late, headwind all the way Sir."

George leant forward and looked up through the open hatch and into the aircraft. "Is the pilot coming down?"

"Pilot?" queried the young ATA girl. "I am the Pilot Sir."

George stood silent for a moment, looking at the girl and trying to comprehend what she had just said.

"You mean you just landed this thing, in these conditions," said George looking up through the entrance hatch again. "Where's your crew?"

"There's just me Sir," smiled the young girl.

"Can I ask what your name is?" said George, still quite amazed.

"It's Frances Sir."

"Well Frances, I take my hat off to you. That was one excellent piece of flying if you don't mind me saying so."

"Thank you, Sir."

"Where did you learn to fly like that?" asked George.

"ATA training and being thrown in the deep end, I guess. They're big planes, but they're quite easy to fly Sir."

"I'll remember that, what do you think Henry?"

"I think she's wonderful," said Henry, smiling at Frances.

"Don't embarrass the girl, Henry, I'm talking about the plane," George replied.

"It's alright Sir, I get lots of comments," responded Frances.

George looked at Henry and Frances standing next to each other and the hair on the back of his neck bristled as he saw them looking dreamily into each other's eyes.

-

In that short space-time moment, as Frances and Henry looked at each other, their time slowed. In an instant of imbalance, their auras glowed, joined, and consumed each other's as a flow of universal consciousness raced between them, and the dual poles of yin-yang balanced their emotions and space-time conscious accelerated away. George thought he had stood still for a moment, watching Henry and Frances while a premonition of a fish out of water, flapping and gasping for air flashed through his mind before time accelerated and the prickly sensation on the back of his neck went as quick as it came.

-

"Here's your car," said George, distracted as an air force blue Standard 10 pulled up at the edge of the dispersal pan. "I'll come with you to admin and get the paperwork sorted. Henry, see to things here will you, give the crew chance to have a look around before the Erk's start crawling all over her. I'll escort Frances to admin and catch up with you later, in the pub."

"Will do Skip," replied Henry, feeling as if he was being pushed out.

George held the car's rear door open for Frances to get in, put her kit bag on the front seat and climbed in the back, next to Frances. The car set off round the taxi track, heading for the admin office just as a fleet of Erk's maintenance vehicles started to arrive and surround the Lancaster Bomber.

George sat quietly on the back seat for a moment as the car pulled away. His mind raced, thinking about singing and became confused about the image of the fish. He wondered where the thoughts were coming from, what they meant, and why he should be thinking of such things.

"Everything alright Sir?" asked Frances, looking at the thoughtful expression on George's face.

"Yes, I just remembered something I have to do," fibbed George. "Sorry about that and about Henry's comment too. Not sure what he was meaning there, hope that wasn't embarrassing for you?"

"No, no harm done Sir, he's quite nice actually."

"Oh, there you are then, no harm done," said George, smiling, with an inquisitive look on his face. "Should I inform Henry he's ...quite nice?"

"No Sir, please, that would be embarrassing," said Frances, smiling back.

"Look it's Sunday tomorrow and we have a day's stand down, we'll be going to the pub tonight, the crew, and Henry of course and... well, listen to me, I'm ranting on and..."

"I don't have to report back until Monday morning Sir," Frances interrupted.

"You don't? Well, that's a coincidence," replied George, beginning to feel flustered with the situation. "Then perhaps you would like to join us, you can tell us about our new plane?"

"That would be nice, thank you," smiled Frances, looking at the relieved expression on George's face and the slow twisting of his fingers in his lap.

"Right," sighed George, in relief. "I'll make arrangements and see you tonight then, Kings Head, seven-o-clock. Ah, here we are at admin too," concluded George as the car came to a stop outside a block of office buildings.

Frances went into the Admin Office to complete the manufactures delivery papers for George's plane. George went and arranged an extra night's accommodation for Frances, and then headed back to his quarters, just along Cheapside.

George walked down the corridor towards his room and was about to barge through the door when he noticed the nameplate of another officer on the wall, by the side of the door opposite his room. The door was open. George simultaneously read the name and knocked once on the doorframe.

"Oh, hello," greeted the surprised officer stepping into the open doorway. "Flight Lieutenant Holdsworth."

"Flight Lieutenant Finch," replied George, looking at the lieutenant and his kitbag thrown on his bed. "George," he said, dropping the formality and putting out his right hand to shake while making polite conversation. "You just arrived?"

"Denis," the Lieutenant replied, shaking George's hand. "Yes, just as that Lanc was landing, actually."

"Oh right, that was my Lanc actually, I watched her come in," said George proudly. "It was flown in by a young ATA, on her own can you believe."

"Yes, they're amazing with what they have to do," replied Denis. "They deliver planes all over the country, any plane anywhere, apparently, and always on their own."

"Well, she knew her stuff putting that plane on the ground, let me tell you. Where have you come from Denis?" said George going into his own room, sitting on his bed, and unfastening his shoelaces.

"Not far, I've just transferred over from 103 at Elsham," replied Denis, stepping across the corridor to stand in George's doorway.

"Yes, some of your Erk's are here too. What about your crew?" asked George, standing up and pulling off his shirt.

"My crew bought it when I crash-landed. 100 squadron is re-forming, so here I am. The war goes on," commented Denis, still standing in George's doorway.

"Sorry to hear that. Look we're down the pub later; you're welcome to join us," concluded George, as he stood in front of Denis, holding his towel and hinting he wanted to pass through the doorway.

"Thanks yes, I'll get ready," replied Denis, stepping back into his own doorway and allowing George to head down the corridor. "What time?"

"When you're ready," said George loudly, without looking back.

It was almost seven when George and Denis entered The King's Head and joined George's crew.

"Hey Skip, what do you think, isn't she wonderful?" said James excitedly.

"Yes, Henry thinks so too, don't you Henry," replied George.

"Yes Skip, w-wonderful," laughed Henry.

"Alright everyone, this is Flight Lieutenant Holdsworth; he just transferred in, needs a crew if you know anyone still looking."

"Lieutenant, do you have another name?" asked Mr President.

"That's Flight Lieutenant," Denis responded. "But you can call me Denis, seeing as we're off-site."

"Will do Flight Lieutenant Denis," replied Mr President.

If he was trying to be funny the crew were not impressed. The Flight Lieutenant's comment had put everyone on edge and the crew mostly ignored him for the rest of the evening.

"Hey Skipper, we've been thinking, like you said," began James.

"Let him have a drink first James, he's just walked through the door," interrupted Charles.

"Will someone get the Skipper a drink, so I can continue," called James, getting exasperated. "Listen up everyone this is important. Skip, about the name for our plane, the motif for the squadron is the skull and crossbones and its motto is 'do not stir up a hornet's nest', and our uniforms are blue, so, Collins has come up with calling our plane 'Blue Hornet'... what do you think?" James put forward, almost running out of breath, trying to say so much at once. "We could have a blue hornet flying out of a skull, with Blue Hornet painted underneath."

"Collins thought of this, you say?" questioned George.

"Yes Skip," replied James, smiling nonchalantly.

"Where are you Collins? Step forward," requested George.

"Here Skip," said Collins, looking shy and reluctantly being pushed forward by his crewmates.

"Is everyone in agreement?" asked George, looking at each of the crew's attentive face. "No one wants 'Duck Skip'?"

The crew noisily jeered at George's comment and chorused their agreement in support of Collins.

"Then you've just named our plane Mr Collins, well done, I like the name too by the way," confirmed George.

"Here's to Blue Hornet," called Charles, raising his glass. "Long may she fly."

"Blue Hornet," repeated the crew in unison, raising their glasses and cheering.

"Well done Collins, here's to you buddy, I said the Skipper would like it," said 'W' holding up his drink.

"However," said George loudly with a grin on his face, gaining everyone's attention. "None of you seem to have realised, the plane's squadron identity is HW-D, so we are stuck with D, Duck, whether we want it or not."

The crew abruptly groaned and moaned at the prospect of being stuck with D, Duck as their plane's identity in the squadron.

"We could have D, Donald," said 'W'.

"Or D, Danger," James injected into the jeering comments of the airmen.

"Henry," said George quietly in Henry's ear, distracting him from the rest of the hackling crew. "I invited Frances, the ATA girl, remember? I said about seven. Well, she's not here, maybe you would step outside, see that she's not lost."

"Yes Sir, right away Skip," replied Henry, suddenly all excited.

"She should be coming from the WAAF's accommodation down Cheapside," added George.

"I'll find her Skip."

"I'm sure you will," George replied.

"A jovial crew you have got together George," said Denis. "They mix together well and you seem to socialise with them more than other Skippers."

"Nothing to do with me, they got themselves together and picked me, if the truth is known," George replied. "Yes, we get on well; I think that's the main thing in a crew, all for one, one for all as they say. But we all know our place when needs be Denis."

"Well here's to you, you're crew and Blue Hornet," Denis expressed, holding up his drink. "I like the name, but it's typical to be stuck with the 'Duck' identity."

"Yes, a good name choice I think, ironic about the 'D' though, especially when you consider the confusing 'Duck Skip' suggestion," replied George with a grin on his face.

At that moment, the blackout curtain swished open, and an attractive dark-haired woman walked into the bar, followed by Henry. The bar went quiet for a moment while everyone looked to see who had entered before going back to their conversations.

Henry guided Frances towards his crew colleagues who were still standing in silence, their eyes glued on Frances as she approached.

"Gentlemen," said George. "This is Frances, she's responsible for flying our plane here today, so a round of appreciation please, and just make her feel welcome."

The crew responded with applause and whistles, circled around Frances, and blocked off Henry to the back of the group.

"Henry, get the girl a Martini, she's thirsty," said 'W', looking back over his shoulder.

Henry pushed forward trying to get through the circle and closer to Frances.

"Henry, the Martini," repeated 'W' over his shoulder. "Where's your hospitality?"

George laughed as Henry sighed dejectedly and went to the bar. The evening continued with each of the crew vying for an opportunity to chat with Frances. Denis made conversation with someone when he could, and George mixed in, chatting with his crew and others around him. As time passed by George eventually called order with his crew.

"Gents, and lady," began George, to a cheery reception at the inclusion of Frances in his opening comment. "Order gentlemen, a bit of quiet if you please. Tomorrow is Sunday, and we have it to ourselves as you know. I'll be attending church in the morning, if anyone cares to join me and we can check over Blue Hornet in the afternoon if anyone is interested?"

"Can I join you at church, if that's alright?" asked Frances.

"Me too, and me," chorused Charles and Collins.

"What about you Henry?" asked George.

"No, n-not for me thanks, Skipper. I'll see you in the afternoon though."

"Anyone else?" asked George.

No more of the crew were interested in attending church but they all volunteered to meet in the afternoon to inspect Blue Hornet.

"Right, I'll say goodnight and see you tomorrow then. Henry, make sure Frances gets back safely will you," said George, to the disappointment of all his crew, with the exception of Henry. "Frances, I'll pick you up for church."

"Right, thank you," replied Frances.

Denis had no interest in calling it a night when he could lay in bed the next morning and said goodnight as George left the bar.

Blue Hornet

The following morning George was up and ready early, he was too early for church so made his way to the Intelligence Office. There they have up to date information and news of the war's progress, items of interest for aircrew, a small library, and 'Window', a wall-based newspaper giving news of squadron crews, welfare notes and sporting activities. It was also a focal point for crews to meet and socialise as they went about their business. This particular morning though George found himself alone and he guessed everyone was being like Denis and taking a lay-in.

The Watch Office and Control Tower however were busy, and George noted from the pinned-up papers covering the notice boards of the Intelligence Office that two more planes were due to arrive that morning. From reading the notices, George got the feeling things were about to change on the base. Five planes had already arrived, plus two more that morning, flying was bound to commence soon, he thought.

He noted the time and began to make his way to church and pick up Frances.

Things were slowly coming to life as he passed casually through the technical site of the airbase.

He stopped at the Guardhouse at the main gate and spoke a few casual words with the guards, who also looked to be taking it slow and easy as if that was the imposed mood for the morning. George turned right outside the main gate and walked casually along Cheapside towards Waltham village. He noted the strong wind of the previous day had dropped and even the countryside was still and quiet with just a hint of frost covering the fields. The quiet before the storm, thought George as he walked casually along.

Frances was at the gate waiting when George arrived at the WAAF's accommodation site.

"Morning Sir," greeted Frances with a smile.

"Morning," smiled George. "Please, call me George, we're not on business."

"Thank you, George," responded Frances.

"How did last night go, did Henry get you back safely?" asked George as they began walking casually along Cheapside together.

"Yes, he was charming; we spent ages talking after we left the pub."

"You both seem to get on well together."

"It's like we know each other if you know what I mean."

"Yes, I have a similar feeling, funnily enough."

"You do!" responded Frances with surprise.

"Yes, I've only known Henry these past few days since arriving here, but it seems like I've known him for years."

"Isn't that strange, don't you think, the two of us thinking we know Henry?"

"Now you put it like that, it is quite a coincident I guess, two people, feeling the same way," said George, thoughtfully. "I thought he would come this morning, to church I mean."

"I asked him last night if he would come, but he said he's not interested in the church," replied Frances.

"You don't have to be interested in the church, it's what you believe that matters," George contributed.

"Well, I'm a believer, but I only go to church because I like to sing," admitted Frances.

"Pardon," replied George, suddenly stunned. "What did you just say?"

"I only go to church because I like to sing," repeated Frances. "Is that wrong, you look shocked?"

"No, not at all," gasped George. "You, you like to sing? You have surprised me."

"Well, I do, I belong to the choir at home," said Frances defending herself. "Why would it surprise you?"

"You don't surprise me, it's you... well, you have surprised me, you sing," spluttered George, trying to grasp the realisation of Frances's comment.

"Why should my singing surprise you George, I don't understand?"

George stopped on the corner of Kirkgate and looked at Frances.

"I've been thinking about singing for a couple of days now, and now you have turned up," explained George.

"Well I'm not a teacher George, I just sing in the choir," replied Frances, looking confused.

"No, you don't understand," replied George. "I've not been having thoughts that I want to start singing, I've just been thinking about singing and the tune Greensleeves, and now here you are, a singer."

"Oh," said Frances, slowly. "That is weird?"

"Well, I'm not sure about weird, but it feels strange to me," replied George.

"No, it's weird because I'm only here because I swapped my plane delivery. One of the girls wanted to take my delivery so we swapped, and it was her plane that I flew here," explained Frances. "I wasn't scheduled to come to Waltham."

"Really? That is strange, it's like we were destined to meet," replied George.

"I'm not sure about that, but I'm pleased I came, I've met Henry and you, of course, and I had a good time last night. I'm not sure it's supposed to mean anything. Things just happen sometimes, I guess."

"Here, turn right up Kirkgate, it comes out by the church, saves us walking round," said George, guiding Frances in the right direction as they resumed walking. "What about us both feeling like we know Henry?"

"Yes, I admit that's a little strange, I guess," said Frances. "In fact, it all seems a little bit strange when you think about it."

"You don't have anything to do with herbs, do you?" inquired George.

"No, why? They're something you put in cooking and there is some old wife's tale about how they can heal and things," replied Frances. "But that's as much as I know."

"They just popped into my head that's all," stated George, laughing.

"Well, they're nothing to do with me, I'm sure about that, I can't even stand the smell of lavender, it makes me go all goose-pimply," laughed Frances. "Maybe they're another mystery for you to solve, George."

Maybe," replied George. "At least I've got the singing resolved, thanks to you."

"Nothing to do with me George, I just flew your plane here."

"After you swapped deliveries," commented George.

"That's amused me too George," said Frances gaining George's attention. "The paperwork said I'm to deliver the plane to RAF Grimsby, and apart from the marker out by the runway everything else here is about Waltham."

"Yes, I thought that when I arrived. I guess it's because Grimsby is so far away, but I think it's always been like that, everyone just calls it Waltham," explained George thoughtfully as the church came in to view. "What are you doing after the service?"

"Henry said he would meet me and go for a walk, then I have to think about getting back," replied Frances.

"Right, I'll say my farewells after church then," said George, with a hint of sadness.

"I'm sure I'll come again, I'm going to try to, even if I have to swap a delivery," stated Frances, smiling.

"That would be nice," replied George, smiling in return. "Here we are, look there's Charles and Collins, by the door, let's go inside," George added as they arrived at the church.

Polite morning greetings were exchanged between George and Frances, and Charles and Collins as they all went in the side entrance of the old Norman Church. George fell silent and respectful as he entered the doorway, it was the oldest building he had been in.

He walked across the vestibule then turned right at the centre of the nave and looked down the aisle at the stained-glass windows, reflecting the early morning sunlight in colourful stripes onto the altar below. The organ played softly as they made their way slowly down the aisle looking to find vacant pews. George sat quietly, his right hand cupped in his left palm, thumb tips touching, and resting in his lap. He looked up at the high beamed roof and the flags and regalia adorning the walls and high spaces.

A gentle murmur of conversation hummed from the congregation, like chanting Buddhist monks as they waited for the service to commence. George relaxed and felt peaceful, calm and at home in the quiet ambience. He waited for the bell to ring and noticed there was more aircrew in the congregation than local villagers, which surprised him. Charles gave George a service hymn book.

During the hymns, George listened for Frances's voice as the congregation sang and sure enough, her voice was louder and sweeter than most others.

Following the church service, George said his farewell to Frances, had a quick drink in The King's Head with Charles and Collins and then made his way back to the Intelligence Office to catch up on the gossip before making his way to the dispersal pan and Blue Hornet.

Three Lancaster Bombers now occupied dispersal pans next to each other, their tail down and nose high up in the air. Several other Lancs were on dispersal pans scattered around the base's taxi track and Waltham airfield was beginning to look like a bomber station. George was in admiration of the command the planes imposed as he approached his aircraft. The two newly arrived planes from that morning were parked on pans on either side of Blue Hornet and attended to by Erks. James waved excitedly from Blue Hornet's cockpit window.

George waved in return, reflecting on James' eagerness to be in the plane and his positive approach towards fighting Jerry. He also thought about why James protected his full identity and hoped this plane inspection would present just the opportunity for him to find out.

"How long have you been here?" George called up to James, who now had his head stuck out of the cockpit side window. "Are there any others with you?"

"About an hour," replied James, with a big grin on his face, looking down at George. "There's just me so far, come on up, I'll show you around, Skipper."

"I believe you could too," replied George, ducking his head as he walked under the wing and towards the entrance hatch.

He suddenly shuddered and paused for a moment. The hair on the back of his neck bristled as he remembered Frances previously coming down the ladder to surprise him, and then standing together with Henry.

George shook off the sensation and began to climb the ladder to enter the plane, crouching forward as he walked steadily up the incline towards the cockpit. He stopped briefly and his breathing became deep and laboured as if the plane's cramped fuselage was closing in around him.

"It's a bit tight Skipper," said James, from the pilot's seat. "Mind your head."

George climbed into the flight engineer's position on the right of the cockpit and pulled down the folding seat. "What do you think James?" sighed George as he slumped quite breathless into the seat. "Fancy being a pilot, do you?"

"That would be nice Skipper, I'd love to be able to fly," replied James, suddenly realising. "Sorry Skip, I'm in your seat."

"No, it's alright, stay where you are," said George, catching his breath and recomposing himself.

"You alright Skip?"

"Yes, just a bit of claustrophobia that's all. It comes occasionally when I'm in a tight situation for some reason. How long have you been away from home James?" George asked, diverting the conversation away from himself.

"About six months Skip. I volunteered to come here. Well not specifically Waltham, just to come and fight, I guess. I got posted here."

"Is this your first placement?" asked George.

"Yes Skip, I got good results bomb aiming during training, so I got made up as front gunner and bomb aimer and sent here."

"That's impressive," smiled George, complimenting James and encouraging his enthusiasm. "Why are you so eager to get at Jerry, you seem impatient and act as if you can't wait?"

"I like fighting, it excites me, it keeps you alert and on edge and I want to win the war," answered James.

"But fisticuffs and brawling are a lot different to what we're going to be doing James," replied George, surprised by James' answer.

"It will still be exciting though Skip," said James, with a big grin on his face.

George looked at James with his smile and bright eager expression just talking about fighting Jerry. "What's with your one name bit James; don't you like your surname?"

"Oh, I just had a rough time with it during school; that's how the fighting started. All the teasing and stuff, I developed a complex about it and got into a few fights over it, so I try not to use it. It's crazy really, 'cos I don't mind my name, I quite like it actually. It's just a habit I continue when I meet new people. Once they get to know me as James, it all goes away."

"I had to ask James, I thought there was a problem," smiled George.

"No Skipper, no problem, just me keeping on with some kids' stuff."

How old are you, James?" asked George.

"Nineteen Skip."

"All grown-up then," said George, suggestively.

"Yes Skip, all grown-up," James replied, looking at George with a tight thoughtful smile.

"So do you think you'll be comfortable down there?" asked George, changing the subject and looking down into the front gunner's position in the nose of the aircraft.

"I'm sure we'll soon be finding out," replied James.

"Well you climb down there, see how it fits, and let me have a sit in my seat," suggested George, now eager to have a feel of being in the pilot's seat.

"Sure thing Skipper, it'll be a tight thing moving around though."

It took a little manoeuvring to change positions, but George eventually got to sit in his pilot's seat. He held onto the control column and looked out of the side window, pressed the foot pedals with his feet, then sat up straight and looked all around him to see just what sort of view he commanded through the Lancaster's large canopy.

George looked at the controls laid out before him, put his finger on the artificial horizon indicator, and ran it along the white horizontal line displayed on the instrument. He stretched out his right arm and grasped the throttle levers, moving them back and forth just a little as he held the joystick with his left hand, imagining he was at the controls, flying.

Lost in his thoughts he gently touched the main compass with his fingertip, he was facing due west.

"Feels good, don't you think?" interrupted James.

"Yes, it feels good James," replied George, coming back to reality and looking out of the cockpit window. "Here come the others," stated George, observing the rest of his crew alighting from the back of an Erk's maintenance truck at the edge of Blue Hornet's dispersal pan.

"Permission to come aboard Skipper," called Mr President, making his way towards the plane.

"That's the n-navy, you dummy," said Henry, laughing, along with 'W' and Charles.

"Yes come on up," said George out of the window, smiling at his jovial crew.

"I'm just being polite," replied Mr President, approaching the entrance hatch and the first to climb the ladder. "It's a bit cramped in here you guys, there's hardly room to swing a cat,"

"So long as you can swing that machine gun that's all that m-matters," replied Henry, following Mr President up the entrance ladder.

"Age before beauty," said Charles, allowing Collins up the ladder before himself.

"You've got that one wrong too," called Henry, overhearing Charles's gesture.

"No, I'm the one with the beauty," replied Charles.

"Not from where I'm looking," laughed Henry.

"I think the bombs have got more room than we have," called Mr President, squeezing into his upper gunner's position, three-quarters along the length of the aircraft. "It looks like me and you are on our own at the back Collins," continued Mr President as Collins squeezed past, on his way to the rear gun turret.

"How many canons do you have?" Collins asked Mr President as he passed.

"Twin 303 Browning machine guns with three-sixty vision, so keep your head down," replied Mr President. "What about you?"

"Four of the same, with about one-eighty vision I reckon," said Collins.

"At least you have a seat," smiled Mr President. "I just have a hammock."

"Gee, thanks buddy, one I can't get out of until we land," replied Collins.

"No worries pal, I'll talk to you, keep you company," said Mr President, fiddling around with his machine guns.

"Like you said, we're on our own at the back Mr President."

"What are you two scheming?" asked 'W', as he entered the plane's fuselage and the last one up the ladder.

"Man's talk," replied Mr President.

"Yeah, right, I don't see any men though," smirked 'W' turning his back on the two gunners and climbing the incline to reach his wireless station.

'W's radio position was directly behind Henry's, only facing forward towards his wireless sets. Henry's location was facing sideways, looking down the port wing, between 'W's radios and the armour plating protecting the back of George's pilot seat. Both positions had tables, though 'W's was somewhat smaller, and his radio unit acted as a barrier between him and Henry.

"Is everyone at their station?" George called out to the crew.

A flurry of responses came echoing along the plane's fuselage.

"Well, this is where the action will take place and we'll be spending a lot of time in these positions. Like you have commented, some of them are a little cramped, so let's get used to them. Getting in and out looks like we could do with some sort of order set up to make things easy, so we are not climbing over one another. Collins, can you hear me at the back there?"

"Loud and clear Skipper."

"You're going to be first in, last out. I think yours is the most difficult position to get in and out of, so that should give you time... Mr President," George called down the plane.

"Here Skip."

"I know you're there Adams, I've been listening to you."

"Yes Skip."

"You're next.

"Got ya Skip, will do."

"James, you follow the President, that will give you time to get settled in the front before me, and then Charley gets in. 'W', Henry, you two can choose, your positions are easily accessible and don't affect anyone so you can follow up at the rear. What do you think everyone, should we give it a go?"

The crew responded positively, but quietly and without their usual banter, releasing themselves from their locations, exiting the plane and assembling outside, beside the entrance hatch, quietly and without too much trouble.

"Well, that went pretty smoothly for a first attempt," commented George. "But I don't think getting out is as problematic as getting in. So, let us give getting on-board ago," said George, encouraging the crew once more into action, though seemingly just for his own amusement and satisfaction of doing something on the plane. "Can you remember your position everyone? Collins, off you go," said George, enthusiastically.

Again, the crew responded quietly and positively and the entrance order exercise worked well.

"Any problems anyone," asked George, calling down the silent fuselage of the aircraft.

"What about the emergency exits, Skip?" asked Collins, in a monotone voice. "Are we going to try those today, mine looks pretty complicated Skip?"

"We'll leave that for another day, Collins, I'm sure there will be some drill or training on escape hatches."

George sensed the quiet mood of despondency in the crew. He realised that as enthusiastic as the crew may have been to inspect Blue Hornet, exercises of entering and exiting the aircraft was not their idea of having an afternoon off, and he quickly responded.

"However, right now I could do with a drink, anyone cares to join me?" called George, noting the instant change of urgency and return of banter as the crew rushed to exit the plane.

The crew responded favourably to George's last suggestion, resumed their conversation of banter, and headed off along the taxi track in the direction of the Crew's Mess.

-

Walking along, listening to the chatter and joviality of his crew, George felt the eternal energy of Chi lift his bodily vibration and the flow of universal conscious flood his subconscious mind with a calm warm sensation of feeling good about himself.

-

"I think tomorrow will be a different day," said George, happy with his surroundings, a smile on his face and a lightness in his stride as he walked along the taxi track with his crew.

Fly High

The evening passed slowly, and the Crew's Mess was quiet after the loud and boisterous merriment of the previous night in The King's Head with Frances present. Henry was also subdued and possibly Frances was on his mind too, she had made quite an impact on him. George wanted some time to himself and decided to make it an early night; he made his excuses about leaving early and left his crew to continue their evening.

The evening was dark, still and quiet, with hardly any wind. A little like the morning's weather, only the frost was just beginning and felt like it would be much colder than the morning's frost. Hands in his pockets George walked steadily down Cheapside towards his accommodation hut.

He thought about the arrival of Frances and her link with singing and though Frances had just accepted the occurrence as one of those things that sometimes happen, George thought there was something more about it.

Where did the herbs fit in, for example, there was no solution to them, and did they have any association with Frances, or is that another mystery to solve, as Frances had suggested.

He wondered about that. And what about the fish, that's a strange one, what is happening to me, what has a fish got to do with anything. Henry, was he a connection between them or was it just a coincidence they both had similar feelings about him? Then there was his déjà vu incident, had all this happened before, just what was happening thought George? Maybe it is the new surroundings, meeting his new crew, Frances, and other new faces, and the arrival of Blue Hornet. Maybe arriving at Waltham he found things exciting and overstimulating his mind.

Arriving at his accommodation hut, George made his way to his room and made himself comfortable. He lay stretched out on his bed, hands behind his head and continued to think about the recent events he had experienced until he wearily drifted off to sleep.

George woke up suddenly, thinking Denis had returned drunk or something as his bed was banging and shaking against the wall of his room. George flicked on the light, went across the corridor, and knocked on Denis's door. The banging continued so George tried the handle. The door opened, Denis lay shaking and sweating in his bed. George entered the room and gently shook Denis by the shoulder.

"Hey, wake up," said George. "You're having a bad dream buddy, wake up."

Denis woke up with a start, laying in his bed trembling and breathing heavily, a searching expression of anxiety in his eyes.

"You're alright Denis, you've had a bad dream by the sound of things," said George, realising he was still dressed and had been asleep in his uniform.

Denis looked at George, then slowly around the room, searching for items of recognition to reassure himself of where he was. His eyes rested looking up at the lightbulb in the centre of the ceiling before he spoke. "Yes, yes I'm alright."

"Would you like some water?" asked George, still standing by Denis' bed, pulling down his doublet and straightening his uniform.

"Thank you, that would be good," replied Denis, partially sitting and leaning back, resting back on his elbows. "Did I wake you?"

"Don't worry about that. It's you I'm worried about, that was some dream, the whole room was shaking," exaggerated George while getting Denis some water.

"Sorry about that," said Denis, slowly sitting up, swinging his legs over the side of his bed, and taking the glass of water from George.

"How's that, feeling better?"

"Yes, I'm alright," said Denis, sipping at the water, taking a deep breath and sighing as he slowly exhaled, allowing his body to relax and his breathing to return to a more normal rhythm.

"What was that about?" asked George, curiously, sitting on a chair by the table. "If you want to talk about it, it's alright by me. I was always taught that it's sometimes better to talk about things than bottle them up."

Denis sat quietly for a moment; the expression on his face was one of deep thought, deciding whether to say something or not.

"Have you ever left your body?" asked Denis.

"Excuse me?" responded George, shocked by what Denis had just said. "Left your body, what do you mean?"

"When I crashed, I wasn't flying the plane, I was watching it," said Denis.

"What do you mean you were watching it? I'm not with you Denis."

"I wasn't in my body; I was floating outside, watching my plane crash."

"I don't think I understand, how were you floating, you'll have to explain it, just tell me what happened?" said George, still surprised, leaning forward, resting his elbows on his knees, and looking at Denis.

"I was already shot-up, limping home. My two gunmen were already gone from when the fighter hit. Both port engines were down but we were doing fine. Len my engineer, he was hit, he probably could have made it, I don't know. I was losing height slowly but not enough power to regain anything I lost. When I saw the Humber, I went for it. Oh, that was a good feeling let me tell you, we were home, only I was too low. I prayed with every bone in my body to make it home, and that's when it happened, I just floated out of my body."

George had not moved, he concentrated on every word Denis spoke.

"I could see myself in the cockpit fighting to gain height. I watched as the plane hit the top of a tree and nosedived into the ground. I saw myself thrown out through the canopy as it smashed off, and I hit the ground."

Denis paused thoughtfully for a moment as if reliving the moment. The room was silent.

"When I came round, I was in the back of the ambulance with medics round me; I hardly had a scratch."

"And your crew, what about the rest of your crew?" asked George.

"All killed, their bodies were laying lined up in the grass. I could see them from the ambulance."

George remained quiet after Denis had stopped talking.

"Why should I be the one who survived? The other guys had done their bit. I don't understand how I was able to be outside my body watching what was happening. That was scary George, I was scared and my crew died because of me not doing my job," said Denis.

Denis sat quietly for a moment looking at the floor.

"I don't know what happened to you Denis, but you can't blame yourself for your crew. Maybe you would have crashed anyway, who knows what might have happened," George answered slowly and sympathetically.

"And we're just expected to carry on."

"We have to Denis, it's expected if we want to end this war," replied George, sensitively. "Have you flown a plane since your cash?"

"No, not having a crew I was a surplus pilot, that's why I'm here, to get a new crew and off you go again," explained Denis, with an angry tone in his last few words.

"Well, I'm sorry about what happened Denis," said George, noticing the anger. "You're not the first to crash or lose a crew. I don't know what to say about your out of body experience, though I am curious about that. However, we will be flying here soon, so maybe that will help you when you get a plane. At least you're alive, that's one way to look at it."

"Yes, I'm alive, if that's what you call it," replied Denis, still looking at the floor.

"I'll put the light out then," stated George, wanting to go back to sleep. "I'll give you a shout in the morning."

It was Denis who woke George the following morning. They dressed and ate and together they made their way to the briefing room.

"Sorry about last night," said Denis.

"That's alright Denis, we all handle things in different ways, and it's not happened to me yet, so I don't know how I'll react. Sorry if I seemed a bit brash, I'm not that good in those situations."

"That's alright, at least you listened. Things like that, how you feel and such are not really talked about, you're expected to get on with it. Which is alright when you're busy flying and occupied, but when you're not, and you spend time thinking about it, it gets to you George," replied Denis.

"How many operations' have you flown Denis?"

"Nine."

"Just the one for me, so far," contributed George. "And that was in a Wellington, I've not flown a Lancaster yet."

"You'll like it, they're quite easy to handle and have good manoeuvrability. You can shake off a fighter if you're lucky, and I've heard of guy's who have barrel rolled their way out of trouble in a Lanc," said Denis.

"Well let's hope you get a plane soon and they get you back up there. By the sound of you, I think you just miss it Denis and like you say, you've had too much time to think about things," stated George.

"Maybe," replied Denis, thoughtfully. "Maybe you're right about that."

George was also right about Monday being a different day. Flying was announced at the morning's briefing and a schedule of training activities were presented that ranged from take-off and landing, formation flying, dummy bomb runs, and flying with fighter escort, all to be conducted for both day and night-time flying.

"And remember," concluded the station wing commander at the end of the briefing. "These might be training flights for us, but should you encounter enemy aircraft, Jerry will see you as a target. Therefore, you will be armed to defend yourselves and you should take appropriate action. Good luck, now let's get to it, gentlemen."

Crews taking part that day, which included George, Blue Hornet and crew, were kitted out with flying suits, boots and parachutes, with transport laid on for the first take-off scheduled for eleven hundred hours. Blue Hornet waited on its dispersal pan with its eight Browning machine guns loaded with live rounds of ammunition.

Flight Lieutenant Denis Holdsworth was also assigned to Blue Hornet for the day, to pass on his experience while his own aircraft arrived later that afternoon.

The station's crew locker and drying rooms were suddenly a hive of activity. Here crews changed into their flying suits, any personal items that could be seen as useful to the enemy were stored in allocated lockers until the return of the assigned locker owner. Wet flying suits could be dried in the drying room ready for the next occasion and crews were collected and transported to and from their relevant aircraft and returned to the locker room for each operational sortie.

All take-off and landings are recorded on a large blackboard in the Watch Office. Crew briefing and de-briefing is conducted before and after each sortie and takes place in the Briefing Room, located in the Watch Office, with any useful detail or observation raised being passed on to Group HQ.

George and his crew filed out of the locker room, suitably kitted out in flying suit, helmet, and boots, with parachute clipped on over their suits. An Erk from Blue Hornet's maintenance team waved from his Crossley QA Tender parked along the road just off the taxi track, waiting to transport them to Blue Hornet waiting on her dispersal pan.

"This way guys," said Charles recognising the Erk, waiting in the blue maintenance truck.

George and the crew followed Charles's lead, headed for the blue Tender and climbed into the back. Charles gave a quick bang on the side of the tailgate once everyone was on board and the Erk began to drive off.

George gave another loud bang on the tailgate and the truck abruptly stopped. "We've forgotten Denis, Flight Lieutenant Holdsworth," announced George.

The crew fell silent and looked at George.

"It's an order, he's on board to pass on his experience," explained George, sensing the reaction from his crew. "And I think you should give him another chance," continued George, remembering the nightmare encounter of the previous night.

Charles jumped out of the truck and walked along the road in front of the locker room looking for Denis.

"Flight Lieutenant," said Charles as he found Denis. "This way Sir."

Charles let the lieutenant climb into the truck first and then banged on the tailgate once he had climbed on board.

"Morning chaps," said Denis, a little less formal, feeling a little conspicuous.

"Morning Sir," chorused the crew, in unison and with lively spirited voices.

George looked around at the occupants in the rear of the truck. "Good Morning, everyone," he said, with a reassuring smile.

The blue coloured Tender pulled up at the edge of Blue Hornet's dispersal pan, everyone alighted, and Charles banged on the tailgate before heading for the entrance ladder protruding from the underbelly of the Lancaster Bomber.

The crew lined up at the bottom of the ladder and entered the bomber in an orderly organised manner. Henry offered Denis to enter before himself and everyone calmly took to their position. An extra seat had been fitted behind Charles for Flight Lieutenant Holdsworth.

Rather than sit down Denis stood between George and Charles.

"I'm impressed," said Denis, loudly, so everyone could hear. "I thought you just performed as though you were an experienced crew, and not like airmen who have not flown in a Lancaster before. I'm with you today to pass on my experience, but it looks like I have just learned the first lesson from you all, well done. I'm sure the rest of the exercise will go as smoothly, gentlemen."

Denis leaned forward and talked over George's shoulder about start-up procedures. Erk's were still working and preparing the plane for take-off and one Erk was passing instruction through the side window of the canopy.

The crew took heart from the flight lieutenant's comment as they settled into their positions; the jovial banter had gone, replaced by a more attentive mood as they prepared for take-off.

"What position are we for take-off?" asked Denis.

"Four," replied George. "After take-off, we do one complete landing, then taxi round for another take-off. We then do two more passes, and just touch down and take-off in one pass through. Then it's a final land and taxi back to our pan."

"And there are five planes in total taking part," confirmed Denis.

"Yes, three before us, and one behind."

"Do you feel nervous?" asked Denis.

"A little anxious, for the first occasion, and in a new Lancaster, yes," replied George.

"I guess that's normal, it will soon pass once you get going and you will be fine," replied Denis. "I'll not interfere, George, you're a pilot, you know what to do, just enjoy it while you can, it will only get more difficult from today."

George paid attention to engine start-up procedure with the Erk providing assistance through the canopy window while Charles attended to throttle control as the first Merlin engine fired up and roared life into Blue Hornet.

The second, third and fourth engine thundered into life, Charles worked hard paying attention to engine speeds and hydraulic pressure, propeller pitch and a precautionary check on fuel level. George was in communication with flight control and the Erk shouting in his left ear through the window.

Each member of the crew was both, anxious and excited, at the same time anticipating their first flight together as a crewmember of Blue Hornet

George signalled out of the window for wheel chocks to be taken away and the Lancaster Bomber rolled steadily forward off her dispersal pan. George guided the plane into position along the taxi track, fourth in line as they filed round to runway 18/36.

The last bomber dropped into line as the procession passed its dispersal pan and George began to feel what it would be like in a real operational situation.

At the tail end of Blue Hornet, Collins watched nervously and quietly as the fifth Lancaster pulled onto the taxi track and rolled up towards him. He felt small and helpless low down in Blue Hornet's tail. The nose of the following Lancaster towered high above him, its huge wings spread wide as if about to wrap around him and squeeze him onto the spinning blades of four gigantic shredders. Collins pushed backwards against the armour plating protecting his back as the plane got a little closer. Suddenly he noticed the bomb aimer through the nosecone canopy waving to him, Collins relaxed and waved back.

The bomber procession came to a standstill at the end of runway 18/36 awaiting take-off instructions. Blue Hornet stopped in line, its propellers spinning. George grabbed a quiet moment, he let the occasion progress around him while he relaxed and took one or two deep breaths. He thought about what he was about to do and quietly prayed for help and guidance in the tasks he was shortly to perform and sent his prayer out into the universe.

One by one, the planes in front taxied to the runway and zoomed off with a roar of thunder. Once the plane before him had raced off down the runway, George rolled Blue Hornet into position at the end of the long concrete strip. George concentrated on what he was doing and sat patiently waiting for the last instruction. He rubbed his sweaty palms together and twiddled with his fingers as he waited.

"D, Duck, clear for take-off," echoed through his headphones.

"Here we go boys," George repeated to his crew through the plane's intercom.

Blue Hornet accelerated down the runway, bumping and shaking, its four Merlin engines growling at full throttle, vibrations resonated down the empty fuselage as the Lancaster Bomber sped faster and faster down the grey strip of concrete laying in a quiet corner of a Lincolnshire field. Effortlessly the plane lifted into the air and the ground sank quickly away from the aircraft.

Within moments the sea was visible over the starboard wing, the town of Grimsby lay dead ahead, and slightly to starboard and the River Humber stretched east to west across the plane's flight path.

The Lancaster's bumping and shaking had disappeared, vibrations were minimal, and the fierce growling of the Merlin engines feathered down to a smooth resonant humming in the ears.

"Steer to zero-nine-five-degree, Skip," said Henry on the intercom.

George banked round to zero-nine-five-degree, flew along the River Humber and out to sea.

"That must be Grimsby down there Collins," said George, over the intercom.

"Probably Skip, I can't see it yet, I'm looking the other way, I can still see Waltham. Is that what you have to look for when you're landing Skipper?" replied Collins.

"What's that Collins?" asked George.

"That narrow strip of runway."

"Yes, not much to aim for is it," replied George.

"I hope you know where it is Henry, cos it doesn't look like much from where I am," said Collins.

"Don't worry Collins, I know w-where it is," replied Henry, with an assuring tone in his voice.

"Boom," said James into the intercom.

"What's happening James?" asked George, sounding alarmed.

"I just blew up the docks Skip," replied James. "I thought I'd practice while I'm up here."

"Just be patient James, you'll get your chance," said George. "And keep your eyes peeled everyone. Hull is just up the river remember, and they get plenty of attention from Jerry. We don't want some lone fighter on our tail on our first day out."

"We're looking Skip, don't worry," confirmed Mr President.

"Nice to hear it," George replied.

George continued to follow Henry's navigational instructions, flying in a large circular clockwise direction, and they were soon on their return flight path for runway 18/36 and their first landing.

"Steady at that," instructed Henry.

"Can you see it Skip?" Collins asked from his tail gun position. "Can you see the runway?"

"Don't worry, we know where it is, we can see it," replied Henry.

George followed Henry's instruction and the runway began to come quicker and quicker. Charles prepared and dropped the landing gear, and in no time at all the narrow landing strip was almost upon them. As the start of the concrete runway disappeared under the nose of Blue Hornet, George bumped the bomber down on the ground, steered a straight line along the concrete strip and applied the brakes.

"Chore-blimey Skip that was a bit of a bump," remarked Henry.

"Sorry chaps, not used to having so much plane under me," replied George.

Blue Hornet gradually lost speed and at the end of the runway, George turned the plane onto the taxi track, continued round the airbase until he was back at the take-off position for runway 18/36, and waited for instructions.

As George waited, his mind was full of anticipation, paying attention to instruments, and his position on the runway, his concentration was intense. Amongst his thoughts, a flash of universal conscious passed through his mind...

-

'fly high'.

-

Eventually, George received instruction from the control tower and took off again down the runway.

George performed his first pass through landing and take-off reasonably well considering the wind speed had increased and started to gust. For his second run, the wind was head-on and gusting quite strongly. Blue Hornet began the final turn and lined up for landing. George concentrated and focused on his approach and airspeed, one minute too fast, the next minute not fast enough, causing the giant Lancaster to lose height. George wanted to accelerate and regain the height lost, but just as he was about to reach for the throttles.

"Watch your ground speed," Denis commented.

George was distracted towards his ground speed indicator. Simultaneously and quite coincidentally, the wind gust dropped and the Lancaster Bomber lost more height, with the runway approaching quickly. George pulled back on the throttles, accelerated and maintained height, then closed his eyes as a subconscious flash of Denis's crash experience passed through his mind.

"Bloody hell Skipper, mind the tree," called James from his front gunner position below George's seat, "I'm down here remember."

Blue Hornet's landing gear brushed through the tree's top branches as she flew quickly onward towards that narrow strip of runway, lying not too far away in the quiet corner of a Lincolnshire field.

Tao accelerated time, George's physical movements slowed. The eternal energy of Chi raised his vibration rate until his subconscious melted into the wisdom of his conscious. His vibration increased higher and faster until he vanished into space-time consciousness that carried him across the parallel.

Parallel Two

Tao

Is 'The Natural Order Of The Universe'

It Holds The Universal Blueprint

Of All Things In Existence

-

Chi

Is 'The Eternal Life Force'

This Binds Together And Animates

All Things

In The Universe

February
1645
Rushton

By the way of Tao and the energy of Chi...

His horse stabbed its front hoofs into the soft turf just before the edge of the dyke and turned a sharp left. William flew out of the saddle in slow motion and closed his eyes tight as he went headlong into the top of the Hawthorn hedge before falling to the bottom of the dyke, while his horse galloped off over the Northamptonshire field.

He lay motionless holding his breath, half in and half out of the cold water, hoping the chasing patrol of Roundhead Cavalry would not see he was no longer on his horse and would continue to chase after it. The distant drum of galloping hooves got louder as they drew closer to his position in the dyke. William took a deep breath and turned his face into the murky water. The rumble of hooves stopped abruptly at the edge of the dyke, William's heart was beating wildly in anticipation, then, exhilaration as the thunder of hooves continued the other side of the hedge and quickly died away.

William lifted his head and gasped for air, water dripped from his nose and chin and his hair was wet, bedraggled, and full of mud. He took a deep breath and began to relax.

It was then that the splinters of Hawthorn spines began to pain his body. He moved slowly and uneasily, painfully trying to sit upon the slope of the dyke. A long spine was stuck through his bottom lip, another into his right cheek, many others poked through his leather doublet and into his shoulders, arms and down his back. His right ankle throbbed from twisting as his foot pulled awkwardly from his stirrup. His doublet and breeches were wet and torn, his black knee-length boots full of cold murky dyke water, but he was alive and free of the patrol.

He began to wipe the water from his face, then winced as his hand caught the thorn sticking in his sore cheek. He gritted his teeth, squeezed his eyes closed and slowly pulled the spine from his face. William opened his tear-filled eyes and looked at the long thorn, felt the tender spot on the inside of his cheek with his tongue and flicked the offending barb into the water of the dyke.

He tried slowly repeating the process to remove the thorn from his lip. However, this was more painful and difficult as his lip pulled and stretched when he tried to draw the spine out. He gritted his teeth, and determined he was going to remove the thorn; he pulled and stretched his lip outwards with one hand and simultaneously pulled down and outwards on the thorn with his other. His eyes watered as the spine slowly withdrew.

William started to remove his doublet but the multitude of thorns penetrating the garment made it too unbearable. Any slight movement he made agitated the thorns that pricked and jabbed further into his skin.

William sat there in the dyke; his feet in the cold flowing water, moaning and groaning at each attempt he made to remove his doublet.

Suddenly he heard singing.

"Greensleeves was my heart of gold."

He sat still and quiet, listening. It was a woman's voice.

"And who but my lady Greensleeves."

William sat patiently waiting for her to come into view. Her voice was sweet and melodic as she walked along, relaxed and familiar with where she was. She must be a local woman thought William, for her to sing so loudly as she walked. The woman came into view, she wore a thick dark brown woollen shawl draped over her shoulders, partly concealing her brown frock covered in the front by a dirty white apron, a pair of simple brown shoes and a white headscarf bonnet tied under her chin to keep her ears warm. She was carrying a large woven basket covered over with a beige napkin.

As she got closer William recognised her, it was Mary, a local peasant woman, who lived and worked on his father's estate and helped in the church. William allowed her to get almost alongside him before he spoke.

"Mary help me, come and help me, Mary," called William, agonising over the thorns penetrating his flesh.

The woman stopped in fright, her singing hushed.

"Who is there, what do you want?" replied Mary, seeing no one, not knowing where to look, her sweet voice now trembling and quivering.

"Tis I, William Rockingham, Mary, no one is here to harm you. I need help," William called from the dyke.

Mary stepped closer to the edge of the dyke and recognised her master bleeding and looking a mess sitting in the bottom of the dyke.

"Sire, what has happened to you?" questioned Mary, her sweet melodic voice returning. Putting down her basket, she stepped carefully to the edge of the dyke.

"I have fallen from my horse and landed in this mess."

"Oh Master, thou should be careful," said Mary, concerned for her master's welfare. "Allow me to help thee, Sire."

Mary removed her shoes, hitched up her dress to her knees, and scrambled down into the dyke. Standing in the steady flow of the icy water she gently got William to lean forward and began delicately removing the multitude of spines protruding from his doublet and body.

"Sire, you are indeed a mess, there are many thorns," said Mary, softly humming and singing and chatting idly about nothing as she busied away.

"You sing sweetly Mary," William commented between grunts and groans as Mary removed each thorn. "Though do you not think it a little daring to be singing so loud in the woods?"

"'Tis for the Green-Wood Man, Sire."

With the thorn's removed Mary helped her master climb up the side of the dyke. He leaned heavily on Mary's shoulder as his ankle was quite strained and could not bear too much weight. Mary sat him in the grass at the edge of the dyke, pulled a blade from the hem of her apron, and disappeared down the track into a small coppice area. She returned moments later with a makeshift staff to help William walk.

"If you would permit me, Sire, I could help with your injuries, stop the pain, and clean them before they turn bad Sire," said Mary.

"Turn bad, what do you mean?"

"Your injuries are many and your skin is torn. They can get diseased Sire and cause you much pain and discomfort. I can help stop that Sire if you would allow it," said Mary.

"How can you do such a thing, you are not a doctor?"

"I know the power of the plants, Sire," answered Mary. "My mother taught me before she passed."

"The power of plants you say. I have heard of such things before but that is sorcerer's magic," suggested William.

"No Sire, I beg your pardon, I am just a simple herbalist, I know nothing of magic Sire," explained Mary, panicking at her master's suggestion and reference to her knowing sorcerer's magic.

"What must you do, how?" William asked, with a thoughtful glare at Mary.

"I just apply a potion from the plants' Sire. It is knowing which plant to apply, Sire."

"And you know how to apply this... this potion?" said William.

"Oh, yes Sire. I know many potions."

"Very well, I will permit you to apply potions to my wounds, Mary. I am already in great pain and you have been helpful to remove the thorns. If you can relieve the pain and I see no magic, I will be grateful," said William. "But this shall be our secret Mary; we could be hanged for sorcery if this were to be discovered."

"I have herbs in my basket now Sire," suggested Mary.

"Not here, someone may see," replied William sharply. "The lodge is along the road, you can perform your deed there, as long as I can reach there."

Mary helped William to his feet and gave him the staff to support himself and take his weight as he walked. The lodge was not far along the track road, but far enough for William to begin to shiver in the cold February air.

As they reached the lodge, William became cautious to the snorting of a horse, hoping it may be his own. It sounded close by. He stopped, took hold of Mary's arm, and guided her to the wall at the side of the track. William looked carefully into the bushes and undergrowth surrounding the lodge. There, on the far side of the lodge were two horses, tethered amongst the bushes.

"Shh," said William, putting his finger over his lips while looking at Mary.

Mary remained silent as William, as quickly and quietly as he could manage, guided her through the gate and into the dense undergrowth surrounding the lodge. He moved slowly and steadily through the shrubs, twigs and branches until he could see both the doorway of the lodge and the two tethered horses. He pulled Mary's arm down and she squatted beside him, looking at the lodge, her wicker basket by her side.

The Gothic style, triangular-shaped lodge looked very sinister standing alone inside the most north-westerly corner of the walled boundary of Rushton Hall, part of William Rockingham's father's estate. The lodge, built of brick and stone, and laid to form horizontal lines round the three-sided building; was designed by his great grandfather. There were three floors, with three windows on each floor, each of the three sides had three gables, and there are geometric patterns of three round each window. The one exception to everything being in three's is, there is only one door.

The lodge is little used by the family now and had it not been for William's injuries, he would not have noticed this activity taking place in his father's lodge.

William waited, the injuries on his body were becoming sore and irritable, he was beginning to shiver in his wet clothes, and he was yielding to the pain his injuries were inflicting as the holes in his back dried and tightened.

Suddenly he heard the lodge door open, two sturdy men, whom he did not recognise came down the flight of steps leading from the doorway. Their attire looked normal; a wide-brimmed hat, doublet and cape, ruffled breeches, gauntlets, and long knee-length boots, nothing that would arouse suspicion, other than they were hiding their horses and coming out of the private property. They stopped at the bottom of the steps, turned, and paused, talking to another man or possibly men, who William could not see. The two men placed their right fist into their left palm that gripped the fist, like some sort of gesture or salute. Then they turned, got on their horse, rode past William and Mary hiding in the undergrowth and out of the lodge gate.

Mary moved to stand up, but William caught her arm and prevented her from moving. He put his shaking finger across his blue lips, looked at Mary and pointed to the lodge doorway. Mary remained squatting, her eyes watching the partly open doorway.

William heard the door creak open one more time, and this time he did recognise the man who came out.

"Reverend Franklin," whispered William Rockingham.

-

A pulse of space-time conscious surged through William's thoughts in a single heartbeat. He felt like he knew what was happening, as if this was a moment of true time and he was in a time loop. He knew that what he saw happening was meant to happen and he knew what would happen next. As quick as the loop opened it closed and William had a feeling that momentarily time had stopped.

-

Mary's eyes and mouth simultaneously opened wide, and she slowly sucked in a gasping mouthful of cool dry air, as she too recognised Father Franklin, despite him not wearing his ecclesiastic robes, but the clothes of gentlemen.

William watched the reverend walk to the pathway that leads over the estate towards the hall, rather than take the normal highway running parallel with the estate wall. As he reached the bushes at the perimeter of the lawn that surrounded the lodge, Father Franklin suddenly stopped to check and look around, as if he had heard someone or something. William bobbed his head down thinking he had been seen. When he raised his head again to look, Father Franklin, now dressed in his ecclesiastic robe, was walking away, along the private pathway over the estate, unaware that he had been seen.

"He must have hidden them so he would not be so easily recognised?" William whispered to himself, thoughtfully. "But what has he been doing, and who were the other two men?"

Mary had not moved throughout the whole event, but she had seen everything.

"You must not say anything to anyone about what you have just seen Mary. Do I make myself clear about this?" said William, with a strong threatening tone. "You could bring trouble upon yourself if you speak of this."

"Yes Sire," replied Mary, quietly. "Not one word shall pass my lips Sire."

"Good, now let us go inside the lodge out of this cold and you can apply your potions, I am in great pain already," said William, hobbling with his staff towards the lodge doorway as they both cautiously entered.

The Mystery of the Lodge

Inside, William quickly sat on a chair by a small round table in the centre of the hexagonal-shaped room to rest his ankle. The light coming through the patterned windows made the room feel small and dingy. Mary asked William to turn and sit so he could lean forward over the back of the chair so that she could tend to his wounds.

"Sire, your wounds are many and bad, I cannot tend them properly," said Mary, concerned by the sight of his injuries. "I do not have what is needed, Sire."

"Then go and get what you need, I cannot leave here like this," William replied. "I cannot walk further, my back pains me, and I'm dammed cold."

"My cottage is not far Sire, I will go quickly to fetch what is needed Sire," said Mary, as she picked up her basket and rushed out of the lodge.

"And be quick woman, I do not have time to sit around here," commanded William, his tone reflecting more his discomfort than any anger towards Mary.

Mary lived in a small thatched, timber-framed cottage on the far side of the estate, along the bank of the Ise River; one of several cottages that house some of the staff that worked on the Rushton Hall Estate. She shared the cottage with Miriam, who works in the kitchen, and had recently wed Michael, one of William's gardeners.

William hobbled to close the door Mary had left open. He watched Mary until she disappeared; singing sweetly along the same pathway Father Franklin had just departed. William stepped back inside the lodge and closed the door. Gently shivering he returned to the chair and leaned slowly back, thoughtfully and carefully resting his pains against the upright of the chair.

William twiddled with his fingers resting in his lap; he slowly looked round the dimly lit, hexagon-shaped room. Its circular patterned windows with a central cross let in little light, and he was becoming cold, irritated by his growing pains, and impatient with the endless waiting.

He began to wonder just what Father Franklin had been doing and he slowly stood up. William shuffled around the room looking to see if he could find any clues as to why the men had been in the lodge. Two corners of the room contained small triangular closets that produced the hexagonal shape of the central room. The closets were empty of anything suspicious.

In the third corner, by the entrance, was a spiral stairway leading to the upper floor and basement.

He made his way down the spiral stairway into the basement. William knew there was a hidden entrance to a tunnel in the basement of the lodge that leads to Rushton Hall. It was a secret escape route. Was that their interest... to be at the lodge? William thought.

His father had taken him through the tunnel on one occasion when he was a boy. He remembered it being dark and damp, with water pools along the floor in places. The air was stale and the torches only burned dimly. William had used it one more time, out of curiosity, to see if it was still possible to use. William checked the doorway entrance for signs of use. Nothing was disturbed, and he left it that way, so as not to disclose its whereabouts and existence. He noticed rows of hooks in the ceiling timbers but found no clues as to the reason Father Franklin had been in the lodge and returned to his chair on the entrance floor.

William was just sitting down when he heard Mary's voice, singing. The entrance door burst opened and she stepped into the dingy room.

"I have been as fast as I could travel, Sire," gasped Mary, her breasts rising and falling with the rhythm of her breath, and beads of perspiration forming on her brow.

Mary put her basket down by the side of the chair occupied by William, who had repositioned himself so he could lean forward over the chair back and allow Mary access to his wounds.

"Mary, can we please do this quickly, I am cold," sighed William.

"Please Sire you must be patient, your wounds are many, I do not want you to suffer Sire," she replied earnestly.

Mary removed his doublet, raised his blooded polka-dot shirt over his head, and lifted a jar of what looked like onions in syrup from her basket. Mary was about to remove the top from the jar and dip a clean piece of cotton cloth into the potion.

"What are they?" asked William, curiously, looking at the jar with both an unsure and inquisitive expression on his face, forgetting how cold he was feeling. "They look like onions."

"They are onions Sire," replied Mary, with a smile on her face. "They will clean your wounds and stop infection Sire."

Mary removed the lid from the jar, as a sharp, sickly aroma filled William's nostrils and watered his eyes. Mary dipped a cotton cloth into the syrup and gently wiped and cleaned the wounds on William's back and shoulders as tears ran down William's cheeks. At first, William felt a sharp tingle at each wound as Mary soothed the syrupy lotion over his punctured skin, then as the tingle sensation died away, so did the intensity of the pain. Mary took her time and gently cleaned William's injuries. She put down the jar of onions and picked out a small bottle of light brown, thick creamy liquid from her basket.

"This potion will stop infection to your injuries Sire, and it will help with the healing," Mary informed William, with a smile on her face. "It is a potion of St. William's Wart and Comfrey Sire."

The explanation meant nothing to William, other than the reference to his name. He was already feeling better, relaxing while leaning over the back of his chair. The stinging pain across his back was already fading away, his eyes no longer watered and he had even forgotten how cold he was.

Mary hummed a tune while soothing the potion into William's body and dabbed the potion onto his cheek and lip sores.

"Mary, who is the Green-Wood Man?" asked William.

"The 'Man of the Green Wood' Sire."

"Yes, but who is he?"

"I am finished now Sire," said Mary, gently pulling William's blooded shirt back down over his wounds and requesting

William to remove his boot from his injured foot. To which William insisted Mary's help was required, and together pulling, while William whimpered and groaned at the pain, they managed to remove his boot.

Mary removed his stocking and saw that his ankle was indeed, quite swollen, both from the sprain and from the remains of dyke water that had been squelching in his boot. Mary dried his foot and leg and took a cabbage leaf from her basket. She squeezed and crumpled the leaf, placed it on the table and banged it with her clenched hand until it was quite limp and sodden with its own milky juices.

William became distracted from his question regarding the Green-Wood Man and watched in amazement at what was happening to the cabbage leaf.

Mary lifted William's swollen foot and wiped the cabbage leaf around his ankle so that it was moist with the juice from the leaf. She then took a piece of long cotton bandage from her basket, wrapped the cabbage leaf around William's ankle, and wound the bandage tightly round the leaf.

William was feeling better about his ankle, though not able to re-fit his boot, due to the cabbage bandage around his foot.

Mary took liberty as she placed the boot from William on the table, then she removed the blade from her apron and cut the leg of the boot from the foot of the boot, before handing back what now looked like a shoe.

William was not amused; he pulled on the shoe and stomped around the dingy room of the lodge cursing at Mary for destroying what was a perfectly good riding boot when suddenly he stopped. He had been so engrossed in chastising Mary without realising he was walking and moving quite freely, almost without pain.

"Well, you seem to have worked magic, Mary. My pains have almost gone and look; I am walking, well, much better than I was able, thank you to you, Mary. But what do I do now, how do I explain or hide these injuries and this magical healing?" Said William complimenting Mary while thinking of what could follow.

"Please, it is not magic Sire, and I do not know what you should do Sire," said Mary, talking rapidly and panicking about William's reference to her performing magic.

"Go home Mary, say nothing to anyone, and I mean anyone, Mary," instructed William, thoughtfully. "Wait... your potions; do I need more of your potions?"

"In two- or three-days' Sire."

"Very well, as I say, Mary, go home and I shall see you here in three days, just after the noon bell Mary," suggested William. "Take the pathway over the estate; as did Father Franklin, I shall travel along the main road to the hall. No one will be suspicious about me walking alone there and we shall not run the risk of being seen together."

William watched Mary leave the lodge, and then sat down again on the chair by the table in the centre of the dingy room, passing time before he would leave. William fiddled with his cold fingers and tapped the cut off leg of his boot on the table while he waited, thinking about Father Franklin. He was just about to stand up when he dropped the fine leather bootleg to the floor.

He leaned down to retrieve his bootleg and paused, looking at the floor under the table. A triangle had been marked on the floor and only partly scuffed out. Sufficient marking remained for a triangle to be identified. William sat up slowly and thoughtfully, he had found his clue, but what did it represent, what was its meaning, other than possibly magic had taken place.

Standing up, William moved the table from the centre of the room and stared at the remains of the markings, aligned to the outer walls of the triangular shape of the lodge that confirmed the marking was a triangle. William scuffed out the remaining marks with his foot and put back the table. He did not want this seen by anyone, and that included Father Franklin and his men. He did not want them to realise they had left traces of their activities.

William made his way out of the lodge towards the gate by the main road; he stopped and looked at himself walking with a makeshift staff, carrying the leg of a riding boot, wearing one boot and one shoe, his breeches wet, his doublet torn and bloody, his lip swollen from where the thorn had penetrated, his hair wet and matted with mud, and minus his wide-brimmed hat.

This was not the noble style of a gentleman, he thought, or the condition in which the son of Rushton Hall should present himself but was indeed the style of a suspicious character. He quickly turned around and walked the more private, estate owned pathway to Rushton Hall, that Mary and Father Franklin had travelled, not long previously.

As William approached the perimeter of the lawn circling the lodge, and the point where Father Franklin had stopped.

-

A flash of subconscious thought told him to stop and look.

-

There in the undergrowth, he saw something glinting. He cleared away the scrub with his staff, and there lay a wood and silver ecclesial cross of the church. The same one Father Franklin always wore around his neck. William picked up the cross and necklace, smiled, looked at it thoughtfully and put it in his pocket.

Approaching the hall, William moved stealthily, avoiding detection. He quickly collected a hessian sack from the garden before stealing his way to his room. He tiptoed in quietly through the doorway in the southwest wing of the hall, moved quickly up the wooden stairway that turned around three sides of an oak-panelled wall, and into his suite of rooms that occupied a quiet corner of the hall.

Once in his room, William stood by the fire to warm through before he undressed and put on a change of clothing. He retrieved Father Franklin's cross from his pocket and placed it in a locked drawer of his dressing table. He put his torn and tousled clothes into the hessian bag, along with the cut off leg of his boot, and threw the bag into the corner of his dressing room. William then rang for his valet to run him a bath but declined any further assistance from the valet to keep his injuries and the presence of Mary's dressing unseen.

William relaxed in his bathtub, his bandaged foot hanging out over the side. He reflected on his eventful day, the secret he now held with Mary applying plant potions to his body, the mysterious magical activities of Father Franklin and the eventful escape from the patrolling Roundhead Cavalry.

The Civil War

This is England, civil war is raging, with skirmishes breaking out here and there as troops rally to position to gain ground, Whigs fighting Roundheads.

Law and order are in disarray throughout the land, with justice laundered and harshly applied or neglected and abandoned, as seen fit by those in authority and power. The church and people's beliefs fragmented into confusion, determined as Protestant, infiltrated by Catholicism or Presbyterians, and compromised by episcopacy or rising Puritanism, or any other faction of faith that could raise a following.

Amongst this chaotic hysteria of disorder, there lay the clandestine following of cunning folk, tellers to whom the common people of the land turned to for support, aid, and guidance in their lives. Occasionally, relied upon to ply their magic against the evil wickedness of witches and sorcerers.

Rushton Hall is the seat of Lord Rockingham, a royalist estate surrounded by a high boundary wall that stands in Rockingham Forest; royal hunting land, that stretches from Market Harborough to Stamford.

The Church of Rushton St. Peter stands to the front of Rushton Hall, situated at the south-eastern corner, and caters for the cluster of hamlets within the estate's grounds. All Saints' Church, however, located within the village of Rushton, stands across the field from Rushton Hall's grand main entrance gates, and caters for a much larger parish.

Mary's cottage and four other shepherd and gardener's cottages lay to the south of the estate's western boundary alongside the Ise River, with Rushton Hall's Triangular Lodge marking the northern limit.

Rushton Hall, within the local region, is renowned for its food and its garden's display an array of beautiful plants and trees. Its reputation for food stems from Mary's mother who was the cook at the hall before she suddenly passed away. She was responsible for establishing the kitchen garden, with its herbs and collection of fruits and vegetables. Her recipes are still used and though Mary has not been blessed with her mother's cooking skills, she has maintained and expanded the herb garden beyond that of her mothers.

The garden is William Rockingham's fanatical pastime, and he searches far and wide for the exotic displays his garden imbues on visitors.

William woke early from his bed and dressed quickly. His injuries across his back were stiff, though not pained, and he made his way urgently to the stables. Through all the endeavours of the previous day, William had forgotten about his loose horse. Had it now returned to its stable, was it still running free and roaming the Northamptonshire countryside, or had it been caught and enlisted into Cromwell's Roundhead Cavalry?

William walked through the west corridor of the hall that overlooked his exotic gardens, and into the tradesmen's north wing. He passed through the busy kitchen; causing work to stop, followed by curtsy and bow of heads, then out to the north courtyard, across the cobbles, and into the stables. As he approached his horse's stable, he noticed he was walking almost pain-free, though with a slight limp. He smiled to himself, as he thought of Mary's remedies, and beamed with delight when his horse poked its nose over the stable door.

The stable boy stepped out of another stall further down the row of stables.

"Sire," greeted the young boy, a smile on his face, relieved to see his master.

"When did he return?" asked William, standing before the horse and rubbing its soft nostrils.

"Feeding time, they always turn up for feeding Sire," replied the groom. "He had a sweat on Sire, he had been running, that is for sure."

The young groom did not enquire as to why the horse returned alone, or if his master had been injured or just fallen off.

"And he is alright now?" inquired William, looking at the stable boy.

"Yes, Sire, fine and dandy."

"Make sure he has plenty of water," William instructed, as he limped out of the stables.

"Will you need him today, Sire?" the stable boy called after his master.

"Not today," William called back, without looking.

Without further hesitation, William walked swiftly across the east-facing front wing of the hall, towards the church. He was determined to confront Father Franklin, put him to task, and see how he responds to innuendoes from the previous day's events, during a contrived conversation.

William quickly crossed the courtyard, with its expansive wall-to-wall lawn and large circular carriage driveway that allowed coaches to draw up to the front of the hall in a grand manner. He passed through the gateway leading onto the patio that fronted Rushton St. Peters' church, just as Father Franklin came out of the church door, dressed in his black and white ecclesiastic robes.

"William, Sire, you are l-limping," commented the observant Father Franklin.

William was instantly thrown off guard, as he continued towards the Rector.

"Yes, Father, something spooked my horse and I went off sideways," replied William, thinking quickly, and walking at a slower, less determined pace.

"Yes, I believe it w-was your horse I saw, it came in through the g-gates and straight round to the s-stables. Amazing how they know to come home; are you hurt?" asked Father Franklin, smiling. "Other than your ankle, I mean."

"No, I'm fine thank you Reverend," said William, feeling as though his idea to confront Father Franklin had reversed, and he was now the one needing to find answers to the questions being asked.

"But your lip and your cheek, it looks like you landed on your f-face Sire," commented Father Franklin. "They are quite swollen."

William ran his tongue along his bottom lip; he felt no pain from the thorn penetrations. He had forgotten about them, and any attention the swelling of his face may attract. He had only been thinking how well Mary's potions were working with regard to not feeling pain, rather than how he may look.

"A couple of scratches," William replied, casually.

Quickly he realised where he had been and wondered what the stable lad and kitchen staff might have thought when looking at him. It was done now; people will just associate his injuries with him falling from his horse, which, will now be no secret to anyone in the household, as such accidents happen. However, it is the healing by Mary's potions that he needs to be kept secret.

"Did you w-want to see me about something?" asked the reverend. "Only I was just going over to All Saints."

"No Father, just coming for a moment of quiet prayer," William replied, truly annoyed with himself for allowing Father Franklin to avoid his questions.

"Then I bid you g-good morning Sire," said Father Franklin, departing towards the hall's main drive and entrance gate.

"Yes, good morning Reverend," said William, surprised to see Father Franklin was wearing his wood and silver cross, or one that looked very much similar.

William entered the church. A few quiet moments in the still ambience of God's house were just what William needed to calm his frustration. He would have to listen to his father and learn more of his conversation and debating skills if he was to follow his father into politics, but more urgently and importantly, if he was going to determine the alternate pastimes of Father Franklin.

William wondered how the reverend could respond so calm and quick to divert his intentions to trap the vicar and learn his secrets. But then Father Franklin was none the wiser as to William's knowledge of his previous day's activities, as he had walked away from the lodge not realising he had been seen.

Perhaps the reverend was just being himself with his smile and polite conversation. But what about his cross, he knows that is missing, despite wearing a replacement. Hmm... though no one else will realise that, thought William.

He remained sitting on the pew, looking down the aisle at the fine, colourfully embroidered cloth that covered the altar, the large ornate silver candlesticks supporting tall white candles positioned at either end of the altar, the large plain silver cross, taller than the candles, took centre position. William listened to the silence; he enjoyed spending time in the quiet ambience of the church, allowing time to ponder and his thoughts to drift.

Why would Father Franklin, a man of the church, have alternative and suspicious interests? He is there as God's representative to the parish congregation, to guide, to listen, to advise. There should be no substitute or conflicting interest, he is there as an example for us all. But then, what are we all to believe? Not so long ago, the countries faith was of Catholic belief, until Henry, in his loss of temper with Rome and the Pope, determines the country shall become Protestant. How can that be? His selfish destruction of the Abby's and Monasteries, the enforced changes to the country's faith, it's the people's religious belief, should we all just change our religious belief to suit the whim of one man so that he can get married? Now we have Presbyterians and Puritans each plying for recognition and the rise of Episcopacy, do they all have Gods too? It all sounds manmade somehow, what about the cunning folk, do they have a God? William pondered.

And who is this Green-Wood Man? Of course, then there are witches and sorcerers that are roaming our land, both reassuringly helpful and alluringly evil with their influence upon the common folk, do they also have a God, or is Satan their God? William paused for a moment and smiled to himself.

Satan, he is there in whichever religion you may believe or follow. Surely if there is only one Satan, there can only be one God, or perhaps we are just supposed to follow what we believe is right. Take Cromwell, he is doing what he believes is right. One arrogant Roundhead, just like Henry, fighting for what he believes, and the country is at war with itself. Such are the private wars and whims that transform the history of our future. What times we are living, everything is changing. Even Father Franklin does not appear to be what he represents.

The church door opened, and sunlight cut through the quiet stillness and William's thoughts. It was his mother, Josephine, arriving for her daily and secret moments of Catholic prayer, in her Protestant church.

William smiled as she sat beside him on the end of the pew. Together they prayed, his mother with her Catholic belief, William, not knowing what to believe, other than what he thinks is right.

The rest of the day William spent with his gardeners in his beloved garden. He walked and talked, pointed and gestured instruction to his head gardener. On the northern edge of the garden, William had created a large circular dome mound; he had covered it with evergreen shrubs and bushes that changed the colour of their foliage with the changing of the seasons.

Cherry trees were interspersed amongst the shrubs for the colourful display of their pink and white spring blossom. Running around the mound William had constructed a stone gravel pathway that spiralled thirty feet to the top of the mound where he had installed a small semi-circular white stone seat with white decorative trelliswork to shelter the seat from the wind.

William was proud of his creation and spent the evening sitting on the seat, relaxing and looking out over his garden, convalescing from his injuries.

On the third morning, William returned to his garden and casually strolled the lawn pathways running between the exotic flowerbeds. He ambled along the bank of the Ise River and then crossed the small meadow where his horse wandered freely, head down, munching the sweet grass. William crossed into the larger pasture, where his sheep roamed. He began walking purposefully; consciously checking his surroundings as he limped briskly along the worn pathway that headed towards the lodge.

The mid-day bell tolled from Rushton St. Peters' Church as William entered the lodge. Mary jumped in surprise and stopped singing as the door opened.

"Oh, Sire, you gave me fright," greeted Mary.

"You are early Mary," stated William, breathing heavily. "Did anyone see you coming here?"

"No Sire, I was careful not to be seen, like you asked Sire."

"Come along then, let us get these potions applied, and get out of here. We certainly do not want to be caught together in this place," instructed William.

Mary sat William down on the chair facing her so she could attend to William's face and dab his wounds and swelling with the same brown creamy liquid as she had done previously.

"They look much better today Sire," smiled Mary.

Mary lifted William's foot and removed his buckled shoe, blue stocking, and the previous soggy potion dressing.

She took another cabbage leaf from her basket and proceeded to destroy it before wrapping it around his ankle and securing it tightly with a clean bandage.

"There is talk in the kitchen about Father Franklin Sire," began Mary.

"Father Franklin, talk, talk about what?" questioned William, attentively.

"They say he is something to do with the cunning folk Sire."

"Cunning folk, they say, who say, how is he involved?" asked William, his mind racing inquisitively.

"I am not sure Sire, I do not talk of gossip Sire, it gets you nowhere, but they say he has been seen talking to a teller by the Market House in Rowell Sire," Mary continued.

"We need to find out Mary," said William, thoughtfully. "In Rowell you say?"

"Beg your pardon Sire," Mary said, putting William's foot to the ground.

"We need to find out what Father Franklin is doing talking with cunning folk in Rowell," repeated William.

"No Sire, your back, I must do your back now Sire," smiled Mary, paying more attention to William's injuries than his conversation.

Mary turned William's sitting position round on the chair, helped remove his doublet, lifted his clean white shirt, and began applying the onion syrup.

"That's much-improved Sire," said Mary looking at William's wounds.

"Mary, we have to find out just what Father Franklin is doing," William stated, looking at Mary over his shoulder and gaining her attention. "While you are working in the kitchen, ask where you can get your fortune told."

"Everyone knows that Sire, Jon the Shepherd will tell you your fortune Sire," Mary replied, with a knowing smile on her face.

"Well say you have lost your mother's wedding ring," suggested William. "And you want to find it. Cunning folk do that sort of thing don't they?"

"I will ask Sire," replied Mary, pulling William's shirt down over his wounds.

"Have you finished?"

"Yes Sire, you are healing fine. One more time and you will be healed, Sire."

"Then let us meet again here in three days, at the same time, and remember Mary, not a word to anyone," said William. "In the meantime, I will try to talk with Father Franklin."

William let Mary leave the lodge first, then followed some minutes later. When he arrived back at Rushton Hall, he spoke encouragingly with his mother, Josephine, suggesting she invites Father Franklin to dinner. He did not want the reverend to think he had been invited for any purpose other than a social occasion. An invite from his mother would be less formal for a social occasion, and knowing how the reverend loves his food, William knew Father Franklin would not refuse such an invitation.

On the evening of the dinner, Josephine wore a silk, pale blue gown, with wide ruffled sleeves down to her elbows, a low neckline that was complemented by a silver, diamond-studded necklace with a large central blue sapphire. Her dark auburn hair was flat and straight across the top of her head, parted along the middle, and combed tightly on either side to curls and twisting locks that hung to her shoulders. Josephine sat at the head of the table; to her left Father Franklin perched on the edge of his chair in his ecclesiastic robes. His wood and silver cross replacement hanging round his neck.

William, sat to her right; dressed in a fine embroidered grey doublet with open seamed sleeves that exposed an inner lining of a light blue stripe down his arm to match the colour of his mother's gown. A white lace collar protruded around his neck, his grey baggy breeches stopped just below his knees with a blue bow, and his dark grey stockings extended to his blue buckled shoes.

Only one end of the long banquet table was set for dinner, a large silver candelabrum festooned with candles cast light onto the table and reflected off the silver cutlery. The three diners face reflected soft and mellow in the glow of the candlelight, emphasised by the room's darkness beyond the table and the candle's glimmer.

White gloved hands, with platter and condiments, reached into the candlelight serving wild pheasant and hare from the fields, vegetables from the garden, and wine from the cellar before returning into the darkness that surrounded the table.

Conversation was pleasant and topical with moments of silence and short occasions of laughter, as the food gradually disappeared from their plates.

"If you will excuse me, I shall retire and leave you gentlemen to talk," said Josephine, rising from the table.

"Good n-night Ma'am, thank you for your h-hospitality, it was a delightful evening," replied Father Franklin.

"Good night Mother, sleep well," answered William, half standing up as his mother left the table.

Josephine gave a small bow of her head towards William and faded into the room's darkness beyond the candlelight of the table.

"More wine Father?" said William, poring without waiting for an answer, and settling back into his chair. "Tell me, Father, what is your opinion of this civil war we are all struggling to avoid?"

"I have n-no opinion of such matters William, Sire. I am a clergyman engaged in the activities of Our Lord, n-not the squabbling of politicians," replied Father Franklin. "What will be, w-will be, W-William."

"I wondered what you might know, I have heard cavalry troops have been seen in the area, as close as Glendon Hall I believe."

"I am not aware of that William, that is close by," contributed Father Franklin, thoughtfully. "Close by indeed."

"Do you have any knowledge regarding cunning folk, Father, are they a growing religious group?" asked William, boldly. "We do seem to have sufficient fractions of religion fragmenting our Protestant faith, Father."

"They are not a religion Sire," smiled Father Franklin, correcting William's comment. "It is an ancient following, men and some women, common folk, who are believed to have magical powers for telling fortunes, treasure hunters, and the likes."

William took a sip of his wine, hopefully encouraging the reverend to drink more of his, and loosen his tongue.

"Can they perform such magic, Father?" questioned William.

"I believe some are better than others, and folk do go to these tellers, Sire," informed Father Franklin. "When they are not satisfied by the church that is."

"Do you know of any such tellers?" William asked. "Your contact with folk through the church must surely provide you with such gossip and hearsay knowledge, Father."

"I know Jon, one of your s-shepherds, tells fortunes, Sire," the reverend quickly replied with a clever smirk, before taking more of his wine.

"How would you know these folk, do they have a sign, a cross, a triangle, perhaps?" William enquired, hesitantly and suggestively. "How would I know one of my shepherds tells fortunes, for I surely did not?"

Father Franklin hesitated and sipped more of his wine. "As you rightly say William, gossip, through w-word of mouth and gossip, as we are gossiping now," replied Father Franklin. "Though I know not of any s-sign, most definitely not the cross, and n-not a triangle," he quickly added, beginning to feel a little flustered by the wine and uncomfortable with the questions.

"I understand a cross may not be their sign, Father, but why not a triangle, common folk can read and understand signs, if not the written word," William reasoned. "Perhaps you know of a triangle sign, our lodge, for example, it is triangular, and we have little understanding of its mystery or the use my grandfather may have implied in its design?" William added.

"William, the time, it is g-getting late, I have engagements in the m-morning, Sire," replied Father Franklin, his stammer becoming more apparent and he became jittery in avoiding William's remarks and suggestions. Standing up he stepped away from the table, cutting his host's questions short. "Perhaps another t-time we can c-continue William," Father Franklin concluded politely.

"Another time Father," said William, accepting the reverend's excuse to leave.

After Father Franklin's departure, William remained at the table. He leaned back in his chair, fiddling with his fingers in his lap, and sipping his wine. He had touched a sore point with his reference to triangular signs and the lodge that Father Franklin did not want to answer. William felt slightly elated with the revelation he had achieved and disappointed that he had not been able to progress further than that which he already knew. Perhaps Mary will have news to report from her kitchen gossiping.

Trinity

The following day William repeated his casual but observant stroll across the Rushton Hall estate to meet Mary at the lodge by mid-day, ensuring he was not seen on the way. However, it was some time before Mary made her appearance.

"Sorry I am late Sire, Jon the Shepherd insisted on talking," said Mary as she walked through the lodge door.

"Not to worry Mary, let us get started with the potion. Did you find anything out about Father Franklin and the cunning folk?" William replied as Mary began attending to his injuries.

"Jon the Shepherd has said that the reverend meets a man who is a teller, in Rowell, and he gave me this," informed Mary, putting her hand in the pocket of her apron and offering William a small piece of folded parchment.

William took the piece of parchment and opened it as Mary continued applying the onion syrup to his wounds. Written on the paper were the words, 'Sator arepo tenet opera rotas'.

"What does it mean?" asked William, looking at the words, suddenly realising they read the same backwards.

"I do not know Sire, I cannot read, Jon the Shepherd said to keep it with me, and I will find my mother's ring," answered Mary. "Which would be interesting Sire as she never had one!"

"That is all?" asked William, ignoring Mary's wry comment.

"He did say the charm's magic would also protect against curses and keep evil away, and it cost me one halfpenny Sire."

"Oh, yes Mary, I shall return the halfpenny," William responded, thoughtfully, wondering what he should do now as he has not learned much about the reason for Father Franklin being in his father's lodge.

"Thank you Sire and your wounds are healing well, after three more days you can remove the bandage from your ankle, there is nothing more I can do Sire."

"You have been most helpful Mary, thank you, I shall reward you in some way. Now, did Jon the Shepherd say..." William stopped talking, looked at Mary, and put a finger over his lips, as he heard horses arriving outside the lodge.

"Mary go into the basement, hide behind the wall under the stairway," William instructed, pushing Mary towards the spiral stairway. "Quickly."

"But I have to be at the church Sire," said Mary, dithering. "There is a christening,"

"Well, you cannot leave at the moment, now quickly, go to the basement and be quiet."

William nervously cracked open the lodge door as Mary made her way down the spiral stairway to the basement. He saw the same two sturdy men who were previously at the lodge, still mounted and pulling at their rains, their horses circling, as they tried to get the horse to stand and face the direction towards Father Franklin, whom he could not see, but could unmistakeably hear talking.

"Gentlemen, w-we w-will have to cancel today, the lodge is not a safe place for us at the moment, someone m-must have seen something. W-William Rockingham has been asking questions as if he suspects something."

William shuddered and his heart skipped a beat at the mention of his name.

"And I have misplaced my cross. I have searched for it everywhere, it has to be here at the lodge, but I cannot find it I have looked. Gentlemen, I have a christening I must attend later this afternoon; we can meet another time at the rectory, I will send word. Now go, get away from here," Father Franklin spoke, urgently and anxiously concerning his missing cross.

The two horsemen did not reply. William heard the mixed rhythmic thudding of hooves trotting out through the lodge gateway and gallop off down the track. Unsure of what Father Franklin may do, William quickly and carefully closed the lodge door and went down into the basement and hid under the stairway beside Mary.

William felt trapped, there was nowhere else to hide, if Father Franklin came looking for his missing cross down in the basement, he and Mary would be discovered. William leaned back against the wall. He looked at Mary and put his finger across his lips for her to be quiet and stood there waiting in the silence, listening to his heart pounding.

Time passed slowly and there had been no sound of Father Franklin coming into the lodge.

"Wait here," William whispered, as he purposefully and quietly made his way up the spiral stairway. There was no sign of Father Franklin and William breathed a sigh of relief. He slowly opened the lodge door and looked out into the leafy undergrowth and shrubs surrounding the lodge; Father Franklin had gone.

"You can come up now," William called out to Mary. "They have all gone."

Mary came steadily up the stairway looking a little shaken and anxious.

"This charm you have been given, why did Jon the Shepherd give it to you?" asked William.

"You said I should ask about my mother's wedding ring Sire."

"Yes, ask in the kitchen I said, not go to a teller," reasoned William, handing back the charm. "Here, you keep this, keep it safe, you may need it."

"The kitchen folk said I should ask Jon the Shepherd Sire, so that is what I done," Mary replied. "He said Father Franklin and those men have been at the lodge for quite some weeks."

"No wonder there is gossip in the kitchen Mary if my shepherd knows the whereabouts and activities of Farther Franklin; I dare say it is common knowledge around the kitchen. Did Jon the Shepherd say anything more; he seems to know quite a lot about what goes on around here?"

"No Sire," Mary replied.

"You say you have a christening this afternoon Mary. Father Franklin just mentioned the same."

"Yes, Sire, I must help in the church and fetch christening water from the holy spring. It is for Miriam and Michael, they were married just last year Sire, you remember. Their child will be christened today Sire," Mary informed William.

"Yes I remember now, my mother will also be attending," smiled William thoughtfully. "Now run along, be careful at the christening, and don't be late, otherwise Father Franklin may ask you questions why. And thank you for your kindness to heal my wounds, it will be our secret Mary. I will send for you if I need you further."

"Thank you, Sire, the charm has worked too Sire," said Mary as she began to make her way out of the lodge.

"What do you mean the charm has worked?" asked William, bemused.

"The charm Sire, we were not discovered, it has protected us, Sire," stressed Mary, feeling safe as a look of wonder appeared on her face. "That is magic don't you think Sire?"

William paused and thought about Mary's magical assumption regarding Jon the Shephard's charm.

"I think perhaps we were lucky that Father Franklin did not enter the lodge, Mary," replied William, slowly and thoughtfully.

"Jon the Shepherd said it will keep evil away Sire, and Father Franklin did not find us, Sire."

"It would appear to be so Mary. Now off you go for the christening, and remember, not a word about this to anyone, and keep the charm with you, it may keep Father Franklin from asking you questions if you are late."

William gave Mary time to cross the estate's meadow and reach her cottage by the bank of the River Ise before he left the lodge.

He thought of Jon the Shepherd being a teller, one of the cunning folk; he thought about the charm he had given Mary and wondered if it was the charm that kept Father Franklin from coming into the lodge, and questioned what other magic it could possess. He crossed through the estate back to his rooms, curious about how much gossip his shepherd might know and if he knew the meanings of triangles?

William's frustration was returning, he was not having much success with his suspicions about Father Franklin, when a flash of wisdom entered his subconscious thoughts.

-

'Father Benedict'.

-

Why didn't I think of him sooner? William thought to himself. He is a good friend of fathers and has a great knowledge of many subjects; he may just know something about triangles and cunning folk. William's spirits lifted and he decided he would visit Father Benedict to see if he could help.

-

The next morning William rode to Rowell, arriving in the small square on the main Market Harborough coach road. In the centre of the square, stood a large stone crucifix bordered on two sides by link cottages; and behind it a short straight cobbled road that leads to the Church of Holy Trinity.

Cottages run down its left side and the graveyard extends from the church down its right. William rode slowly along the cobbles and hitched his horse to the rail beside the stone water trough at the side of the church gate. He walked the short pathway lined by gravestones leading to the door and entered the church, as his horse sucked thirstily at the water in the trough.

William crossed the vestibule and stood by the first row of pews, looked down the aisle towards the altar, knelt on one knee, and whispered a short prayer.

"William Rockingham my son, welcome," greeted an excited Father Benedict, coming from behind the vestibule to meet William as he rose from his prayer.

"Father Benedict," William replied, politely bowing his head while shaking hands enthusiastically.

"What brings you to my parish William, business, or pleasure?"

"It is always a pleasure Father," William replied, smiling broadly. "Though I must confess, I have come seeking guidance too."

"Guidance you say, then you have come to the right place my son, guidance is our speciality. How can I be of help?"

"I have some difficult questions I hope you are able to help me with Father."

"Then perhaps we should go to the rectory, it is more private and I can provide you with refreshment after your journey," replied Father Benedict.

Together, William and Father Benedict left the church and made their way to the rectory. William left his horse tethered to the water trough as he and Father Benedict turned right immediately out of the church gate and crossed Rowell marketplace. Dominating the large, cobbled square was the old market house; a strange building with unique edges, and a strange vertical hollow, design in such a way that people say it is a cross.

Though it is also the building where Father Franklin has been seen talking with cunning folk. They continued walking diagonally to the left, across the square, passed the front of The King's Head Inn, a busy drinking and coaching house. They crossed the road again diagonally left to enter a large detached three-story building that fronted almost onto the dirt road and just a little away from the hectic market square.

Father Benedict led William into his study. He arranged for drinks to be served before he sat down in a comfortable leather chair behind a large oak desk, from where Father Benedict had a clear view into Rowell marketplace. He gestured for William to sit opposite on an equally comfortable leather chair, though not as grand as Father Benedict's.

"Now William you may ask me your questions, and hopefully I will be able to provide you with answers."

"Father, I have recently come across cunning folk. One of my shepherds is a teller, I am told. Do you know anything about these people, should I be worried, are they dangerous?"

"William, cunning folk or tellers as you rightly say, have been around for years, in fact, hundreds of years. They are mainly Christian men, sometimes women, from parish congregations. They are most commonly sort after and employed to use their magical powers..."

"How do they use their power, their magic?" interrupted William excitedly.

"Usually for **fortune-telling** and treasure hunting, sometimes for healing."

"Healing, I can vouch for..." William interrupted, then realising what he was saying cut his comment short. "Sorry, do go on Father."

"Sometimes they use tellers to locate missing persons, or criminals and stolen property, occasionally to influence people to fall in love," Father Benedict answered, looking at William with a thoughtful expression on his face. "They are used for many things common folk are unsure about in their life or want to know. Cunning folk have quite some respect from the local people William."

"Is the church involved with cunning folk Father?"

"The church is not interested in treasure hunting or fortune-telling William. Perhaps that is why there are cunning folk. Though as I say, many of them are from local parishes and are known to both the clergy and congregation."

"Are they used for magic?"

"It has been known for them occasionally to use their magic to combat the evil of witchcraft and sorcerers. But, as I have said, that is occasionally."

There was a soft tap on the office door, quietly a maid entered the room and served mugs of warm ale. William watched impatiently, twiddling his fingers as she placed a brown ceramic mug on the desk in front of him.

"How is your mother these days William, it is quite some time since I saw her last?" asked Father Benedict, quickly changing the conversation.

"She is well thank you, Father, so kind of you to ask."

"Please send her my regards and your father."

"He is at parliament, as usual."

"If I know Lord Rockingham he is a busy man in such times, William," responded Father Benedict as the maid left the room.

"Yes, I sometimes wonder for his safety in such a position Father."

"He is highly regarded by the King and the House, William. I am sure his safety would not come into question. Now, where were we with your questions?"

"Thank you, Father. These cunning folk, how are these people regarded, Father? My shepherd, whom I have learned is a teller, he seems no different to another folk."

"There is almost no persecution of cunning folk by the common people William. They regard them as useful, as opposed to witches who can be as evil as they can be helpful, and sorcerers, who are mostly seen as harmful and evil. You seem to be quite disturbed by these folk William, has something happened?" Farther Benedict enquired.

"Is there another side, where do they get their magical power?" William asked, ignoring Father Benedict's concerned question.

"There is some belief that the power and magic of cunning folk has a spiritual dimension with connections to the mysteries of the universe," Father Benedict replied. "Though that is not a belief shared by myself, or the church."

William sat quiet and sipped his ale following Father Benedict's last remark.

"William, has something happened, you seem quite distressed?"

"One moment Father and I will explain. What about triangles, what do you know of these Father? What magic do they possess, what are they used for?"

The room fell silent as Father Benedict hesitated, took a long sip of ale, and thought for a moment before answering. William sat patiently twiddling his fingers, watching Father Benedict.

"A triangle is a symbol, a sign, William, a symbol for trinities. The church has the trinity of the Father, Son, and Holy Spirit. This church, for example, is the Church of Holy Trinity. I believe the cunning folk use the trinity of mind, body, spirit, and sometimes people refer to the trinity of past, present, and future. There is also a trinity from the east, where life, death, and rebirth is a belief of the common folk in a spiritual nature figure of a Green-Wood Man that is believed to be a protector of the forest. As you can see, a triangle represents a symbol of belief William.

Many folk cannot read but will understand the meaning of a sign or symbol as you know."

"What about the use of a triangle symbol?" asked William.

"The use of a symbol, you mean to use a triangle in a ritual?" questioned Father Benedict.

"Yes, to use one in a ritual," repeated William, becoming excited about the progress he was making with Father Benedict.

"Now you are getting into the mystery of magic and conjurers. Something has happened; tell me, William, what have you seen?"

"Please Father tell me what you know, then I will answer your questions."

"Very well William, but this does not leave this room, do I make myself clear. If it were not for your father, I would not be having this conversation."

"Thank you, Father, I understand."

"Triangles William, represent strength, a triangle pointing up for example can represent male energy or the elements of air and fire, it can also represent ascension to the spiritual world. A triangle pointing down represents female energy and characteristics, the elements of earth and water, and descents into the physical world. Some say the triangle can be used as a summoning symbol when scratched upon the floor but is beyond my knowledge William. That is the knowledge of witches and sorcerers."

William remained quiet again, a little depleted by Father Benedict's reply but continued deep in thought while he drank his mug of ale.

"Does that answer your question, William?" asked Father Benedict, quietly.

"What would a triangle scratched on the floor summon?" William replied.

"It could be knowledge, it could be for healing, or it could be some other magical or spiritual mystery," suggested Father Benedict. "You have seen such a symbol?"

"Yes, father."

"Where?"

"On the floor of the lodge Father."

Now Father Benedict remained silent, becoming restless in his posture. Then leaning forward with a grimaced expression, he continued. "That lodge, it has always been contentious, attracting mystery and magic. The shape of it is a triangle you have realised, full of threes and references to the trinity and triangular mystery and magic. When did you see this triangle scribed in the floor?" asked Father Benedict, quietly agitated by the reference to the lodge.

"About two weeks ago Father."

"And nothing since?"

"No Father, I think I have disturbed them," William replied.

"Who are these people, do you know them?" questioned Father Benedict.

"I would rather not say at this time Father, I need more evidence."

"Well let me know when you need further guidance, my son, we cannot have evil spirits wandering around the country, can we," smiled Father Benedict.

William smiled in return and thanked Father Benedict for his time, help, and the refreshing ale. "You have been most helpful Father, thank you."

As he left the rectory, William crossed the road back into the marketplace, aware that Father Benedict may still be watching him through his study window. He wandered around the square scrutinising the activity around the imposing market house, hoping he would see Father Franklin or one of his sturdy accomplices. William quickly realised that he would not know what to say or how to confront them if he had seen them and set off to retrieve his horse and return home to Rushton Hall.

As he slowly journeyed homeward, William thought he heard pistol shots and charging cavalry. He spurred his horse into a gallop, deciding to leave the road and head for the woods. He approached a deep dyke between him and the safety of the woods and kicked his horse on into the jump...

His body suddenly tensed as he remembered his last attempt to jump a dyke. In the blink of an eye, a deep pulse of universal consciousness surged through his subconscious mind. Time accelerated and William floated over the dyke in slow motion... he closed his eyes and space-time conscious accelerated him across the parallel.

Parallel Three

Time And Consciousness
Are Parallel

One Cannot Exist
Without The Other

Time
Manifests
Consciousness
Manifests
Thought

Thought Is Consciousness
Nothing Ever Happens Without
First There Is Thought

February

1943
Waltham

George opened his eyes, his subconscious thoughts were floating in universal consciousness, and all around him was accelerating and racing quickly past…

George pulled himself together, focused his concentration, gripped the bomber's steering column, and steadily pulled back on the throttles. Blue Hornet slowly accelerated; with a bump and a puff of black tyre smoke, she momentarily touched her wheels on the narrow strip of Waltham's concrete runway and raised her nose skyward.

For those watching from the Control Tower's balcony it looked like a display of brilliant low-level flying, for George however, it was a sigh of relief as he and his aircraft climbed high into the sky.

"Bloody hell Skipper," repeated James, following his near-miss with the tree. "That's one life gone, only eight left."

"That was close Skip," said Charles, with relief in his voice, his hand resting on top of George's hand, still clutching the throttle levers.

"Let's hope that's not what those watching on the control tower thought," replied George, looking across at Charles.

"I had visions of déjà vu there for a moment," said Denis.

"Yes, sorry about that," replied George. "I'll try harder next time. I guess that's what practise is for; I knew I should have been flying higher."

The crew all realised what had happened and kept their thoughts silent. Henry gave out direction instructions and George flew the bomber round for the final landing. Having learned a lesson, he gave himself more height and flew high during his approach, then brought Blue Hornet down at a steeper descent rate closer to the runway, levelled out, and landed smoothly along concrete runway 18/36.

Once Blue Hornet touched down the crew responded with whooping and cheering to show their support for their skipper.

"Thank you, gentlemen, thank you. I think we could all do with a drink after that little escapade," said George over the intercom. "The crew's mess at seven anyone?"

George's suggestion was followed by more cheering and jeering as Blue Hornet taxied round to her dispersal pan.

As he disembarked from his aircraft George noticed twigs from the tree were still stuck in Blue Hornet's landing gear, and there was no way that was going to be missed by the maintenance Erks. At the debriefing session, George confessed to flying through the top of the tree and received verbal caution from his squadron leader and a recommendation to be more careful.

George left the debriefing session and went to his room for some quiet time and to rest. However, it was not long before there was knocking at his door. George rolled off his bed and cracked opened the door sufficiently for him to poke his head out into the corridor. It was Denis.

"Oh, sorry to disturb you George, didn't think you would be resting."

"That's alright, how can I help?" asked George, paying no proper attention.

"No help, just to let you know I've got my new plane. It flew in during our training session this afternoon," said Denis, with a big smile on his face.

"Well good for you Denis," replied George, paying a little more attention.

"It was flown in by Frances," said Denis, cutting George short. "The lady who was here on Saturday night, she said to tell you she would meet you in The King's Head."

"Oh, right," said George, paying attention and allowing his door to open a little wider. "Thanks for the message, are you coming?"

"Not sure at the moment, I've got a crew meeting first," smiled Denis.

"It's all happening for you Denis," replied George, smiling back.

"All for one and one for all," replied Denis, quoting a comment George had made to him when referring to his crew.

"Hey, that's the spirit, go get 'em, Denis. See you in the pub, if you can make it, and bring the crew," said George enthusiastically.

"We'll see," responded Denis, hesitantly and thoughtfully.

As soon as he was ready, George marched swiftly along Cheapside on his way to The King's Head, hoping he would arrive before others of his crew and he could have some time alone with Frances. If she was there, he thought anxiously.

George slowed his marching pace and began dawdling as he slowly approached the WAAF's accommodation site, anticipating he would meet Frances at the annexe gate. He looked down Cheapside towards the junction by the blacksmiths to see if she had left ahead of him, but she was not visible. George took one or two steps backwards and forwards at the gate of the WAAF's accommodation building, passing time in the hope that Frances would emerge from the annexe.

George looked at his wristwatch; it was approaching seven. He turned and faced the gate and looked at the annexe building entrance door, deciding Frances must have already left and was waiting in the pub. George became agitated and noticed his heart had begun to race excitedly and he was becoming anxious at the thought of missing an opportunity to chat with Frances alone. He resumed his marching pace, setting off towards the junction by the blacksmiths at the end of Cheapside.

As he marched along, he thought he heard his name between his deep energetic breaths. There it was again, but this time he did hear someone calling.

"George." He slowed his pace and turned to look behind. Frances was waving and calling and in an instant, George felt an excitement and calmness wash over him at the sight of Frances running towards him. He took a long deep breath and recomposed himself as Frances approached.

"Crikey, you're in a rush," said Frances as she caught up.

"I didn't want to be late," replied George, thinking of a cover-up and looking at his wristwatch. "It's seven-o-clock. I didn't want you to sit alone in the pub. Henry doesn't know you are here and we arranged to meet in the crew mess, so I've sent word for them to come to the pub. They may not arrive at seven so I came early. Well, I thought I was early."

"Well, you didn't give me much time to come out of the annexe. By the time I came out you were marching off," said Frances as they began walking.

"You saw me then?" replied George, sheepishly.

"Yes, I saw you, hanging around, looking at your watch."

"Really," gasped George, in a surprised tone, and feeling self-conscious.

"Yes, I was looking for you, hoping we could walk together."

"Really," repeated George, even more, surprised by Frances' reply. "I thought the same, but thought I had missed you," he confessed.

"Really," replied Frances. "That was nice of you George, thank you," she added, putting her arm through George's arm and holding onto his wrist as they walked along.

"Are you cold?" asked George, startled by Frances' gesture with her arm.

"No why."

"No reason," replied George as a broad and happy smile spread across his face.

"Are you comfortable with my arm through yours?"

"Not a problem," said George, smiling and turning to look at Frances. "I'm surprised you're back so quick actually. I wasn't expecting you to return so soon, though I'm pleased you have. Did you swap a delivery?"

Frances laughed. "No, I was scheduled to come this time and so excited when I was told about coming," replied Frances, giving an affectionate squeeze onto George's arm.

"I'm sure Henry will be pleased and surprised when he sees you."

"I hope so," replied Frances. "I couldn't wait to get here and see him again. What about you George, do you have someone special?"

"Yes, sort of... yes, yes I have someone," spluttered George, caught off guard by the question.

"What do you mean, sort of?" questioned Frances, turning her head to look up at George.

"It's complicated."

"Why, what's her name?" quizzed Frances, eagerly.

"Jean."

"Where is she?"

"Portsmouth, I think."

"You can tell me to mind my own business if you like," smiled Frances as they walked along Cheapside, snuggled together arm in arm against the evening chill.

"No, it's alright, I've not spoken about her, or to her, for some time now I think about it, so it feels a little strange all of a sudden," said George.

"Why haven't you spoken with her, is there something wrong?"

"I'm not sure, just circumstances, I guess. She moved to Portsmouth, and I came here," replied George. "I think we have spoken once since she moved."

"How long is it since she moved?"

"Hmm, nearly three months now."

"Three months, George that's terrible. You can't not speak to someone for three months, that's awful," gasped Frances. "Why did she go to Portsmouth?"

"She's in the WRNS, it's where she has been stationed."

"You could write, have you written to her?" asked Frances as they rounded the corner by the blacksmiths and headed towards The King's Head.

"Yes I've written, several times."

"And?" questioned Frances.

"And what?" replied George, curiously.

"And what did she say, she must have replied, surely?"

"Yes, I've had one reply but that was not long after she went to Portsmouth."

Frances paused and thought quietly for a moment. "How long have you known her George?" Frances eventually enquired.

"Nearly a year now. We are supposed to be engaged; well, we have planned to get married, after the war that is. Jean wanted to hold off the engagement until after the war, just in case, she said. That was before she moved. I got posted here and that is how it has been left. The war and the armed forces will determine the outcome I guess," contributed George. "It hasn't changed how I feel about her. Things are just difficult with the war on."

Frances squeezed and hugged tightly onto George's arm as they approached The King's Head.

"Well, I think you should... "

Frances paused her conversation as they entered the pub. George went to the bar for drinks and Frances claimed seats by the fire in the crew's usual corner. Fortunately, for George, no other members of his crew had arrived, and it took a while to be served before George returned with the drinks and took a seat next to Frances. She looked at George while taking a sip of her Martini.

"George, don't you think that's strange, her not replying?" Frances said as she resumed the conversation. "I mean, I couldn't wait to come back here and see Henry and when I saw I was scheduled for a delivery today, well, I was over the moon with excitement. And I would certainly be writing to Henry if I had to wait three months without seeing him."

"I never thought about it like that," replied George, thoughtfully. "I do think of Jean quite a lot but flying, transferring to Waltham, now all the training exercises, there never seems to be any time. Though I think you are right, I would have thought she would send more than one letter in three months."

"Write to her George; find out if things have changed between you."

"I will," said George. "You're right, I'll write this week before we start flying sorties. What about you and Henry, is it..." George cut his sentence short as, on mass, his crew burst into the bar and made a be-line straight towards their skipper and his attractive companion.

They pulled chairs up to the table, surrounding both Frances and George, preventing any opportunity to escape. All talking at once, their comments were confusing and distracting and it was impossible to respond to anyone's particular remark, other than to blurt it out and hope someone heard what was said. George sat back in his chair and smiled at the sudden burst of enthusiastic chatter, most of which was intended for Frances. He took a sip of his beer as he realised his opportunity to talk alone with Frances had passed and he would have to wait for another occasion to ask his questions.

Echo

Frances departed early the next morning, having spent an exciting and raucous evening with the crew, and romantic moments alone with Henry. George and the crew gathered for a social breakfast before resuming their take-off and landing training, with the addition of formation flying in the afternoon.

"Left a bit Skip, we're getting a little close to Echo," said Charles, looking out of the plane's large cockpit canopy at the Lancaster Bomber flying on their starboard side.

"Will do... he's falling back, I can't see him," replied George as he steered Blue Hornet a little to port. "It's not easy this flying formation lark, I wouldn't want to be in Echo's position in the middle of the pack. It's tough enough where we are, what it's going to be like at night in the dark, I shudder to think."

"We'll get there Skip, one way or another, we'll get there," Charles answered in a reassuring voice. "A few more days of this and..."

"S-starboard turn coming up Skip," said Henry through the intercom.

"Thank you, Henry. Mr President, are you there? Keep a lookout for anyone turning wide in our direction, you too Charles," requested George. "And keep your eyes peeled for Jerry everyone, we don't want him crashing the party."

Charles stuck his arm out and put his thumb up above the throttle levers to show he had understood George's instruction.

"Will do Skipper," answered Mr President over the intercom.

"Sure thing Skip," added Collins from the tail end of the plane.

"You alright back there Collins?" asked George

"I could do with a drink Skip."

"You said you don't drink, you're too young," said 'W' butting in through the intercom.

"Just water, I mean, I'm thirsty."

"You hear that everyone, he's thirsty," responded 'W'. "I'll get you a proper drink later, make a man of you."

"T-turn coming up any moment Skip," repeated Henry.

"Thank you, Henry, we're ready," replied George. "Keep your eyes peeled boys."

The squadron leader's instruction came through over the radio and George began a slow starboard turn to one-seven-five degree.

The port side wing lifted skyward, and the starboard wing simultaneously dipped to the wide expanse of dark blue sea as Blue Hornet banked round to one-seven-five degree. George watched the plane in front, maintaining distance as both planes slowly turned.

George fell into a trance like concentration and watched as the blue sea rose into view through the right-hand side of the cockpit canopy, tilting the line of the horizon and forming the image of a cross with the angle of the wide wingspan of the leading Lancaster.

-

The premonition of a fish out of water, flapping, and gasping for air flashed through George's mind.

-

Mr President looked up through the top of his gun turret at the dark black underside of Echo fuselage, which now appeared to be flying above him.

"Echo's getting close Skipper," said Mr President through his intercom.

George shook his head and let the premonition go, returning his attention to flying Blue Hornet. "Roger that," George replied through the intercom.

Charles looked up through the top of the cockpit canopy, but Echo was not in view. He shuffled round in his seat to see Echo but was unsuccessful.

As the squadron of Lancaster's continued their starboard turn Echo continually swung wider out of formation and closer to Blue Hornet. Slowly the air turbulence between the two planes began to shake Blue Hornet, and the roar of Echo's four Rolls Royce Merlin engines revolving at full throttle above them became very audible.

Through the front gun canopy of Echo , Mr President could see the panic-stricken face of the bomb aimer flapping his arms about as the two giant aircraft came steadily closer and closer together.

"Get out of here Skip, go left, go left," yelled Mr President, suddenly and urgently through his intercom. "Dive Skip dive."

The premonition of the fish flapping and gasping for air flashed through George's mind as he listened to Mr President's yelling through the intercom.

"Bloody hell Skip dive, dive," repeated Collins, shouting from Blue Hornet's tail end as the large black wings and fuselage of Echo suddenly appeared directly above him, accompanied by four roaring Merlin engines.

The premonition disappeared as George instantly turned Blue Hornet to port and dived out of formation, away from Echo 's encroachment into their flight path.

"We were nearly taken out there, Skip. Echo was feet away, coming wide towards us Skip," explained Mr President.

"Well done, good call Mr President, you too Collins," answered George as he steered clear of the squadron formation and put Blue Hornet on to a level course, while Charles balanced engine revs and propeller pitch.

"My pleasure Skip," replied Mr President slowly, with relief in his voice. "My pleasure."

"We can all thank you both for that one. Maybe I should be the one to buy you that drink Collins," added George.

"I'm suddenly thirsty too for some reason Skip," replied Mr President.

George chuckled to himself. He thought no more about the premonition and radioed his reason for breaking formation to the squadron leader. He then went to resume Blue Hornet's place within the squadron's formation. Charles waved at Echo through the large cockpit canopy. Echo's pilot saluted in apology and put his thumb up in reply.

Back on the ground, the crew lockers and drying rooms were buzzing with talk about the afternoon's flying and in particular the near-miss between Echo and Blue Hornet. Echo's pilot sort out George amongst the melee of airmen and apologised for his wandering off course. Steadily, one by one the aircrew left the locker room and headed to their billets and the crew's mess, where their boisterous chatter continued into the night.

"You coming to the m-mess Skip?" asked Henry, on his way out of the locker room.

"I'll come for a quick one," replied George, following Henry. "I want to write a letter so it will be quick, and I need to thank Collins and the President too, buy them that drink I promised. That was some call they made Henry."

"I don't know Skip, I didn't see anything, I just felt the buffeting and heard the engines roaring just as they began shouting."

"Me too, Echo was too far back for me or Charles to see her. I just put the plane into a dive, not what I expected on a training flight. Well, we'll soon find out what happened when we hear all about it from our two heroes."

That conversation was in full swing as George and Henry entered the crew's mess. The room was wide, tables and chairs scattered the floor, the bar was directly opposite the entrance door and stretched along most of the wall, leaving room for a makeshift stage at the left-hand end of the room. Airmen lined the bar shouting and jeering and facing the stage where Collins and Mr President were running round with their arms stretched out turning circles in unison, demonstrating the near-miss of the two Lancaster's.

"Will you look at these two," George commented, his attention drawn towards the lively activity his two crewmen were performing on the stage.

Henry laughed as he made his way to the bar. "Beer Skipper?" he asked.

"Just a half," smiled George, watching the antics of his two crewmen.

Suddenly the focus of attention swung in George's direction as his presence in the mess became noticed. A loud cheer and applause spread around the room. George raised his hand in the air and smiled in acknowledgement.

"I guess everyone knows about the incident by now," said George.

"It could have been worse by the s-sound of it," replied Henry.

George gestured in the direction of the stage with a nod of his head. "Well, thanks to those two it wasn't."

"Cheers," said Henry, turning from the bar and passing George his beer.

"Cheers, so how are things with you and Frances, the two of you seem to be hitting it off?" quizzed George, changing the conversation.

"Like I said in the beginning, she's w-wonderful."

"Seriously wonderful, or just wonderfully, wonderful," laughed George.

"Well, as you say Skip, we're hitting it off quite well," smiled Henry, teasingly. "Actually, to be serious, we're both quite taken by one another. I mean, c-coming out of the blue like that, I can't really believe it myself yet."

"Yes, it was quite noticeable at the time."

"What do you mean?"

"The two of you under the plane, you stood staring at one another for what seemed like an eternity, as if you were transfixed."

"I don't know what you mean," said Henry, with an enquiring expression on his face.

"When Frances came out of the plane it was like the whole world stopped turning and only the two of you existed."

"I don't remember it being like that," said Henry.

"Believe me, I was watching."

"I remember thinking how w-wonderful she looked."

"Yes, and you said as much too," laughed George.

"Yes, I remember saying that, it just came out."

"So, it's serious between you both?"

"I think so, it's happened so fast and it's as if we have known each other for ages."

"Yes, that's what Frances said too."

"You've talked to her?" questioned Henry, a little surprised.

"Yes, Sunday before church and last night, before you arrived at the pub, we had quite a little chat."

"Oh really, she never said, what did she say?"

"I'll tell you some other time," said George, as other members of the crew began to gather round.

"Hey, there you are Skipper, are you having another beer?" interrupted Charles.

"No, I'll get these, I promised Collins a drink, and then I must go actually, things to do," replied George.

"Where's your lady friend Henry, not here tonight?" asked Mr President.

"Yeah, she's here that often I thought she was part of our crew," said "W".

"Unfortunately, n-not," replied Henry.

"Unfortunately, not what?" taunted 'W'. "Not here, or not crew?"

George bought the crew a round of drinks and once they had concluded their stage performance, he thanked Collins and Mr President for their life-saving action before he departed.

On his way off base, Denis was just coming out of the guardhouse, as George arrived to check out.

"You going to the billet George?" asked Denis.

"Yes, it's been a busy day, one way, or another."

The two pilots walked together briskly along Cheapside, swapping polite pleasantries of conversation, including comments regarding George's near-miss. Their walking pace soon began to slow as their tête-à-tête developed.

"Denis," said George, "I remember you saying you had a déjà vu moment when I flew through the top of the tree the other day. Was that for real?"

"No nothing, just a comment George, I was relating to my crash that's all."

"Yes, I realise that, but it made me think about your experience of leaving your body, and I wondered if that was how it happened."

"I can't say, George, why do you ask?"

"I had a déjà vu moment myself the other day."

"Really, well I guess they do happen to people from time to time."

"Yes, I was standing in front of my crew when suddenly I thought I had been somewhere as if time had stood still for a moment or two. Was that how it was for you, how it happened I mean?" asked George.

"I don't think so, I didn't feel anything, one moment I was flying the plane, the next I was floating about watching it crash. I didn't feel as if I had been anywhere, or that time had stopped if that's what you're asking?"

"I don't know what I'm asking Denis, just trying to understand it really. Why do you think it happened?"

"What, me out of my body or your déjà vu?" Denis questioned.

"You out of your body, and my déjà vu, both, I don't know Denis, I'm curious to understand these things, what do you think?"

"Well it's never happened to me before, and I hope it never happens again as it was quite scary, but, I will say this, I was in a frightening situation and scared about crashing and dying and I just seemed to be on my own, there was just me."

"What do you mean just you, what about your crew?"

"There was just me, my thoughts, my conscious if you like. There was nothing else."

"But you were in a plane with a crew."

"Yes, but in that final moment as I left my body nothing else mattered. I had no feeling, I could see the crew, the plane, the tree, I could even see myself. It felt like there was just me, nothing physical, just me, my spirit if you like, floating in the air, watching."

"That's different to my déjà vu, a lot different. How long did it last Denis?"

"How long does it take when you know you're going to crash," replied Denis. "I don't know, five, ten seconds, perhaps a little longer, I'm not sure."

"That's what I mean Denis, you know you were out of your body for that amount of time, but my déjà vu cannot have lasted for more than a second, two at the most, but to me it seemed like I was somewhere else for ages, at the time it felt like years. That can't be true though, because what would my crew be doing if I was away for all that time. Come to that, what would my crew be thinking if I had disappeared in front of them."

"I think leaving my body was like a safety device. I was so scared and tense it was like a stress release," added Denis.

"Why do you say that?"

"When I was out of my body, I was calm, almost without emotion, I had no concern about what I saw happening, even though it was my crew suffering and dying."

"That's the difference, you watched everything, did you think you were about to die?"

"Yes, I saw everything until I was thrown clear of the plane. I thought I was going to die when I was flying the plane, but I can't remember thinking that when I was out of it. During the time I was floating, I just watched, I can't remember thinking anything."

"I guess you still remember it to Denis if you get the occasional nightmare about it."

"I did but that's not so bad now, like you said George, I had too much time to think."

"Yes, sorry to go on about it, a little insensitive of me really, sorry. I'm just curious about these things that's all."

"It's alright George, talking about it has helped me."

"Well, it has given me food for thought Denis," replied George. "Come on, let's get a march on and get back to our billet and out of this cold, I still have a letter to write."

Back in his room, George sat on the edge of his bed, leaned forward, put his head in his hands, and thought about Jean and Frances, and the letter he said he would write.

He wondered why Jean had not replied to his previous letters, had something changed, and was there something wrong, as Frances had suggested. Why was he feeling so affectionate about Frances when she was clearly enjoying building her relationship with Henry, thought George?

Then his thoughts changed to the conversation he had just had with Denis. Where did he go, did he go anywhere, leaving your body is definitely different to déjà vu.

Confused, George stood up, put on his heavy blue overcoat, and walked out of his room. He marched quickly down Cheapside, past the WAAF's accommodation annexe, past the Temperance Hall canteen, turned right into Kirkgate, and arrived at All-Saints Parish Church.

Bombs Away

George quietly opened the heavy wooden door and stepped inside the old church. It was dark and shadowed, what light remained from the setting sun would soon be gone. George crossed quickly to the nave and sat on the end of the first pew. He looked down the aisle and listened to the silence.

George liked the still and quiet atmosphere; it somehow felt natural to him, the feeling of emptiness that surrounded him. He breathed slow and shallow while regaining his breath, so as not to disturb the quiet harmony of the old sanctuary. Habitually he cupped his hands resting on his lap, right in left, and touching his thumbs together. He sat quietly letting the day drain away and his thoughts wander. With all the hustle and bustle of the formation of 100 Squadron and the training, he had missed his quiet times. George slowly relaxed into the ambience of the Norman church and felt in tune with the spiritual atmosphere that had evolved through the centuries of predecessors' prayer and worship.

He focused his thoughts on his conversation with Denis, and his déjà vu experience and sent them out into the universe.

He sat peacefully still, wondering how he could possibly experience leaving his body, or understand his experience of déjà vu.

What must he do in order to experience these phenomena, what wisdom must he learn? Patience, he must be patient, let the answer come.

Gradually, George became quiet and motionless, and time passed as he relaxed deeper and deeper into the spiritual atmosphere that surrounded him.

Slowly George opened his eyes, the sun had set, and darkness filled the inside of the old Norman church, He remained seated for a moment to regain his composure and gain his bearings. George felt calm and relaxed about himself as he fumbled along, holding onto the back of the pew to find his way out. Against the white of the church wall, he could make out the dark shape of the large entrance door, stepping carefully towards it. Outside the wind was blowing and the air was cold. George shivered against the dark chill as he gradually returned to feeling like himself. He pulled the collar of his heavy blue RAF overcoat up round his ears and quickly made his way downhill towards The King's Head.

George entered the pub and was standing quietly at the bar, just receiving his beer when Henry emerged behind the counter. The two men looked in surprise at each other.

"Didn't expect to see you serving drinks Henry," said George.

"George, this is H-Horace, he's the owner," replied Henry, turning to look at a red-faced, portly man who immediately appeared behind Henry. "Horace, this is George, my Skipper."

The two men reached over the bar and shook hands.

"Just been showing your man the hounds," said Horace.

"Hounds?" questioned George.

"Fox Hounds," replied Horace, "I keep the hounds for the local hunt, out the back yard."

"Didn't know you were a hunting man Henry," said George, his feeling of relaxed harmony slowly disappearing in the moment of discord.

"I'm n-not really, it just came up in conversation with H-Horace, and he kindly took me out to see them. What are you doing here, you said you were letter writing?"

"Me, oh, I just popped out for a nightcap, busy day again tomorrow," replied George.

Horace excused himself from the two airmen and Henry came round to the front of the bar to join George standing by the fire.

"Interesting man, Horace," said Henry. "He's heavily involved with the fox hunt; he stables the horses over the road as well as keeping the hounds."

"It's very English, fox hunting," replied George.

"Yes, part of country life," said Henry, sensing the atmosphere between them was a little strained.

"How did you get to know Horace, I didn't know you came here so regular?"

"Just talking," replied Henry, avoiding part of George's question. "He asked about my accent and the next thing we have things in common to discuss."

"Do you fox hunt, Henry? Oxford sounds like the sort of place fox hunting would take place, it's a very English city too."

"I have friends who participate, other than that I have no connection, though I do like the horses. Cricket is more my thing," answered Henry, trying to soften the atmosphere.

"Ah, Cricket, now there you go again Henry, another very English pastime, and one that I have no understanding of."

"I know what you mean George; it can be confusing, silly mid-on and googlies, that sort of thing."

"There you are Henry, you have lost me already," said George taking a sip of his beer and changing the subject. "How about flying, are you prepared for tomorrow, we have more formation flying, with bomb practice thrown in, I believe?"

"Yes, always ready for that Skipper. I think James is excited about that too."

"Well, I'll leave you to it then Henry, as you say, I have a letter to write."

George finished the last drop of his beer and moved to place his empty glass on the bar.

"You were going to let me know what Frances had said about me," Henry anxiously enquired.

"Some other time Henry, it's nothing to worry about," said George, putting his glass down and heading for the bar door. "See you at o-eight-hundred."

"Yes, o-eight-hundred Skip," replied Henry, thoughtfully.

-

The zero-nine-hundred take-off was incident-free and James was excited as Blue Hornet climbed into the sky above RAF Grimsby. The morning briefing had been straight forward, rendezvous off the coast above Scarborough, fly in formation back to the Humber and bomb to the markers on the coastal flats south of the Humber estuary.

George banked round to three-one-zero degree while climbing to ten thousand feet as he flew inland along the River Humber. Blue Hornet bumped and shook as a strong north-easterly wind and thick patchy cloud continually blew and buffeted the Lancaster westward. George paid attention to direction and kept adjusting course.

"We need to be incident-free this trip Skip, we've lost two lives already and we haven't been to Germany yet," stated Mr President, casually, while looking out of his upper gun turret.

"Or even seen a German, come to that," added Collins, through his intercom.

"Well, you better keep your eyes peeled and make sure we don't see one today either," replied George, busy at the plane's controls.

"How are you feeling James, are you ready with your bombing finger?" said 'W'. "We're doing all this just for you today you know."

"I'm ready, but we're only taking photographs today 'W', there are no bombs on board," replied James.

"Yeah, I know that, but you still need to be on the ball with your aiming," added 'W'. "We don't want a miss."

"No problem with my aiming boys, it feels like we're actually getting ready to do something today, I can't wait," said James.

"All in good time James, all in good time," laughed George, knowing how excited James was about today's exercise.

"Turn coming up S-skip," came Henry's voice through the intercom. "James keep a lookout for the main road going east to Scarborough, we can fly along it Skipper, it will take us to the rendezvous point."

"Standing by," said George.

"Will do Henry," replied James. "How will I know which is the main road?"

"You'll see the city of York with its minster to the left and the main road runs east all the way to Scarborough.

"Got it, Henry, I can see York and the church dead ahead now."

"Just where they're supposed to be at the moment, James."

Blue Hornet began bumping and buffeting as it passed through dense cloud and air turbulence. George gripped the steering column and turned back on course.

"Can we get out of this cloud Skip, it's difficult to see down there?" asked James.

"Just a patch of cloud and turbulence James, it'll pass soon," said George, reassuringly.

"You'll see better if you keep your eyes open James," added 'W'.

"You keep to your radio 'W'. We're busy finding our way right now. There it is, I've got the road Henry, right below us now, almost," replied James, as Blue Hornet emerged from the cloud and he saw the ground, ten thousand feet below suddenly become visible.

"Turn to zero-four-four degrees Skipper, keep the hills to your left and follow the road," smiled Henry, happy with his achievement.

"Turning now," said George.

George turned Blue Hornet to zero-four-four degrees, and head-on into the wind. Charlie adjusted engine revs and propeller pitch to give more thrust, but he could do nothing to smooth out the aircraft's shaking and bouncing as she flew on eastward to the rendezvous point.

"You still with us Collins? You're quiet at the back there," asked George into his intercom.

"I'm here Skip, keeping a watch out. All's quiet, apart from 'W' chatting his head off."

"Yeah, well said Collins," replied James.

"Hey, I was just lending support James," 'W' responded.

"Well, it didn't sound like support," said James.

"Let's have some order guy's," interrupted George.

"Two planes coming in at four-o-clock Skip," announced Mr President, swinging his turret round to point his two 303 Browning machine guns at the incoming aircraft.

"Are they ours, the coast is dead ahead, maybe they're heading to the rendezvous point like us," asked George?

"Another one right behind at six-o-clock Skipper," Collins called out, quickly gripping the handles of his four 303 Browning's in readiness.

"They look like Lancaster's Skip," replied Mr President.

"Yes, they're Lancs, they're ours," confirmed Charlie, turning to look out of the cockpit canopy.

"Take it easy boys, they're ours, I have two more ahead of us," George contributed.

"Copy that Skip, two Lancs dead ahead," added James.

"Keep an eye on them, Mr President, you too Collins," requested George.

"Will do Skip," echoed the two gunners.

"Call 'A' Alfa will you 'W', let our leader know we're here and ask what he wants us to do," George requested.

'W' relayed the order through to 'A' Alpha.

"Take your position, D-Duck, fly course one-two-zero degree," came the squadron leader's radio reply.

George turned D-Duck to one-two-zero and took position within the growing formation of Lancaster Bombers. As Blue

Hornet turned to the new bearing the buffeting and shaking began to smooth out as the wind started to come from behind the aircraft.

"Keep your eyes peeled boys, there are planes all over the place at the moment, and remember, Mr President doesn't want any near-miss incidents today," George announced. "He's worried we're losing too many lives."

"Why does he call us Duck, he knows we are Blue Hornet?" 'W' grumbled in his Welsh accent through the intercom.

"Protocol 'W', protocol, don't you have that in Wales?" replied George.

"Of course we do Skip, but... "

"Then you know why he calls us Duck," confirmed George, interrupting.

"We have Echo alongside again Skip," Charles informed George, looking out of the starboard side of the canopy and waving at the pilot.

"Keep a watch on his movements, Charles, we don't want him getting too close," replied George.

"Hey Henry, how's that ATA Sheila you're seeing, is it serious?" asked Mr President.

"Yeah, are the two of you together?" added 'W'.

"W-why do you want to know?"

"I think she likes my Aussie charm," replied Mr President, teasing Henry.

"W-well you have no chance there Mr President, you and charm don't quite go together, so I have no worries on that score."

"Hey, good reply there Henry, how about Welsh, do you reckon I stand a chance?" enquired 'W'.

Blue Hornet suddenly erupted with cheers and laughter at 'W's comment.

"Leave it alone 'W', she's spoken for," laughed Henry.

"You going to marry her then?" asked Mr President. "I will if you don't."

Henry did not answer he remained silent at his navigation table. 'W' put his head round the side of his wireless units and looked at Henry leaning over his maps and compass.

"He's blushing boys, he's gone bright red," said 'W' through the intercom.

"Woo Henry, are you going to marry her, you are, aren't you, you're going to marry her Henry?" quizzed Mr President.

Blue Hornet's intercom went quiet as the crew held their breath and the roar of four Rolls Royce engines echoed in anticipation through the long empty fuselage.

"Come on Henry spit it out boy-oh, yes, or no?" prompted 'W'.

Henry lifted his head from his map table and smiled at 'W'. "Maybe," he said quietly into his intercom.

George felt his heart miss a beat and Blue Hornet's fuselage filled with jeering and cheering. "Come on everyone, let's not get carried away here, let's have a bit of order, we have a job to do," he said speaking loudly into the intercom. "You can quiz Henry all you like when our job is done."

"This is leader, this is leader," said the radio, bringing silence and order to the crew. "New course one-eight-zero degree in five minutes. Repeat, one-eight-zero degree in five minutes. Peel off single file to targets at one-minute intervals."

"Here we go Skip," said James excitedly.

"Just be patient James, all in good time," George replied.

"Yeah, we don't want you recording a miss James," added 'W'.

George waited five minutes and turned to one-eight-zero degree; Blue Hornet was fourth in line for the bombing run. The north-easterly wind was still blowing strongly and the big Lancaster Bomber was slowly drifting towards Yorkshire's coastline. George corrected his flightpath a couple of degrees to compensate for the wind and flew a perfect one-eighty degree. Charles trimmed the propellers, reducing speed to two hundred and fifty miles per hour in order to maintain the distance between the leading bombers.

Blue Hornet's crew became quiet, concentrating, anticipating.

"Crickey Skipper, have you slowed down," said James anxiously, peering through his bombing sights.

"Patience James, patience, just keeping distance."

Slowly the Humber estuary came into view. Spurn Point Lighthouse reached out from the river's northern coastline, perched on the end of a curving sandbank like the nail of a single claw scratching at the shipping in the estuary. Bull Sand Fort, situated in the Yorkshire water of the estuary, and Haile Sand Fort just off the Lincolnshire shoreline, nestled in the brown murky water of the River Humber, their six-inch cannons and submarine netting protecting the shipping routes and entry to the ports of Hull and Grimsby situated further along the river.

The red flare bombing targets became visible, their swirling smoke drifting over the estuaries southern sand flats of Donna Nook, stretching southward along the east coast of Lincolnshire.

"In you go D-Duck, your turn," said the squadron leader's voice on the radio.

George flew Blue Hornet directly towards the red smoking flares. James lay stretched out in the bomb aimer's position below George's seat in the nose of aircraft. He had a clear view of the ground far below, the red smoke from the triangle of flares drifting westward over the sand dunes that stretched south along the coastline.

"Over to you James, it's all down to you now, you're in control," said George in a calm voice, but inwardly feeling quite nervous in the tense and quiet atmosphere that had overcome his crew.

"About time, thank you Skip, go steady at that," began James peering through his bombsights. "Go left a bit Skip we're drifting with the wind."

"Just be patient James, it will come," said George as he steered left and tried to hold a smooth steady course for James.

"Hold it Skip hold it... nearly there... left a bit more, nearly, nearly... "

Blue Hornet was flying smoothly in the tailwind at ten thousand feet above the triangle of red flair target. The Humber estuary had passed and the red wispy target appeared to approach slowly, despite flying at two hundred and fifty miles per hour.

"Hold it there, Skip... hold it, hold it..."

James pressed the release button. "Bombs gone Skip, bombs away..." said James excitedly, with a big grin on his face.

George continued to fly steady and straight to ensure the photograph was taken correctly, as the rest of the crew cheered and congratulated James.

"That better be a good hit James," said 'W'.

"Right on the button," replied James, smiling to himself.

"I'll get you a drink if it is," answered 'W'.

"I'm going to check the photo James and if it's a miss the drinks are on you," added Mr President.

"It's a hit boys, don't worry about that. I'll have a pint please 'W'," replied James, confidently laughing into his intercom.

George banked Blue Hornet to starboard and out of the bombing flight path.

"Let's go home Henry," said George. "We'll find out the results of James' bomb aiming and who is buying the beer in debriefing tomorrow."

"Steer two-one-zero-degree Skip," instructed Henry.

'W' passed James his pint of beer. "You deserve that one James, that was almost a perfect hit," said 'W'.

"And the Skipper too," replied James. "He did the flying."

"To James and the Skipper on a great achievement," said Charles, holding up his pint of warm ale.

"To James and Skip," chorused Blue Hornet's crew.

"Yes, well done James, Jerry will have something to worry about if you perform like that when we start sorties," George praised.

"I told you, I'm here to win," replied James, holding his pint of beer above his head in response to the applause and cheering from his crewmates.

The crew settled down after praising James and began idly chatting amongst themselves. George and Henry sat down at a table in the centre of the crew mess.

"So, what's all this about marrying Frances?" quizzed George. "I listened to the crew rib you about it while flying back yesterday."

"Yes, encouraging b-bunch aren't they, b-but to me it seems like the right thing to do," replied Henry.

"A bit quick, don't you think? I mean you've only seen her three times."

"Sometimes that's enough to know don't you think?"

"Well, I guess..."

"I knew the first time I saw her if you want the truth."

"Yes, that was quite a moment Henry."

"There you are then, you n-noticed something special too."

"She's a striking girl Henry, I'll give her that and to be honest, I was quite attracted to her myself."

"So that was why you rushed her off in the car."

"No not really, never thought about it, to be honest, just sorting business, and I'm engaged anyway."

"You're engaged, well you're a dark horse, I n-never knew that Skipper."

"No, I've not made it public, I'm not sure about it, to be honest, that's what my letter was about."

"About what?"

"About being engaged, my letter was to Jean my fiancé. She hasn't written for some time now."

"Why, is there something wrong?"

"I'm not sure, that's why I have written, it's a long story Henry, I'll fill you in when I know what to tell you. In the meantime, I'd appreciate it if you keep it under your hat."

"My lips are s-sealed Skipper."

"So does Frances know anything about your intentions to marry her?"

"I don't think so, I've not said anything to her. I only decided yesterday when Mr President and 'W' quizzed me about her. I said maybe to shut them up, then when I thought about it, I liked the idea. We both feel the same way, and it's like we just know each other, so I'm going to ask her the next time I see her."

"Well I wish you luck Henry, it seems to be fashionable to marry quickly under such difficult circumstances. Jean thinks we should wait until the war has ended, just in case. I'm not sure which way is right, to be honest."

"I think it's what you both want, and I've not asked Frances yet so I don't know what she will say. What did she say to you, has she said anything about me?"

"No, not really, she has just said similar things to you, about knowing one another and that she wants to keep seeing you."

"Do you think she will s-say yes?" asked Henry.

"You better ask her that one, old boy," replied George.

A Love Letter

Formation flying and bombing practice continued into mid-February before Frances returned with one of the last remaining Lancaster's for delivery to 100 Squadron. RAF Grimsby looked different with snow covering the airfield.

The runways and taxi track stood out black and bold against the white of the countryside and Waltham airbase was on high alert as a consequence. Jerry had raided the city of Hull a couple of times, disposing the last of their payloads over Grimsby as they flew back to Germany.

George headed for The King's Head after his quiet time in All Saints Church. The pub was sparsely populated and George sat by the fire with his glass of beer, silently contemplating the content of the letter he had written for Jean. He glanced up at the blackout curtain as it swished open and his heart skipped a beat as Frances walked into the bar. Excitedly he stood up and waved at Frances, catching her attention as she paused to look round the room for a friendly face.

"Oh, I'm pleased you are here," greeted Frances. "I didn't much fancy sitting on my own."

"Well, hello again, this is a surprise," said George, enthusiastically speaking at the same time, his sombre contemplative thoughts quickly vanishing.

George welcomed Frances with a hug and a kiss on her cheek.

"You have just made my day," added George. "Can I get you something to drink?"

"Made your day, why's that?"

"Oh, no reason, just seeing you is enough."

"That's nice of you to say, George, can I have a Martini please?"

"Coming up," replied George with a smile.

Frances sat down at the table and made herself comfortable as George went to the bar for her drink.

"One Martini," said George, placing the drink on the table and sitting on the chair next to Frances.

"Thank you, George," replied Frances, taking an eager sip of her drink.

"So what brings you here, as if I cannot guess, when did you arrive?"

"Mid-afternoon, I've been waiting in the annexe hoping you would all be in here this evening."

"Well, I had no idea you would be here, and I'm not sure where Henry is. He could be in the crew's mess with the rest of the crew, though I'm sure you're not here to see them."

"Oh, no not especially," sighed Frances, a disappointing expression appearing on her face.

"However, Henry is friendly with the owner of the pub, so he could pop in here any moment," said George, giving some hopeful encouragement to Frances.

"Well, at least you are here," replied Frances.

Henry's intention of proposal quickly passed through George's mind.

"You quite like Henry, don't you?" said George, smiling at Frances's comment.

"Yes, you know I do, why do you ask, has he said something?"

"No, nothing, I just remember the two of you meeting under the plane and how quick you have got together that's all."

"It just seems so natural George; I've never met anyone like him before."

"Love at first sight," stated George.

"Yes, it was, now I come to think about it," said Frances. "What about you George, have you written Jean her letter?" Frances added, shifting the focus of attention.

"Yes, though I haven't posted it yet," answered George, thoughtfully.

"Why not?" questioned Frances, a surprised inquisitive look appearing on her face.

"No reason. I haven't got round to it I guess."

"Is there a problem George, you're looking worried?"

"If I post it, I'm not sure I want to know her answer," said George, looking affectionately into Frances's eyes.

"Why, why not, what are you worried about George, at least you will know, one way or another if she still loves you?"

"What if I don't get the answer I want?"

"Do you think there's a problem with Jean?"

"I don't know, I don't think so."

"If you send her your letter you will know," said Frances, reassuringly.

"I'm not sure I have asked or said the right things. It reads like I'm accusing her," replied George anxiously.

"Well re-write it, George. Don't ask her anything, just send her a love letter, let her know how you feel, how you cannot wait to see her again, her reply will tell you everything," Frances responded, affectionately placing her hand on George's forearm to comfort him.

"That's the bit I'm not looking forward to," replied George. "I watch you and Henry and..."

"... And what?" asked Frances, interrupting George's pause.

"It's just... that you said you would write to Henry if you couldn't see him, well I've done that and only received one reply. You even swapped plane deliveries to come here to see him."

"Hmm, I see what you mean when you say it like that," Frances sympathised.

"Maybe Jean is right and we should wait until after the war has ended, just in case," said George.

"You can't leave it like that George," answered Frances.

"Why not?"

"Because you can't, if you still love her send her a love letter George. Waiting for the end of the war might be too late."

George sat quietly for a moment, drinking his beer. "Alright, I'll write another letter," said George eventually.

"A love letter," replied Frances, looking at George.

"Yes, a love letter," smiled George, nervously fiddling with his fingers.

"And post it this time, this could be the last time I am here for a while, nearly all the planes have been delivered so promise me you'll post it."

"Really?" said George, distracted by Frances's alarming comment. "You've been here so regular I've got used to you being here. I forgot about how many planes are here now,"

George, continued, quietly and thoughtfully. "I'm going to miss your visits."

"George, don't avoid my request, promise me you will post the letter," repeated Frances.

"Yes I promise," replied George, taking a long look at Frances and smiling. "Look, if this is your last visit, I'm sure you must want to see Henry, so I'll nip off and find him, let him know you're here."

"Will you, oh that's so kind of you," said Frances, excitedly.

"Wait here, I'll be back to keep you company if I don't find Henry."

"Thank you, George," replied Frances, standing up to hug and kiss George on the cheek. "I'll miss you if I don't see you again."

"And I'll miss you too," said George, holding onto Frances' warm embrace before setting off to find Henry.

Heavenly Canopy

It was dark and stars filled the heavenly canopy as George steered Blue Hornet round the taxi track and aligned her for take-off along runway 18/36. His heart was beating faster than normal for his first take-off into the night sky. Everything around him appeared different and George reached out to touch each control and instrument to reassure and familiarise himself with their positions within the darkness that surrounded him.

"Everything alright Skip?" said Charles, through the blackness of the cockpit.

"Just checking," replied George, his face dimly lit by the lights emanating from the array of instruments laid out before him. "Funny how everything looks different."

"I think what lies ahead of us, will soon be the norm Skip," replied Charles.

"You may be right about that Charles, but it's of no help for tonight," said George, waiting patiently for control tower instructions and nervously twiddling his fingers. "This one is for the experience of what is to follow."

Control tower take off instructions resounded through Blue Hornet's radio.

"Here we go Charley, my boy," said George as he steadily pulled back on the throttle levers.

Blue Hornet's four Merlin engines roared into life, propelling the invisibly camouflaged Lancaster down Waltham's main runway before disappearing into the night sky.

"Keep your eyes peeled everyone, there's just Echo and Bravo flying with us tonight so let's hope they keep their distance. Good luck everyone," said George through the intercom as Blue Hornet climbed into the darkness.

The crew remained in a sombre mood as Grimsby appeared below the climbing Lancaster, its black roads running between white snow-covered rooftops that made the town clearly visible from the air. A sharp wedge of darkness marked the River Humber cutting into the dapple patterned landscape. Below the white covered fields reflected their snowy brightness, that improved visibility for a first-time night flight while above was a canopy of darkness, speckled by the twinkle of a million stars.

"Steer three-four-zero degree Skip, altitude ten thousand feet," Henry instructed through the intercom.

"Three-four-zero coming up," replied George.

"Can anyone see anything?" asked Mr President from his gun turret on top of the plane's fuselage.

"Yes, lots of white fields and a black sky," replied James.

"Same here," added Collins, through the intercom.

"It's as black as night up here," said Mr President.

"That's because it is night-time," quipped 'W'.

"I'm just saying, that's all," responded Mr President.

"It's damned cold, I know that," said Collins. "Can we go any faster Skip, get me back to my warm bed?"

"All in good time, all in good time," repeated George, peering through the cockpit windscreen. "Can anyone see Echo or Bravo?"

No one replied and Blue Hornet continued on course three-four-zero.

"How do you see anything anyway?" asked Collins, eventually breaking the silence. "Like Mr President said, it's as black as night out there."

"Just look for exhaust sparks or flashes of cockpit and canopy reflections," Charles answered.

"Is that all?" queried Collins.

"That's all I'm afraid unless you get a clear view of something in the light of the moon," replied Charles. "We're camouflaged not to be seen remember, we don't want Jerry spotting us."

George was concentrating, staring through the large cockpit windscreen into the black darkness that surrounded the Lancaster Bomber. His permanent, unwavering attention drawn towards the mesmerising darkness of the night sky laid out before him.

-

For a split moment, time slowed down, and all around him occurred in slow motion. His conscious flooded through his thoughts and heightened his senses. He listened to the drawn muffled chatter of his crew. He felt like he was on autopilot as his thoughts raced and he watched the activities unfolding before him. In his mind's eye, he could see Bravo flying far below Blue Hornet, where he knew it should be.

-

"Turn to course one-one-zero Skipper," instructed Henry.

"Roger that," replied George.

"There's a Lancaster in front of us Skipper, about five hundred feet below, clear as daylight against the snow, going the same way as we are Skip," James reported from his front gunner position located under George's pilot seat.

"Yes I know," replied George, turning to coarse one-one-zero. "Keep an eye on him, James, let me know when he turns."

"Will do Skip."

George suddenly felt elated about what had just occurred, he felt as if something had just confirmed that what was happening around him was meant to happen as if he had passed through some sort of time loop of consciousness, where all things are known.

Slowly the snow-white land of England's east coast passed under the wide wingspan of the enormous Lancaster and only darkness lay ahead. The lone bomber, still clearly visible five hundred feet below Blue Hornet suddenly disappeared as it crossed the line between land and sea. Gradually the night closed in around George and his crew as the snow-covered land began to fall away behind Blue Hornet.

"Holy smoke Skip, that Lanc just disappeared," exclaimed James.

"Yes, I saw it, keep looking for it James, we'll be landing soon and I don't want it surprising us," George requested.

"Will do Skip."

"Collins, keep a lookout for the other Lanc, it must be around somewhere, you too Mr President."

"Copy that Skipper," replied Collins.

The crew of Blue Hornet fell silent as the plane flew onward into the dense darkness of the night. It was difficult to tell where the dark sea ended and the black sky started. George continued to stare into the night, occasionally looking at, and relying on his array of instruments and Henry's instructions to guide him.

"Can you see anything Charles?" asked George, without turning his head to look; his focus remaining staring into the night sky spread out before him.

"Not a thing Skip," replied Charles, gawking out of the cockpit canopy. "I think I can see the coastline out the starboard side Skip, but I'm not sure. The covering of snow makes it a little brighter that's all."

"You can see the odd star if you look up," said George. "Where are we Henry, what's our position?"

"Almost no w-wind tonight Skip, so no problem w-with course. We are about twenty miles off the coast and five miles north of the Humber," informed Henry. "Stay on this course for another fifteen minutes Skip."

"You gunners stay alert now, we're coming up to the Humber, Jerry could be about, they've had a couple of raids at Hull just recently so stay focused," said George into the intercom.

"There's no radio traffic," 'W' reported. "I don't think Jerry is about Skip."

"Thank you 'W', just stay alert boys," repeated George.

Blue Hornet remained on course for another fifteen minutes before George turned her to starboard and headed towards the snowy Lincolnshire coast, just north of The Wash. As the Lanc flew over the coastline, the reflection of the snow-covered fields illuminated the cockpit and gun turret canopies, raising spirits and stimulating the crew into conversation.

"Are we heading home yet Henry?" asked Collins from the tail end of the plane's fuselage.

"S-shortly, one more t-turn and we're homeward bound," replied Henry into the intercom.

"Hey Henry, I hear your girl was here again, did you ask her this time?" enquired Mr President.

"Ask her what?"

"You know what, don't give me that Henry."

"Come on boy-oh, we're all dying to know now," added 'W'.

Henry remained silent concentrating on his navigation duties.

"Did she turn you down Henry?" quizzed Mr President. "Have I still got a chance?"

"Steer zero-one-zero Skip, let's go home," said Henry into the intercom.

"Come on Henry, did you ask her or not, me and 'W' have got a few beers wagered on her reply," prompted Mr President.

"I asked her," responded Henry.

"Come on boys, we're not home yet, let's stay vigilant," interrupted George. "Landing is ten minutes away, we don't want any mishaps at this stage, do we, Mr President."

"No Skip."

George steered the new course, zero-one-zero, and headed towards Waltham. He remembered his tree incident during landing training and remained flying high as the landing lights of runway 18/36 came into view. Visibility suddenly improved as the Lancaster Bomber approached the snow-free runway and familiarity of repeated landings guided George to a perfect touch down. As usual, the crew cheered and complimented their Skipper as they taxied round to Blue Hornet's dispersal pan and her engines were cut.

"So, what did she say Henry?" shouted Mr President as he climbed out from his gun turret.

"The drinks are on me boys," replied Henry, with a big smile on his face.

"She said yes," concluded 'W', looking round his radio set at Henry. "I'm right, right?"

"Yes, you're right 'W', I'm engaged to be married everyone," said Henry, loudly, while shaking 'W's hand.

"I thought I was in with a chance there Henry," said Mr President, standing at the exit ladder.

"N-not a chance mate," Henry replied, climbing out of the plane's fuselage and into the back of the Erk's waiting Crossley truck.

Henry became swamped by compliments and backslapping from each member of the joyous crew as they climbed into the rear of the waiting maintenance vehicle.

As the RAF blue Crossley transported Blue Hornet's jovial crew to the locker and drying room two Lancaster Bombers landed along Waltham's runway 18/36, one behind the other.

"There go Echo and Bravo Skipper," said James.

"Yes, thank you for your keen observation James," replied George.

"Any time Skip."

Training at RAF Grimsby became more intense with everything taking part during daylight and the hours of darkness to simulate real operational activities. Landing, take-off, and formation flying became routine night-time activities, while gunning and navigation training were repeatedly practised throughout the day. Bombing practise became a regular night-time activity that built up to a full-scale rehearsal of a real operation.

Waltham's RAF airbase was beginning to look and sound like an operations station. One last plane was required for delivery in order to complete 100 Squadron's full complement of sixteen aircraft, with two additional planes in reserves.

It was mid-morning on the 11 February 1943 that George found himself passing by the watch office when his attention was suddenly drawn towards a Lancaster Bomber approaching runway 18/36. He realised this was the squadron's last plane for delivery and quickly found his way to the balcony of the control tower to watch it arrive. Mingling amongst the other officers George secretly hoped it would be Frances at the plane's controls. He knew Henry was busy in a training class, unable to greet Frances on her arrival; giving George a chance to meet her and spend some time with her.

As the plane touched down George made his way to the admin office to find out who had been assigned to collect the arriving pilot from the dispersal pan. Armed with the information George made his way out to find the waiting vehicle, a blue Standard 10 staff car. The driver was startled as George climbed in alongside him.

"It's alright, it's a surprise, the pilot is a friend of mine," George informed the driver.

"Yes Sir," replied the driver, looking at George and shrugging his shoulders as he put the car in motion.

The blue staff car set off, away from the flat-roofed admin office, out of the station's busy technical area and along the deserted taxi track that ran around the perimeter of the airfield. They passed by the majestic spectacle of 100 Squadron's full complement of Lancaster Bombers at close hand before arriving at the designated dispersal pan; just as the last arriving Lancaster's propellers stopped revolving.

George alighted from the blue Standard 10 and quickly made his way to the entrance hatch underneath the plane's fuselage. He became a little anxious as he waited patiently for the hatch to open and the ladder to drop down.

"What if it is not Frances?" George suddenly thought.

He listened to the metallic sounds of latches sliding and clicking inside the aircraft until the hatch door eventually dropped open, followed by a yellow metal ladder dropping to the ground. A short pause followed before the uniform of a flying suite began descending the ladder.

"Frances," exclaimed George, loudly and anxiously the very moment he recognised the attractive pilot.

"Oh... George you startled me," said Frances, surprised by George's relieved greeting. "What are you doing here?"

Frances leaned back into the fuselage and pulled her kit bag from inside.

"Here, catch, you can be useful now you're here," laughed Frances.

George took her kit bag and guided her to the waiting staff car as the maintenance Erk's began to swarm over the gleaming new bomber.

"Admin please driver," requested George as he settled beside Frances in the rear of the blue Standard 10.

"How did you know it was me?" asked Frances, relaxing on the back seat.

"I didn't," confessed George. "I just took the chance."

"What if it was someone else delivering the plane?" laughed Frances.

"But it wasn't," smiled George.

"Well, it was a nice thought anyway, thank you. How is everyone?"

"Busy, everyone is fine but busy," replied George. "How long are you here this time?"

"The usual, I catch the early morning train back."

"Well, things are a little different here. Flying and training is intensifying; building up to real operations, you know the sort of thing, and we're flying tonight, so not much time to see Henry I'm afraid."

"Where is Henry?" asked Frances, suddenly feeling dejected.

"He's in the navigation room preparing tonight's flight plan."

"I will have time to see him?" asked Frances, feeling a little anxious.

"Yes, he'll be out for lunch," confirmed George. "And I think you had better join us, see the boys one more time. The number of times you have been here they regard you as one of the crew you know."

"Then I had better not disappoint them," replied Frances, with a smile.

The blue staff car proceeded round the taxi track, delivering Frances to the square block of dark blue admin office on the edge of the airfield's technical area.

"Can you wait five minutes driver, I'd like to deliver the pilot officer to her quarters along Cheapside, once she has finished here?" requested George.

"That was part of my order to do so Sir," replied the driver.

"Well, there we are, all sorted," said George, with a happy smile.

Frances disappeared into the admin office to complete the paperwork for the plane she had just delivered and was soon getting back into the waiting staff car.

"All done," Frances remarked, as she leaned back, relaxing into her seat.

"Drive on please driver," George jovially requested. "The WAAF's annexe along Cheapside please."

The driver smiled as he looked at his two happy passengers in his rear-view mirror before driving off.

"Can I persuade you to take us into the village after we have dropped off the officer's kit bag?" George requested. "It's two minutes up the road, hardly any extra time at all."

"I should really report back Sir," replied the driver.

"I'll be so quick," Frances persuasively added, not knowing why George wanted to go to the village.

"If you're quick," the driver replied, with an uneasy feeling.

"Thank you, you're an angel," said Frances, smiling into the driver's rear-view mirror.

The driver stopped the car at the WAAF's annexe before driving on and arriving at the corner of Kirkgate outside All Saints Church.

"Thank you, driver," said George, as he alighted the blue Standard 10.

"Yes, thank you," added Frances, getting out of the car and wondering why she was standing outside the village church. "What are we doing here?"

"I don't know, I want to talk and I couldn't think of where to go where we wouldn't be interrupted. Sorry, the church jumped into my head on the way," said George, walking along the pathway towards the church door.

"Well, it's a strange place to bring me."

"Maybe, but not for me, I come here quite regularly, actually," replied George, pushing open the large wooden door and stepping inside the quiet ambience of the church.

"Oh, it's very still and quiet," Frances commented. "I've never been in an empty church before."

"I like to come here, to sit and contemplate, think about things, have some time to myself and recharge my batteries," said George, quietly.

"Why, are you religious?"

"No not really, I don't agree with lots of things about the church, but I like to be inside them, it helps me think. This church is the oldest one I've been in; they don't have places as old as this in Canada."

"So, what do you want to talk to me about?"

"Nothing special, I just felt like I should talk with you that's all, and because it could be your last visit, but let me begin by offering my congratulations on your engagement."

"Oh, thank you, George."

"I hope you'll be very happy," said George leaning forward to kiss Frances on her cheek.

"I hope so too, thank you. I guess Henry told you. Do all the crew know?" replied Frances, accepting George's kiss, though not responding similarly.

"Yes, Henry told us all together at the end of one of our training flights. He had no option really; the boys kept on ribbing him until he gave in."

"That sounds like Henry," said Frances. "Keeping it to himself."

"You don't sound too pleased about something," quizzed George. "I thought the two of you were over the moon, happily in love, like you've known each other for years."

"I am, and we are, but there's something I'm just not sure about," Frances replied thoughtfully.

"Like what," asked George.

"This is awkward, I wasn't expecting this. George, we haven't known each other for too long but I trust you and I know I can talk with you, but you mustn't say anything about this to anyone, especially Henry, do you promise."

"I knew there was something we needed to talk about, and yes, I promise, you know I won't say anything to anyone, not even Henry," replied George.

"George," began Frances. "When Henry asked me to marry him, I was over the moon, filled with excitement. We sat together in The King's Head dreaming about what we would do after the war. Well, about five minutes after I said yes, he excused himself and I thought he was going to the toilet, but he disappeared behind the bar, and instantly I got a strange niggling feeling. When he returned he was all apologetic but wouldn't tell me what it was about, he just said it was a bit of business."

"He surprised me the other day too. I went in The King's Head for a quick drink and he appeared from behind the bar counter, talking about fox hunting with the landlord. The thing that struck me was he seemed annoyed that I discovered him behind the bar,"

"I hate it when someone is secretive," said Frances, angrily.

"Wow, Frances stop, please don't use that word," interrupted George.

"What word?" questioned Frances.

"The 'h' word you just used, it's not a nice word, I don't like it."

"Why, what's wrong with it, it expresses my feelings."

"It carries nasty overtones, it's like a witches curse," explained George.

"Well, maybe that is how I feel about secrets."

"You could say you don't like secrets instead, that's much nicer."

"But that doesn't express how strongly I feel about him being secretive, and witches died out years ago George," laughed Frances

"Is that what your niggling feeling is about, Henry having secrets?"

"No, having secrets is annoying and I don't like it," said Frances, teasingly. "I'm not sure what the niggling feeling is, it's just there, and it hasn't gone away."

"Hmm, if you don't know yourself what your niggling doubt is, then I'm not sure how I can help you," George slowly replied.

"It's not a doubt George, it's a feeling, it's like I think I know something, but I don't know what it is, it feels physical if you can understand what I'm trying to say," corrected Frances.

"Are you sure about wanting to get married?" George responded.

"Yes, we are deeply in love with each other and can't wait to get married."

"Well, I hope you both will be very happy, and maybe your niggling doubt, sorry, feeling, is nothing to worry about. Perhaps it's a nervous feeling about getting married that will go away when you're more accustomed to being engaged," concluded George.

"Maybe you're right, though it's strange to have this silly feeling when everything else seems so right, perhaps I should ask a witch about it," remarked Frances. "Enough about me, I wasn't expecting that but I do feel better about it now, thank you for listening. So what about you George, have you written your love letter to Jean?"

"Yes, it just needs posting," replied George. "I'm happy about this letter, you were right, writing a love letter has taken away the accusation that the first letter contained, and I don't feel so worried about sending it this time."

"Well, I hope you do post it, for your sake and Jeans. You can't leave it like it is."

"No, I know, and I'm going to post it this time, promise," George confirmed.

"I'm sure she will reply, George."

"That's what I'm worried about, it's just that..."

"I know why you're stalling George," interrupted Frances. "Why you put yourself out for me and get me to yourself like we are now. I'm flattered, and I cherish our friendship George, but I love Henry and I'm going to marry him."

"Yes, I know and I'm happy for you, really," said George, with a tight-lipped smile, hoping that it hid his feelings. "You're right, it's wrong of me to be like this, I just... well you know what I just. Come on, let me get you back to the NAAFI, we can have something to eat and find Henry for you, he should just about be finished with his training session."

"I'm not going to say goodbye George, I don't want this to be the end, I may have delivered the last plane but I'll come back, I'm determined about that,"

"No, I don't want to say goodbye either, that sounds too final. I'm sure there will be replacements for you to deliver."

George politely concluded his private conversation and escorted Frances back to the NAAFI where they found Henry and the rest of the crew enjoying lunch.

Frances approached Henry from behind and placed her hands over his eyes as the crew quickly recognised who she was and cheered her on. More joyful laughter and cheering erupted as Henry removed her hands then stood and warmly embraced Frances as he discovered whom it was playing tricks.

Blue Hornet's crew continued their banter throughout lunch; each one offering their congratulations and each with hugs and kisses for Frances. NAAFI personnel joined in with greetings and compliments and soon the whole canteen joined in as they learned of the celebration.

Slowly the NAAFI began to empty as people left to return to their duties and Blue Hornet's crew suddenly realised they were saying goodbye to Frances as they departed to resume preparations for the night ahead.

"I'll see you next time then," said George, embracing Frances while kissing her on her cheek. "Don't leave it too long."

"I won't, and thank you, for everything," Frances replied.

"Are you all prepared for tonight Henry?" George asked.

"Yes why?"

"Go spend some time with your fiancé while you can," said George. "I'll cover for you and see you in the briefing room in time for tonight."

"Thank you Skip."

"Thank you, George," said Frances, with a warm smile as she clasped hands with Henry and disappeared out of the NAAFI.

Jerry

The night-time training flight concluded without incident and the next few weeks training for all Lancaster crews at RAF Grimsby became more and more intense, culminating with their first offensive operation taking place on the 4th March 1943.

Eight Lancaster Bombers were selected to drop mines at various locations along the French coast, of which, and unfortunately, two aircraft had not returned. The following day 100 Squadron took part in their first operation over Germany. Their target was the steel plants around the industrial city of Essen in the Ruhr Valley, an area known to Lancaster Bomber crews as 'Happy Valley'.

The next morning was one of sombre mood as news spread around Waltham airfield that two aircraft had not yet returned from the previous night's operation along the French coast, and it came as a stark realisation of what was at stake for the crews preparing for the coming night's operation.

The airfield was busy with maintenance Erk's working on every aircraft, fuel trucks and generator equipment scattered around the Lancaster's dispersal pad, blue tractors pulling snaking trains of bomb trollies loaded with each bomber's payload, engine test runs starting and stopping and belching out plumes of thick black and white smoke all added to the preparation activity.

Henry was in the Navigation Room plotting the course for the night's operation. Charles was mingling amongst the maintenance Erk's around Blue Hornet, making routine pre-flight checks. James, 'W', Collins, and Mr President were in the NAAFI mixing with other crews sitting around, waiting. George was in the Intelligence Office talking of the pending operation with other pilot officers. He looked at the day's schedule pined on the notice board.

13:45 Hrs – Navigator & Bomb Aimer Briefing

14:45 Hrs – Operation Main Briefing

15:45 Hrs – Transport to Communal Site

16:00 Hrs – Operational Tea

16:30 Hrs – Transport to Technical Site

17:15 Hrs – Transport to Aircraft

George made his way to the NAAFI to find his crew and grabbed a mug of tea before sitting at the table.

"Any news?" asked Collins.

"No nothing," George replied.

"No news is good news," 'W' commented.

"Where's Charles?" asked George, ignoring 'W's comment.

"He's out on Blue Hornet, he'll be here soon, it's almost lunch," replied James. "He came out with the three of us while we checked our guns."

"That plane's going to be heavy Skip, the amount of stuff being loaded, I don't know where they're putting it all?" said Mr President.

"I think you're right about that Mr President, what about Henry?" replied George.

"He's plotting our course Skip, well I think that's what he said he was going to do," answered 'W'.

"He's what? We don't know where we're going yet," laughed George.

"You know Henry Skip, always trying to be one step ahead," said Mr President.

"He's love-struck Skip," added 'W'.

"Well, he better get un-love struck when there's work to be done," George commented. "Ah, there you are Charles, everything alright?"

"She's already and waiting Skip," replied Charles as he joined the crew. "Just the bombs to be loaded and she's ready to go."

"Well, that's about it, boys, let's have lunch and we'll regroup at the briefing," George suggested.

George ate quickly and excused himself from the table. He returned to his room along Cheapside and lay quietly on his bed, thinking and talking to himself of what was to come. Am I ready, this is for real this time, there's no room for any mistakes, Jerry would be there, waiting, ready and prepared. All during training Jerry has been fighting for real, they'll know what they're doing.

"Come on, we can do this, we're ready, James is more than ready," smiled George. "He'd go on his own. The others are ready too, they're good lads."

George heard Denis moving about across the corridor. He jumped up off his bed and knocked on Denis's door.

"How are things, Denis?" George said loudly. "Are you ready?"

"Yes, come on in George," Denis replied as he opened his door.

Denis was smartly dressed in his RAF uniform, collar fastened and tie tied.

"Well, you look smart, are you going somewhere?" said George, looking surprised as he stepped into the room.

"Just popping over to see Jerry, old boy. Need to look your best when you're about to teach someone a lesson," laughed Denis.

"Yes, yes, I couldn't agree more, give him a good thrashing I say, old chap," replied George, joining in with the charade.

"What do you think George, are you ready?"

"As ready as I can be, I think. I was just laying on my bed, but it gets you thinking too much. I was pleased when I heard you distract me."

"This is your first, right."

"Second actually, first Lancaster."

"Oh yes, I remember you saying so," smiled Denis.

"Any tips, recommendations?" asked George.

"Just do what you think George, there is no formula, every sortie is different. Remember your training and you're just about there," replied Denis.

"So, what's with your uniform?" asked George, curiously.

"It's my way to prepare myself, George. To let you into a secret, I act the whole thing. From this moment on and until I return, it's an act, George. I don't think I would get through it all otherwise."

"I see what you mean old chap, it's rather like one being on stage," spoke George, in his best theatrical manner.

"Rather old boy, just follow the script," laughed Denis. "Gosh, I think you've got it old chap."

"Give me a shout when you head for the briefing and I'll walk with you," George requested, grinning to himself while returning to his room.

Time passed quickly as George pottered about in his room. He flitted from one pointless task to another to occupy his time before picking up his love letter for Jean. He looked at it thoughtfully, remembering his promise to post it while tapping it on his fingers. A few seconds passed by as he tapped the envelope on his fingertips.

Denis knocked on his door.

"You ready George?"

"Yes coming," replied George, putting the letter back in the cabinet draw.

George sat alongside Denis during the operations main briefing, listening intently to the station's wing commander and his squadron leader as they divulged the operation's information and detail. Their target was the city of Essen and Lancaster's from two other squadrons would be joining 100 Squadron, making forty aircraft in total taking part in the night's operation.

Transport to the NAAFI at the communal site and during tea was buzzing with chatter, all in reference to the target and the squadron's first visit to Happy Valley. Similarly, the transport back to the technical site and the crew lockers was filled with talk about the night ahead as crews changed into their flying suites.

"Hey Charley, don't forget the pigeon," commented 'W'.

"What pigeon?" replied Charles.

"You know the one that has to come with us. You said you would look after it, remember?" said 'W'.

"Yeah, I remember that, Charley. 'W' said he doesn't like pigeons and you said..."

"I know what I said," replied Charles, interrupting Henry.

"I don't see no pigeon," said 'W'.

"That's done by the maintenance Erk's, stupid," laughed Charles. "You don't think we have to run around looking for a bloody pigeon do you."

"Yeah, there you go stupid, the Erk's look after the pigeons," chorused Mr President.

"Hey, less of the stupid, you didn't know that Mr. President," said 'W', defending himself.

"Come on boys, transport in five m-minutes," called Henry. "Remember to leave all personal possessions in your locker."

"Yes Sir, lover boy," quipped Mr President.

"Alright, we've had some fun, let's get going boys," instructed George.

-

The mood of the crew changed as they transferred through the evening darkness along the taxi track to Blue Hornet waiting on her dispersal pan. Alighting the blue Crossley truck, they stood around in quiet thought, grouped together in front of their Lancaster Bomber in almost silence, looking at each other, looking up at the plane's newly painted skull and crossbones' emblem with its blue hornet flying out of one eye socket and the words Blue Hornet neatly painted underneath.

George smiled knowingly at his crew, he observed other crews entering their aircraft, and Collins was the first to react. Without speaking, he slowly passed round each of his crewmembers and silently shook their hand. Then before entering the heavily laden bomber, he looked up at Blue Hornet's new emblem, kissed his hand and slapped the kiss on the bomber's fuselage before climbing the ladder. Mr President watched Collin's performance and followed suit, as did all the crew as they each entered the Lancaster Bomber.

As the crew took their position, the weeks of routine training kicked in and Blue Hornet was soon buzzing in anticipation on her dispersal pad. George slowly pulled back the throttles and the heavily laden bomber slowly moved forward to take her place in the long convoy of Lancaster's proceeding along Waltham's taxi track.

"She's heavy Charles, it took extra thrust to get her moving," said George.

"I can see that, you'll need full throttle and lots of it tonight Skip," replied Charles.

"Make sure the props are at full thrust," commented George.

"Roger that Skip."

"Take-off is into headwind Skip so we should have plenty of airspeed for lift-off," said Henry through the intercom.

"Thanks for that Henry; I think we're going to need it."

It was soon Blue Hornet's turn for take-off and as she moved forward to take her position at the end of runway 18/36, through the darkness George noticed a gathering of waving maintenance Erk's at the opposite edge of the taxi track.

"Look at that Charley, we're getting a send-off, give them a wave."

Charles obliged and returned the wave as George lined up Blue Hornet.

George suddenly felt quite tense as he waited for instruction and began fiddling with his fingers.

"You alright Skip?" said Charles.

"Just impatient," replied George.

D-Duck, you're clear for take-off screeched the radio.

"Here we go Charley boy," said George as together they steadily pulled the four throttle levers fully back, one hand on top of the others.

Blue Hornet lumbered forward, slowly picking up speed as she passed along the narrow strip of concrete runway. Due to the additional payload in her bomb bay, the ride was more a long up and down rollercoaster motion as opposed to the skipping bouncing and shaking feeling the crew were more familiar with during training take-offs with an empty bomb bay.

George watched the runway passing underneath Blue Hornet, keeping one eye on his airspeed indicator. He peered into the darkness looking for the runway markers as the concrete strip accelerated faster and faster. Slowly the up and down motion of the heavy aircraft smoothed out and the plane lifted off the runway. George gently pulled the joystick towards him and Blue Hornet climbed steadily into the night sky above the coastal town of Grimsby.

"We're about fifty feet lower with this bomb load," said George. "Any more weight and we would be taking the tiles of the houses."

"We're clear Skip, that's what counts," replied Charles, reassuringly.

"Course zero-eight-five, w-when you're ready Skip," said Henry. "Keep to five hundred feet Skip, w-we'll be coming down to skim the water soon."

"Roger that," replied George curiously.

"Diversion course first Skipper, we don't want Jerry to know where we're heading and fifty feet above the water should keep us hidden under their radar for some time," continued Henry.

"Roger, Roger, keep your eyes peeled you gunners, this is the real one," said George. "Turning to new course zero-eight-five."

"Roger," replied Henry and the three gunners in unison.

"Who's Roger," asked 'W'?

"You keep to your radio 'W', it's not you," said Mr President.

"And where's the pigeon?" responded 'W'. "Has anyone seen the pigeon?"

"Can anyone see anything?" said James. "We're over the water. We crossed the coast a few minutes ago, now it's just black out there."

"Thanks for that James, you can come down to fifty feet Skip," said Henry.

"Take it steady Skip, you'll have to trust the instruments unless you can see better than I can," commented Charles.

"I'll have to trust in something," replied George.

Let's have a bit of hush boys, give the Skipper chance to concentrate," Charles instructed through his intercom.

"How long do I stay at fifty feet?" asked George.

"About an hour Skip," replied Henry.

"An hour!" remarked George.

"Sorry Skip," said Henry. "Not my choice of route."

Blue Hornet fell quiet as the crew gazed out of their respective canopies, allowing George to concentrate while they searched for any sign of Jerry in the dark sky. Time passed slowly as mile after mile of dark swirling water raced under Blue Hornet's fuselage. The monotonous drone of the plane's four Merlin engines and the continual staring into the empty blackness of the night became drowsing and hallucinating. A squeal and crackle from 'W's radio as he twizzled the frequency dial listening for enemy chatter jolted everyone's attention and interrupted their silent concentration.

"Everyone alright?" asked Charles. "What about you Skip?"

"Yes, everything's fine Charles," replied George. "I think it might be good if someone spoke occasionally, I got the feeling we were all falling asleep."

"We need to start climbing Skipper, rendezvous at eighteen thousand feet is fifteen minutes away," Henry interrupted.

"Alright everyone, we're about to become visible, Jerry will soon pick us up and scramble their fighters so be alert, and remember there are forty other Lancaster's with us, somewhere out there, so let's be vigilant. We don't want any incidents, do we Mr President?" said George, rallying his crew.

"No Sir, no incidents tonight everyone," replied Mr President.

George climbed Blue Hornet to eighteen thousand feet and the three gunners engaged with their weapons and peered into the dark sky.

"N-new course coming up Skipper," warned Henry.

"Roger that."

"I reckon they have spotted us Skip, there's lots of radio traffic all of a sudden," said 'W' into his intercom.

"Thanks for the warning, did you all hear that? Looks like the fun is about to start boys," George commented.

"Let's hope the decoy w-works Skip and they prepare for us in Hamburg, where we are currently heading, and not where we are g-going," said Henry. "We turn before we get to any heavy ground artillery Skip, so it's just the Luftwaffe we need to keep a lookout for."

"Fingers crossed Henry, fingers crossed," replied George.

"Turn to one-eight-five degree Skip," instructed Henry. "We're about ten minutes off the coast, there might be some coastal flack Skip so be prepared, we're not far from Bremerhaven."

"Roger, one-eight-five coming up."

"There should be some cloud cover as we go inland Skip," said, Henry.

The atmosphere inside Blue Hornet was of intense concentration and anticipation as the Lancaster headed on its new course towards Happy Valley and the steel city of Essen.

"I think I can see the coast Skipper," reported James, laid out full length underneath George's seat.

No sooner had James finished talking than the first offensive artillery shells started exploding in the dark sky around Blue Hornet. Bright yellow-orange ack-ack shells began peppering the sky, with swaying searchlights locating and lighting up one or two unfortunate Lancaster's for the artillery to aim at.

Slowly, the brief ground offensive and bright swaying searchlights faded away as D-Duck left the coastline behind. All eyes were now searching the dark sky for evidence of the Luftwaffe's Junker fighters.

"Can anyone see anything?" said Collins from the rear of the aircraft.

"I can see the ground, just make out a few things," answered James.

"I'm pleased about that," said 'W'. "We haven't brought you all this way for you not to see anything."

Suddenly a bright ball of fire exploded in the dark sky to the port side of Blue Hornet. A trail of white and yellow flames began streaming from the ailing Lancaster as it started to fall out of the night sky.

"Holy smoke, where did that come from?" shouted Mr President. "Did you see anything Collins?"

"Not a thing."

"Where's that cloud cover Henry?" said Mr President.

"Stay with it, boys," George calmly said. "We only need to see the one with our name on."

"I'd sooner there wasn't one with our name on Skip," quipped 'W'.

"Amen to that," replied Mr President.

"Target fifteen minutes away Skipper," called Henry.

The crew became quiet, each one concentrating on their task at hand, and speaking only when it was necessary, as Blue Hornet passed in and out of cloud cover. The city of Essen was approaching fast, the Luftwaffe fighters had left the raiding bombers only for the searchlights and ground artillery to take over with their full defensive assault.

George became tense as the ack-ack shells started exploding amongst the bomber's attack formation, and around his bomb-laden Lancaster, now vigorously shaking and rocking as the plane buffeted in the turbulence created by the anti-aircraft shells, as they continued to home in on the objective.

"Target coming up, dead ahead Skip," said Henry into his intercom.

"I can see it, Skipper," confirmed James, laying full length in his bomb aimers' position directly below George's seat.

Two ack-ack shells blasted one after the other close to Blue Hornet. The plane shook violently causing George to grasp the joystick tightly in order to maintain course and altitude and stay in formation.

"Open the bomb doors," ordered George, while fighting at the plane's controls.

"Roger that," replied Charles, shouting nervously into his intercom.

George concentrated hard, wrestling with the joystick as the bomb bay doors opened and a surge of smoky air sucked into the long bottomless fuselage of the raiding bomber.

"Bomb doors open," confirmed Charles.

"Roger," replied George.

"Your turn D-Duck, in you go," rasped the squadron leader's voice over Blue Hornet's radio. "Good luck."

"Tally-hoe boys, here we go," said George, clearly and calmly through the intercom. "Over to you James, it's all down to you now, give them what you've come here for."

"Roger that, you bet Skipper, hold it steady dead ahead Skip," replied James, peering through his bombsights.

In that moment, Blue Hornet fell silent; all that could be heard was James calling his instructions into his intercom.

"Dead ahead Skip, dead ahead."

George gripped the joystick tightly and focused his intense concentration on flying the plane.

His thoughts and physical movements became calm and coordinated as time around him stopped, locked into the still, timeless wuji moment before his future became his history. All around him slowly faded as he passed through the eternal loop of space-time conscious and raced across the parallel.

Parallel Four

The Order Of Time

Is Such

That

The Mass Of The Earth Creates

The Slowing Down Of The Time At Your Feet

While Your Head Is In

The Faster Time Of Your Future

Time

Is A Perception Relative

To Space

Time Can Pass More Slowly In Some Places

And More Quickly In Others

515 BC.
Changbai

Jiang was sitting on the doorstep, daydreaming and scratching the dry dusty ground with a stick. Suddenly startled, he looked up as three men in black and red robes entered the courtyard of his home and walked towards him. Their shaven heads glowed and reflected the hot sun. Jiang knew of these men and was surprised to see them in his courtyard.

"Papa," he called as he slowly got to his feet.

His father's arrival at the doorstep coincided with the three monks. Jiang watched with wide eyes as his father put his hands together across his chest and bowed. The courtyard had fallen silent, only the washing fluttered gently on the lines that stretched between the square block of peasant homes. All attention was towards Jiang. His father took the monks inside the house and before Jiang could follow, the door closed.

Jiang stood looking at the closed door in front of him. He began twiddling his fingers as he waited, impatiently. Gradually he sensed the stillness of the courtyard. He slowly turned and observed everyone standing motionless, staring in his direction.

He inhaled deeply, then leaning forward he opened his mouth wide and screamed long and loud into the courtyard, pointing his stick and arcing from side to side until he had screamed and pointed his stick at everyone and sent them back to their business.

Jiang turned back to the closed door. He knew the meaning of the visit and stood watching, waiting for it to open and to enter. Eventually, the latch lifted and the door swung open. Jiang quickly stood back and to one side allowing the monks to exit, single file. His father followed but remained standing in the doorway. One by one, the monks turned towards Jiang, put their hands together as in prayer, and gave a small bow before they walked out across the courtyard.

"Papa," called Jiang, following his father into the house.

It was three moons later that Jiang's father escorted him along the journey to the temple. His mother had prepared him a small package of dry food wrapped in cloth and tied in a bundle at the end of a long stick that he could carry over his shoulder. She also gave him a small water pouch that he could refill along the way. He had no personal possessions other than the clothes he was wearing.

His departure was a happy and sad occasion, mixed with hugs and kisses, watery eyes and smiling faces. Happy that her son had been selected for a life in the temple, sad that this would be the last time she would see Jiang for a long time. He was just nine years old.

Jiang's father opened the door to begin their journey; outside they were met with all the residents of the housing complex, standing in line across the courtyard, waiting to give their farewell. It was a silent, eerie, and respectful send-off, marked by hands at prayer and bowing of heads as Jiang passed along the long line of friends and neighbours and out of the courtyard of his life.

It was four long days walk before they arrived at the tiny village in the foothills of the Changbai Mountains. A monk was waiting in the square. He greeted Jiang and his father and lead them to a small hut on the outskirt of the village. Here they slept the night before Jiang would depart, alone with the monk on the last climb to the temple.

The monk was outside the hut in meditation when Jiang woke; it was just dawn. He shook his father. "Papa."

Rays of sunlight began to stream horizontally through the small window and onto the opposite wall of the wooden hut. The monk opened the door. "We must leave shortly," he said softly.

Jiang hugged his father tight. "Do I have to go, Papa?"

"You will have a good life, Jiang. Your mother is very proud for you to be chosen to enter the temple. We shall pray for you Jiang, you will always be in our heart," replied his father.

"It is time," said the monk.

Jiang's father put his hands on his sons' shoulders and turned him to face the monk. "Take care of my son," he said quietly and gently pushed Jiang forward towards the monk.

Jiang screwed his head round to look at his father. "I'll pray for you Papa."

The monk reached out, took Jiang by the hand, and began to walk towards the high mountains. As he walked Jiang looked back to his father, he kept turning to look every few steps. Finally, he turned and waved as he slowly disappeared out of sight.

The track to the temple was dusty and well-worn with people randomly spaced along its route, travelling in both directions.

Some making the climb, carrying wood or food destined for the temple, others descending with empty baskets, heading for refills in the village. All would pause and bow as they encountered the red and black robes of a monk along the pathway. Jiang responded similarly and in unison with the monk. These moments of respect broke the monotony of the journey that was otherwise mostly silent. After an hour's climbing, the monk stopped Jiang and suggested they rest a while and take a drink.

"How much further?" asked Jiang.

"From here the path becomes steeper. It will take two more hours."

Jiang sat on a small boulder at the edge of the path. He drank greedily from his water pouch. He wanted to talk but was unsure of speaking as the monk only spoke with few words and remained mostly silent.

The monk was sitting cross-legged on the opposite side of the track, his eyes closed. Suddenly he began a low melodic chant that startled Jiang. He watched the monk and listened to the long murmuring sound emanating from the motionless monk.

Jiang tipped his water pouch in the air and sucked out the warm liquid.

"Drink slowly, take small sips regularly," said the monk, without opening his eyes. "You should save some water now. You will need it as we get higher."

Jiang stopped drinking and looked at the monk as he rose to his feet. "We should continue before the day becomes hot," prompted the monk.

The climb continued in silence. Jiang began stopping and resting as the climb got steeper. His breathing became a deep pant through his open mouth, at steep sections he climbed with hands and feet, and he fell some distance behind. The monk paused and waited for Jiang to catch up.

He smiled as Jiang reached him. "One more rest, we are almost there. You are doing well."

Jiang felt his heart lift; encouraged by the monk's comment and knowing they were nearly there. He remained standing and took a long drink from his almost empty water pouch. He was hot and tired and beads of sweat covered his forehead. Jiang looked up and observed the monk, he was not breathing heavy, nor was there sweat on his brow. He did not look like he had been climbing for almost four hours.

Jiang smiled inwardly, "I will be like him one day."

"Come, soon you will hear the waterfall, then you will arrive at the temple."

There was still some time climbing before Jiang could hear the waterfall. A gentle hissing above his head became louder with each eager step he took. Finally, he reached a small plateau and before him stood the temple. He looked, left and right, he could hear the gentle splashing and pattering of the waterfall, but he could not see it.

"Where is the waterfall?" Jiang asked the monk.

"Patience, first you hear the water, then you see the temple."

Jiang looked at the temple, trying to find the waterfall. The pathway he had just ascended crossed the small plateau and passed through a large tunnel, carved through the solid rock face. Large, heavy wooden gates rested on either side of the entrance, that when closed, formed a formidable protective barrier for the temple. High above the tunnel stood a huge intimidating, defensive looking building, painted red and adorned with flags. Built directly onto the cold imposing mountain, it spanned the tunnelled gateway, its enormous green curling roof hung out over the sheer face of grey rock.

Jiang followed the monk as he passed through the arched tunnel and ascended a long flight of stone steps onto a prodigious stone-tiled courtyard. Either side stood large, majestic buildings, fronted by steps and a single row of carved and decorated pillars that held up the huge green tiled roof. Across the courtyard stood a smaller building with closed shutter doors and bright decorated pillars at each corner. Its curved glazed roof glistened in the sun.

Jiang looked at the building with amazement; he had never seen a temple before. To the right of the building was an intricate ornate paifang gateway. A grey stone step way climbed between tall red columns and disappeared behind the glinting roof and the towering grey rock of the mountain. Three, green roofs spanned the gateway supported by red pillars. The high central roof bridged the stairway, protecting intricate red and gold ornate gates. Two lower roofs extended either side of the stone steps, each protecting a dragon statue that guards the gateway entrance. Jiang looked around trying to see the waterfall. Behind him, was a strange building. From this view inside the temple, it was a large similar-looking building to the ones on either side of the courtyard, but viewed from outside the temple; it was the huge, intimidating building that defended the sanctuary's entrance.

And there, almost hidden in the far left corner of the courtyard Jiang saw the waterfall. Cascading between two rock faces and falling into a small manmade pool that briefly contained the water before it continued down an inaccessible cliff face and on towards the village below.

Jiang was excited, he ran to the pool, as close to the waterfall as he could get. He reached out to let the cool water splash his hands, then wiped his hot face and swished the pool water back and forth. He giggled playfully.

The courtyard became silent; several monks stood motionless looking towards the pool and waterfall. Jiang sensed the stillness of the courtyard; he stopped splashing in the water and thought quickly, then slowly turned to face the courtyard. He put his hands together and bowed in silence.

Jiang remained standing, looking into the courtyard with his hands still clasped together. He watched as the monk walked towards him across the courtyard and wondered what might happen.

"The master is waiting," said the monk, beckoning Jiang to follow, before turning back towards the small central building with the closed shutter doors. Jiang followed, crossing the stone tiles and climbing the five steps that fronted the temple building.

"Wait here," indicated the monk before passing through one of the shuttered doorways.

Jiang stood still looking at the door the monk had passed through. As he waited another monk came and entered the building. Jiang tried to look inside the building as he opened and closed the door, but it happened too quickly for him to see anything. Jiang stood and waited.

The door opened and closed as the second monk came out again. Jiang turned and watched him walk across the courtyard, then turned back to watch the shuttered door. He looked at the decoration on the door and fiddled with his fingers. He was tired and thirsty after his long climb. Jiang remembered his water pouch and drank what was left of the warm water then wearily he sat on the steps in front of the building. The afternoon sun was hot and Jiang's eyes were getting heavy. His young body was tired from the four days walking with his father and almost one day climbing with the monk. His head nodded and lowered slowly to his knees as he gradually went to sleep.

Wang Ling Temple

The next morning Jiang was woken by the monk.

"Quickly, put these clothes on, Master Fu is waiting."

Mystified as to where he was, he did as he was told while looking round the dark room. He pulled on a pair of plain black slacks and tied the waistband, then wriggled into a loose-fitting black jacket that buttoned from under his chin and down the full length of the front.

"Follow me," said the monk, promptly leaving the room.

Jiang followed; through the shadowed building, out across the large-shaded courtyard and up the steps of the same building he last remembered waiting at.

"Wait here."

Jiang stopped and watched the monk disappear through the same door as yesterday. The westerly air was chilled. The eastern sky was pastel blue with evidence of morning sunlight creeping over the Changbai Mountains. Jiang wiped the sleep from his eyes and looked down at himself in his new clothes.

He wriggled his shoulders against the stiffness of the material; he was not used to new clothes and felt a little uncomfortable.

His pants were a little long and he bent to roll up the length of the legs.

As he stood, the monk was standing waiting, holding the shuttered door open. He said nothing, just gestured for Jiang to enter.

The monk followed Jiang into the hall, placed a hand onto his shoulder, and guided him to the centre of the room. He remained standing next to Jiang. The building was still in morning shadow. Dawn stabbed through the door's shutters and cut through the swirling smoke of the burning incense. Red and gold silk cloths lined the wall behind effigies of gods and master's past. Lanterns and prayer scrolls hung from the ceiling. A large black and white yin-yang emblem adorned the centre point of the wall. In front of the symbol was a raised platform covered with red silk blankets and cushions.

There, sat Master Fu. The monk put his hands together and bowed. He turned his head slightly to look at Jiang and gestured for him to bow also. Jiang suddenly realised, clasped his hands, and bowed slowly to the master. Master Fu smiled at Jiang's reaction and bowed in response.

After a moment's silence and with a smile still on his face Master Fu spoke, steadily and softly.

"You have made quite an entrance. Everyone here at Wang Ling Temple now knows of your arrival. I hope your learning will match your youthful spirit. Nonetheless, you are here at Wang Ling Temple because you are the third incarnation of Master Jiguang and we welcome the return of your presence to Wang Ling. In keeping with tradition and throughout this life as a Taoist Monk, you shall receive a new identity. It has been decided by the high master that you shall take the identity of our past master and will be known as Jiguang. There will be a naming ceremony to mark this occasion. Do you understand what I have said?"

"Yes," answered Jiang, fiddling with his fingers behind his back.

"Yes Master," prompted the monk, whispering quickly.

"Yes Master," added Jiang.

"Yes Master Fu," expressed the monk, turning to look at Jiang.

"Yes, Master Fu," repeated Jiang, putting his arms straight by his sides and standing stiff and upright, to attention, as he did when respecting his father's words.

Master Fu smiled and continued. "You shall come here to me each new moon. I shall be your teacher. You will learn the wisdom to be a Taoist Monk again. You shall also be responsible to perform other tasks during your training, for the welfare of the temple. Li Qiang will explain these tasks." Master Fu waved his hand in the direction of the monk standing next to Jiang.

With a sudden warm feeling of belonging, Jiang turned his head, looked up at Li Qiang, and smiled while Master Fu continued. "I think the first step along your path to enlightenment and becoming a monk is for you to learn patience. To help you with this lesson, at the side of this building is the Grand Paifang Gateway. From the gateway are The Five Hundred Steps to Wisdom. At the top of these steps, there is a bell. When you have learned the wisdom of the five hundred steps and demonstrated this wisdom to me, you shall be responsible to ring the Zhong. It is the bell that calls everyone to meditation, and it shall become your responsibility to perform this duty." Master Fu paused. "Do you understand this lesson?"

"Yes, Master Fu," replied Jiang, still wiggling his fingers behind his back.

"Another boy will arrive soon; he will join you in some of your lessons," Master Fu added then paused again. "Monk Li Qiang will show you round the temple, make you welcome and show you your responsibilities. And there will be time for you to practise what you are taught. Do you understand Jiang?"

"Yes, Master Fu."

"Then for today that will be all."

Li Qiang put his hands together and bowed. Jiang quickly copied before he felt a warm hand rest on his shoulder to guide him out of the building and begin walking slowly round the courtyard together. They walked in an anti-clockwise direction. Li Qiang monotonously explained about each building they passed. Like the young boy he was, Jiang swished his hand in the waterfall pool, walked up and down the steps that fronted the buildings round the courtyard and stroked the dragons as they came to the Grand Paifang Gateway of the Five Hundred Steps to Wisdom.

"Now we shall walk the steps to wisdom," said Li Qiang, catching Jiang's attention. "This shall be your first lesson. After, it is your responsibility to walk the steps each day, until you gain their wisdom."

Jiang looked at the steps climbing steeply and curving to the left, round behind the building in which he had met Master Fu. Li Qiang had already started on the walk and Jiang rushed to catch up. The steps were wide, enough for three people but he quickly found the steps were not of even height. Each step was cut to match the gradient of the mountain and Jiang found the steps harder to climb than the previous day's climbing he had made to reach the temple.

The lower height steps he managed quite easily, some higher ones he had to pay attention to keeping his balance as he lifted his foot high enough to make the step. Jiang looked down at the green glazed rooftop as he passed above Master Fu's building. The stairway was now turning sharply to the right, passing behind and between the rugged contours of the mountain, each step taking him higher. Soon he was falling behind Li Qiang and getting out of breath. He tried to go quicker to catch up, but tired even more and eventually lost sight of Li Qiang as he gradually disappeared round the bend ahead. Jiang stopped and sat on a step to rest and catch his breath before he continued. He rounded another bend and there was Li Qiang, waiting under the shade of an old cherry tree on a small level plateau.

As he reached the plateau, Jiang heard the gentle sound of running water. There passing along the side of the stairway was a stream of water, the same water just before it became the waterfall that cascaded into the courtyard far below. Jiang looked down into the courtyard and observed the red-painted buildings on the small plateau, built tight against the mountainside. Above the first curved green tiled roof were a second building and a third that climbed parallel, alongside the steps to wisdom.

Li Qiang pointed to a wooden ladle, attached to a string fastened by the side of the stream. Jiang grasped the ladle, scooped water from the stream and drank, thirstily.

"From here it is polite to let quicker walkers pass," commented Li Qiang as together they resumed negotiating the steps. Jiang noticed the steps were now just wide enough for them to climb side-by-side. Occasionally, so steep and narrow were the steps as they passed through small gaps between the rocks that Jiang had to put his hand against the rock wall to keep from tumbling. Soon

Jiang had fallen behind and the gap was such that Li Qiang was again out of sight. Jiang continued climbing, determined not to stop.

Now alone, he struggled and fought to keep going. He started to think of the past few days walking with his father and remembered complaining how he was tired and wanted to rest. He thought about playing in the square back home with his friends, never thinking of feeling tired. He wondered why all the climbing he had done the previous day, now seemed easy compared to the steps he was climbing.

Jiang sensed someone was following him. He stopped climbing and looked behind, it was Master Fu. Remembering Li Qiang's comment Jiang quickly stood to one side and pressed himself back against the rock wall, allowing Master Fu to pass. The master smiled and bowed as he passed. So smooth and swiftly did Master Fu pass and vanish out of sight that Jiang thought he was flying. Jiang continued his climb and imagined he was Master Fu flying up the steps until tiredness crept back into his legs. He thought about resting when he suddenly spotted Li Qiang. His heart lifted, tiredness faded from his legs and he almost flew up the last few steps.

Jiang's last step was through a lavish arched paifang entrance onto a large spacious tiled courtyard. In the centre was a tall cylindrical, extravagantly decorated steel furnace. It was black, rusting at the bottom where the ever-burning embers had burnt away the colour.

To the right, beyond the furnace, two white tiger carvings guarded a wide elaborate stairway that leads up to the Holy Hall, the Gong, where prayer and rituals were performed. The Gong was majestic, raised high on a separate plateau, overlooking the courtyard, set back against the mountain face. It's enormous curved, green glazed tiled rooftop was decorated with dragons at either end, facing inwards, towards each other. Its strong wooden roof beams adorned with colourful decoration and carvings. Five pillared archways spanned the front of the Gong. To the left of the furnace, on either side of the courtyard, overlooking the lower sections of Wang Ling Temple and facing the western slopes of the high Changbai Mountains, stood two large pavilions. The nearer pavilion housed a great brass bell, a Zhong. On the red coloured floor under the bell, was a black and white yin-yang emblem. In the opposite pavilion hung a large, decorated drum, on the floor, below the drum, was a circular painted emblem of a phoenix and dragon.

Jiang stood looking with amazement; he forgot about his tired legs, he had never seen such a magnificent sight before. He walked round in a little circle looking at the buildings on the courtyard. Jiang noticed, that beyond the paifang entrance, The Five Hundred Steps to Wisdom continued higher up the mountain. He stopped walking and looked back at the bell hanging in the pavilion.

"Is that my bell?" Jiang asked.

Li Qiang smiled. "Yes, that is your bell."

"But there are more steps beyond the gate."

"Yes, they continue, to The Moon Garden. The Five Hundred Steps end here."

"What is The Moon Garden?" asked Jiang.

"First you must master the Five Hundred Steps to Wisdom."

"Can I see The Moon Garden?" questioned Jiang

"First you must have the wisdom," stressed Li Qiang.

"I have mastered five hundred steps," Jiang smiled, pointing. "Look, there is the bell."

"Little wisdom is gained climbing the steps one time," commented Li Qiang.

Jiang ceased with his questions and walked over to look at his bell.

"We should return down the steps, it will soon be time for meditation, but first we must eat," Li Qiang advised, allowing Jiang time to examine his bell.

Having returned to the bottom of the five hundred steps, been shown where to freshen up, and provided with food and refreshment, Jiang found himself climbing the five hundred steps again. This time he was alone, and the steps were busy with monks heading towards the Gong and Jiang seemed to be continually giving way to faster walkers. He eventually reached the top and waited by the paifang at the courtyard entrance, as Li Qiang had instructed. He looked up the steps leading to the Moon Garden, wondering. Then among the monks heading toward the Gong, he noticed one monk walking towards his bell. Jiang stood watching hoping to see the bell ringing, but the monk arrived at the bell's pavilion and also stood there, waiting.

Jiang felt a hand on his shoulder.

"Come, this way," said Li Qiang.

Jiang joined the flow of monks walking towards the Gong. He became a little apprehensive, wondering what was happening, and stayed close to Li Qiang. Once inside the Gong, Jiang was shown to a floor mat at the rear of the hall.

"Wait here until I return. Observe what happens, you should learn our customs. This is all part of your lessons," instructed Li

Qiang before he joined his fellow monks on the main floor of the Gong.

Many of the monks had taken their place with just a few spaces remaining. Suddenly Jiang's bell rang; its deep vibration resonated through the hall. The last of the monks were taking their place. The bell sounded again, and a silent peaceful atmosphere filled the Gong, nothing moved. The bell struck a third time, and the Master's in their long black outer robe covering a white undershirt and pants filed into the hall and took their place on the front row across the Gong floor. The deep boom of the bell struck again, just as the reverberation of the previous ring began to subside, now nothing stirred. Once more the bell sounded, there was a short pause before the high master appeared and sat crossed leg on his raised cushioned podium, his red and black trimmed robe covered him from head to toe, and his plain black hat covered his hair. Again, the bell rang, followed by the slow beat of the drum that hung in the opposite pavilion overlooking Wang Ling Temple. Gradually the drum tempo increased and became a quick repetitive rhythm that boomed and circulated with the incense fragrant atmosphere of the Gong.

Jiang watched intently as the drumming slowed and died, replaced by a gentle humming emanating from the monks. Jiang briefly thought about Li Qiang purring similarly as they climbed the mountain before his thoughts drifted to home. He felt alone, sitting on his mat in this strange place. So much had happened in so few days that he felt lost. He remembered the hugs and soft kisses from his mother as he left his home, the long walk with his father. He thought of his friends playing in the courtyard. Jiang jumped as the monks humming turned to chant and unsuccessfully, he tried to listen to their words. Distracted he looked at the lanterns and prayer flags hanging from the ceiling, similar to the ones hanging in Master Fu's hall. Behind the high master was a large effigy of a fearsome man, a God, Jiang thought to himself. Decorated pillars stood between other elaborate statues on either side of the God. Between the large effigies and the high master was an altar, covered with red and gold silk cloths and adorned with offerings.

Jiang was lost in his thoughts, fiddling with his fingers, and looking round the Gong when suddenly his bell rang out. The monks remained sitting in silence until the final ring of the bell. Jiang paid attention as the monks began to stand and file out of the hall. He anxiously looked for Li Qiang. He was tired and still had to descend the five hundred steps before he could sleep.

At the foot of the steps, Li Qiang guided Jiang towards the huge red pillared hall to the left of the courtyard. They climbed the steps that fronted the hall and entered between the huge, decorated pillars into a large reception room, crossed the floor, and passed through a curtain that covered the entrance to a corridor. At the end of the corridor, Li Qiang pulled back a heavy striped curtain that exposed a small simple room.

"This is your room Jiang, your bed is there in the cupboard," said Li Qiang, with a smile. "Today has been long. It is always difficult the first days and you have done well. In the morning, at the hour of breaking, I will come for you. We must clean the courtyard and the halls, have breakfast and do the washing up. Then we must go to the Gong to recite the scriptures. Life is sometimes hard in the temple, but it is a good life and your lessons with Master Fu will bring great reward." Li Qiang paused. "That is for tomorrow and the future. Now you should sleep."

Li Qiang put his hands together and bowed slowly to Jiang, then departed.

Jiang took his bed from the open-fronted cupboard, rolled out his bamboo mattress, pulled the heavy blanket over his tired body and went to sleep.

Master Fu

The next morning Li Qiang explained the routine tasks, leaving Jiang to sweep and clean the large reception hall before taking him to eat and assist with the washing-up. Jiang was again faced with climbing the five hundred steps in order to attend the reading of the scriptures. Following meditation and having descended the steps, Jiang took part in Tai Chi exercises in the main courtyard in front of Master Fu's hall. After the exercise class, Li Qiang took Jiang into Master Fu's hall and sat him in front of a small altar on one side of the room.

"Remain here until the master comes for your lesson. This is your quiet time. You should learn to sit correctly, relax, practise breathing and meditation," said Li Qiang, putting Jiang into the lotus position as he spoke. "The Master will teach you to read and write. Calligraphy is important for a monk and you will attend this lesson each day after your quiet time. For now, sit quietly, be patient, empty your mind. The Master will come," Li Qiang concluded before leaving Jiang alone in the quiet of Master Fu's elaborately decorated hall.

Jiang sat quietly.

The room was filled with smoke from the burning incense and Jiang watched as the smoke interlaced between the shafts of sunlight streaming into the hall through the slats in the hall's doors. He suddenly became aware of how still and quiet the hall had become. Just the slow drift of the circulating smoke passing through the light and dark stripes that cut across the hall was all that moved. Jiang looked at the large effigies that lined the wall; he looked up at the lanterns and flags, sitting quietly, fiddling his fingers. He started getting fidgety and turned round to look behind him. He wanted to go home and play with his friends. He thought of his mother. He wondered when the master would come, then jumped when he realised, he was already there, sitting on his cushioned podium. Jiang clasped his hands together and bowed his head, hoping he was doing the right thing, the master responded.

Jiang enjoyed his lesson, his calligraphy was not particularly legible for his first attempt, but the master was pleased with his determination to succeed. As the lessons passed there was a marked improvement in his brush strokes, as with his Tai Chi exercises and his commitment to utility responsibilities. His mastering of the five hundred steps showed little progress. However, it was the quiet times Jiang struggled with. He missed his mother and playing with his friend. He spent time by the waterfall playing with the water, and Li Qiang would spend time comforting Jiang, talking and guiding him through his unhappy moments.

"Tomorrow is your first lesson with Master Fu," announced Li Qiang while giving Jiang words of encouragement. "Your first step to wisdom Jiang."

Jiang looked at Li Qiang and smiled.

The following afternoon Li Qiang escorted Jiang to Master Fu's four-pillared hall. His calligraphy lesson was replaced with Master Fu's lesson of wisdom. Jiang sat patiently through his quiet time in front of Master Fu's podium, excited, anticipating what words of wisdom he will receive.

"Welcome to your lessons Jiguang, it is nice to see you again after so long. How do you like being back at Wang Ling?" asked Master Fu, referring more to Jiang as past master Jiguang than to Jiang himself.

"Yes, Master Fu," Jiang replied, unsure of how to answer.

"Good," responded Master Fu, pausing to observe Jiang before continuing. "I am told you are progressing well, Jiguang. I am pleased to hear this," said Master Fu, pausing again. "Now, to begin your lessons I will tell you a story about why you are here and who you are. How would you like that?"

"Yes Master Fu," repeated Jiang.

"In the beginning many moons ago there was Tao, the sauce of the universe, and the stars and universe were in Wuji, a condition of stillness, a state of emptiness. Then one day because of a pivotal action of Taiji that disturbed the delicate balance and stillness of Wuji, there came about the balancing manifestation of Yin-Yang, high and low, light and dark, mother and father. Tao, Jiguang, is the flow, the way of the universe, the source from which all the elements of the universe derive and Chi is the life force, the energy that binds and holds everything in the universe together. Do you understand so far Jiguang?"

"Yes Master Fu," replied Jiang.

"Good, I will continue... within the universe and nature, all things that exist are known and live in cycles, like day and night, the four seasons of spring, summer, autumn, winter, the cycles of the moon. These are renewable cycles of rebirth and decay where the old passes away to be replaced by the new, as in death and life. Within these cycles everything is recycled, nothing goes to waste but is transformed. Now, within our body makeup, our life's existence, our being alive, we have our subconscious that is part of nature, part of the universe and is subject to the natural cycle of life and death. Through our connection to nature, when our body dies, our subconscious is recycled, and transformed into a new rebirth, through the life force of Chi. Within a rebirth Jiang, all your traits and knowledge and the experience of your conscious are recycled within your subconscious. Therefore, Jiguang, that is the reason you are here before me as the third incarnation of Master Jiguang. Now, Jiang, I think you may be wondering how I know you are Master Jiguang? Well, that is because he was known to play with his fingers in the same unmistaken manner that you play with yours," concluded Master Fu. "Do you understand this story Jiguang?"

"Yes Master Fu," replied Jiang.

There was a long pause before Master Fu continued. "That will be all for your lesson today. However, you should remain here in the quiet and think about the lesson I have just given. Think about the story, about how you have come to be here and who you are. Through quiet thinking you will learn to understand," said Master Fu. "But first you should learn to breathe and sit correctly, like a monk," he continued. "That will be most beneficial towards you progressing."

Master Fu corrected Jiang's sitting position, placing him in the crossed leg lotus position and guided him with his breathing before he left Jiang alone to contemplate his first lesson.

Jiang remained sitting in the large hall with its shadowed, silent stillness. The incense laden smoke drifting slowly between the shafts of sunlight, its aroma tingling Jiang's nose with each inhalation of his breath. He thought about the story Master Fu had just told him. He looked at his fingers. 'How can I be Master Jiguang? Why is day and night Yin-Yang?' Jiang sat quietly confused and started feeling hungry. Unsure how long he was supposed to remain in the hall but being hungry was suddenly all he could think about. After taking a quick look around to make sure Master Fu was not watching, he quickly stood up and headed out of the hall in the hope of finding Li Qiang and something to eat before it was time for evening meditation and the climbing of the five hundred steps.

Jiang was full of questions about his first lesson as he ate his evening meal with Li Qiang and his mind was full of thoughts as he lay in his bed trying to sleep.

The next morning followed a similar routine of domestic duties, breakfast, scriptures and meditation, Tai Chi exercise, quiet time and calligraphy, not forgetting the long climb up and down the steps of wisdom, though Jiang's thoughts were not towards performing his tasks and lessons. Throughout the day, Jiang was thinking about Master Fu's story. He wondered how Taiji affected Wuji and how his conscious lives in the universe. He thought about being Master Jiguang and how that could be. Day after day, he had question after question for Li Qiang as he slowly grasped and reasoned some of Master Fu's story.

As the next new moon approached, Jiang's questions became less frequent and he paid more attention to his tasks, in particular his calligraphy and meditation. He talked frequently with Li

Qiang and became quite attached to his friendship without realising his thoughts of home became less frequent.

In the afternoon of the new moon, Jiang sat quietly in Master Fu's smoke-filled hall. He sat correctly in the lotus position, with legs crossed, back straight, breathing through his nose, mouth closed. His hands lay in his lap, his right palm cupped in his left, his thumbs gently touching at their tip.

"Very good Jiguang," said Master Fu quietly from his cushion covered podium. "To begin today's lesson, I will first answer questions from our previous lesson."

Jiang thought for a moment before asking. "What is conscious, Master Fu?"

"Conscious is you Jiguang, it is your thoughts, it is your existence, and it is part of the universe. Your conscious is in two parts. While you are here in this physical body form you have a subconscious that holds all the relevant knowledge you need for you to live and perform tasks and challenges within this life. External to your subconscious is your conscious that is attached and accessible through relaxed focused meditation. Your conscious lives in the universe, in space-time, and is the holder of all knowledge, past, present and the future of your existence," answered Master Fu.

"What is Chi, Master Fu?" asked Jiang, eagerly interrupting while the master paused in silence.

"Chi is the energy that brings the universe to life, it is the life force, the vital energy that binds all things together and sets the universe in motion. Chi is the source of all life, from the slow life cycle of the mountains and the stars to the speed and energy of light, Chi is its life force Jiguang," replied Master Fu. "Let us pause for a moment and think of these wonders. Let us understand their place and the effect they have in our life."

Master Fu stopped talking and sat in silence. Jiang copied, silently trying to understand Master Fu's explanations.

"For today's lesson I will explain the Tao," began Master Fu, breaking the silence. "Tao is the natural order of the universe, a cosmic force which flows through all things. It is the way, where all things and all life is connected in balanced harmony. Tao is the source of the universe, through which all things manifest, it holds all knowledge of all things at all times, past, present and future, it is the path, it is the Tao, and the Tao is you."

Master Fu paused for a moment before continuing. "Here at Wang Ling Temple, through practice and ritual, and by following the way of Tao, we align ourselves spiritually to the cosmic forces and live in balanced harmony, in accordance with the alternating cycles of nature, so that we can gain enlightenment," concluded Master Fu.

"What is enlightenment?" interrupted Jiang.

"Enlightenment is the harmonious and spiritual transcendence of the human subconscious joining with the cosmic conscious of the everlasting universe, by way of the Tao. It is a timeless condition where you transfer from one state of awareness to the higher level of consciousness," replied Master Fu, looking at Jiang, and taking a pause with his teaching.

"That will conclude today's lesson, Jiguang. Now you should sit here and contemplate all we have discussed today. And, you should begin to make time to include and practise your lessons as part of your daily activities, Jiguang. You will learn and understand more when you implement that which you have learned."

"Yes Master Fu," replied Jiang.

After sitting contemplating his lesson, Jiang climbed the five hundred steps to his bell and waited for Li Qiang before entering the Gong. As he approached his mat at the rear of the great hall he was surprised to see another boy sitting in the same place. Jiang sat on his mat and crossed his legs; he turned and smiled at the boy sitting next to him, put his hands together and bowed his head. The boy did not respond but turned his head back to watch the Masters file in across the front of the Gong.

The boy's presence and his reaction to Jiang's greeting distracted Jiang in his thoughts throughout the meditation and he played continually with his fingers. It was not until the ringing of Jiang's bell at the end of the ceremony and the appearance of Li Qiang that Jiang felt comfortable about the boy. As he left the Gong, Jiang faced the boy, put his hands together, and bowed one more time to the boy. This time the boy responded with a nod of his head. Jiang smiled and headed for the five hundred steps with Li Qiang.

It was not until Tai Chi exercises the next morning that Jiang saw the boy again. Jiang noticed the boy was taller and older than himself and tried to watch him as they performed their exercise movements. Jiang observed the mistakes the boy made and remembered how he had made similar errors in his early lessons. Jiang determined that in his free time he would help the boy learn the intricate movements of Tai Chi.

At the end of the lesson, and before Jiang could speak to the boy, he was collected by his guardian monk and guided out of the courtyard. Jiang headed for Master Fu's small hall at the head of the courtyard and at the same time watched as the boy entered the larger hall on the opposite side of the courtyard from the hall he lived in. It was Jiang's quiet time and was now responsible to make his own way to his lessons.

He positioned himself in front of the small altar in the smoky hall and quietened himself in preparation for meditation. As he focused on his breathing, the words of Master Fu entered his mind.

"You will learn and understand more when you implement that which you have learned."

Jiang thought about Master Fu's words, they sounded just like Master Fu was talking to him. What did it mean, where did they come from? Did they come because he had thought about helping the new boy with his Tai Chi? Yes, thought Jiang. If I practise what I am taught I will learn more. If I help the boy, I will also learn. The same as Li Qiang helps me.

Jiang was still thinking about Master Fu's words when the hall door opened and the boy was guided into the hall by his guardian. It was already time for his calligraphy lesson and in the second lesson, he was to be joined by the new boy. Jiang remained quiet and waited for the master to begin the lesson.

At the end of the lesson, the boy had to wait for his guardian to escort him from the hall. Jiang looked at the boy, stood before him and bowed.

"My name is Jiang," he said, introducing himself to the boy.

"Hmm," responded the boy, looking up and down at Jiang. "I ...am Hui," he eventually added, with a quick nod of his head.

"I can help you with your Tai Chi," Jiang offered.

"Hmm, h-how can you do that?" replied Hui.

"To begin your steps are too long, you are out of balance. Take shorter steps and you can transfer your balance more smoothly," said Jiang

"Hmm," Hui responded.

With that, Hui's guardian was at his side ready to escort him away. Jiang was disappointed by Hui's reaction and talked about it over supper with Li Qiang. At the following Tai Chi lesson, Jiang watched Hui as he took shorter steps in his movement, retaining his balance. Jiang smiled.

Jiang worked hard in his lessons and was pleased that Master Fu complimented him on his progress. However, it was several moons later before Jiang encountered Hui again, other than politely tolerating his presence at Tai Chi and calligraphy.

It was at the small plateau on the five hundred steps, Jiang was struggling to climb the steps and in need of refreshment. As he approached the plateau, he noticed Hui sitting under the old cherry tree at the side of the stream. Jiang reached for the wooden ladle to get himself a drink.

"Jiang, I should thank you for your help," said Hui.

Jiang was confused, what did he have to thank him for? "Thank me for what help?" he replied, taking a sip of water from the ladle.

"For my T-Tai Chi."

"Oh, yes, thank you, you are much improved now."

"And I have not been so f-friendly," said Hui, going on to explain. "I have been sent here by my parents, they no longer want me, and I don't want to be here. At those first meetings, in the hall, w-well, I am older and bigger than you and did not expect you to approach m-me as you did."

"That is in the past, and I was worried that you might change my life here, and I don't want that to happen. I like to be here," said Jiang, impatiently. "Please, excuse me, I must progress to the top, I must not be late."

"If you were b-bigger you would be q-quicker," replied Hui.

Hui's comment stuck with Jiang as he continued to climb the steps.

If I am bigger, I would be quicker. If I am bigger, I would be quicker. Jiang wrestled with this thought all the way to the top of the steps, throughout the evening's meditation and as he lay in his bed that night.

The next morning, he spoke with Li Qiang about Hui's comment.

"How can I climb the five hundred steps more quickly? Hui said if I am bigger, I could climb quicker, but that will take a long time. I must first grow and become taller to become quicker, like you and Master Fu," began Jiang.

"It is not about how quickly you walk the steps," replied Li Qiang.

"Then what is it about?"

"It is about patience and wisdom, Jiang."

"Climbing the steps is hard, some steps are difficult, they are almost too big."

"Do not climb the steps, Jiang, walk them," said Li Qiang. "Walking is easier than climbing."

"How do I walk the steps?" asked Jiang.

"Through patience and wisdom," replied Li Qiang.

"That will take until I am older and can make the steps," Jiang commented.

"Now you are gaining wisdom, Jiang," concluded Li Qiang.

Jiang stopped talking and ate his breakfast. He helped with washing the dishes then headed for the five hundred steps and morning meditation.

In his mind, Jiang was determined to walk the steps. He set off steadily, not rushing. He tried to make his steps evenly paced but the steps to wisdom did not support his approach and soon he was back climbing to reach the top in time. Jiang remembered climbing the track to Wang Ling Temple and looking at Li Qiang, observing the lack of perspiration on his brow, and not being out of breath. I will be like him one day, thought Jiang and stuck with his adopted approach each time he walked the steps.

The following day at evening meal Li Qiang informed Jiang that at the next new moon his naming ceremony would take place, along with Hui. Jiang suddenly became anxious and excited, both at the same time. He quizzed Li Qiang instantly as to what would happen and what he should do. At the same time, in his mind, he was excited that this would be his first step to becoming a monk.

Master Jiguang

On the morning of the ceremony Jiang was dressed in similar robes to Li Qiang; a long black outer robe with big baggy arms, a white undershirt and slacks with black slippers. His hair was gathered at the back, covered by a flat-topped hat, tied under his chin. He was excused from the morning's duties and walked up the five hundred steps to the Gong with Li Qiang. Jiang's newly adopted approach to walking the steps seemed to be working. He did not struggle so much, nor fall too far behind Li Qiang. He wondered if it was the effects of the occasion, or perhaps Li Qiang was not walking so fast that he managed the steps so well, but whatever it was, it made him happy.

As they came to the top of the five hundred steps, Jiang noticed the red lanterns, coloured bunting and prayer flags hanging from lines stretched across the courtyard. Large ornate drums on decorated frames were lined in rows across the courtyard, larger ones to the rear, by the pavilions, smaller ones to the front, facing the Gong. Long brass horns were positioned on each side of the two white tigers guarding the steps.

Upon entering the Gong, Li Qiang guided Jiang to the far side of the Great Hall. There, he was placed on one of two small silk-cushioned podiums and told to sit in the lotus position.

Smoke from burning incense drifted through the hanging lanterns and prayer flags. The central altar was full of offerings.

"Remain here throughout the ceremony," instructed Li Qiang.

"What should I do?" asked Jiang anxiously.

"Nothing," replied Li Qiang. "Be patient, that is all."

Jiang waited nervously. He began playing with his fingers, then stopped. He looked down at his hands, opened his palms and stretched his fingers. He thought about Master Jiguang. He thought about becoming Master Jiguang.

The monks began filing into the Gong and taking their positions. Jiang's bell rang, and silence fell upon the hall. The bell rang again, and the masters and high master entered and took their positions. The drum replaced the bell and gentle humming emanating from the monks replaced the drum. Jiang looked at the empty podium next to him. "Hui, where was Hui".

Jiang looked around the hall. He could not find Hui, and wondered where he was, what might have happened to him?

The monks began chanting. Jiang was just thinking the ceremony was not any different to morning meditation when unexpectedly horns out in the courtyard sounded. Their drone flooding across the valley of the Changbai Mountains and resonating through the Gong of Wang Ling Temple. Jiang forgot about Hui. Cymbals crashed and higher-pitched horns shrieked out. The noise was deafening and lasted sometime before silence fell, and the monks resumed their chanting. As the chanting hushed, the high master began reading scriptures, followed by more chanting and more scriptures.

Jiang sat patiently, watching and listening from his podium.

The deep drone of the large horns and the cymbals clash resumed, followed by the high-pitched shrieks of the horns. As the screeching horns and cymbals, ceased, thunderous drumming began from the huge drums lined across the courtyard.

Abruptly, the drumming stopped. In the silence, four monks approached Jiang on his podium. One monk stood at each corner and slowly he felt himself and the podium being lifted. He was carried to the front of the Great Hall and placed in front of the high master. As the four monks retreated, the high master began reading scriptures. Jiang heard the name Jiguang being mentioned several times. Chanting and more scriptures followed before the four monks returned. They paused, one at each corner of Jiguang's podium. Jiang's bell sounded. When his bell stopped, Jiguang was carried out of the Great Hall. He was placed in the bright sunlight, at the centre of the patio area that fronted the Gong. He overlooked the tigers that guarded the wide elaborate steps leading down onto the courtyard.

The monks lined up in rows at the foot of the steps, in front of Jiguang. His bell rang and the monks dropped to their knees, put their hands on the floor in front of them and put their forehead to the ground. They remained bowed until the bell stopped ringing. Once the monks had returned to their standing position the large horns sounded, followed by the cymbals and the small shrieking horns. The noise continued until each monk had filed past and bowed in respect to Jiguang. Shortly after the last monk had filed passed, the rows of drummers began vigorously beating the lines of drums. Their repetitive booming rhythm suddenly stopped and once more Jiguang's bell rang, this time to mark the end of the ceremony.

Li Qiang came and collected Jiguang from his podium. He was tired and thirsty from the ceremony and sitting in the warm sun.

He stopped at the small plateau while descending the five hundred steps with Li Qiang. He grasped the wooden ladle and scooped a drink from the stream.

"Where is Hui?" he asked Li Qiang.

"He has gone. He ran away in the night."

Jiguang was upset to hear what had happened and wondered if he should have been friendlier towards Hui. He wondered where he could have gone.

"Where would he go, what would he do?" Jiguang reasoned.

"Hui is a troubled boy Jiguang. He fights with the demons in his head."

"Demons, what are demons," asked Jiguang?

"Demons are of the spirit world Jiguang. Demons are the bad, the evil influence within life. They live in present time and torment our afterlife, our thoughts. Hui was sent here to help him overcome his demons," Li Qiang explained.

"Why would he run away, it is nice here at Wang Ling, I could help him?"

"Hui would not accept our teachings; he had no belief in the wisdom of Tao or the guidance of angels," replied Li Qiang.

Jiguang struggled to control his young emotions. "What are angels?"

"Angels are our guide; they reside in our future and guide us through our present life and protect us from demons."

"What will happen to Hui? His mama and papa do not want him."

"I cannot answer that Jiguang; it is for Hui to find the answer for himself."

Jiguang's head was full of thoughts and memories of the day and about Hui. He looked down at himself in his ceremonial robe and thought about being a monk, now he thought about demons and about being Master Jiguang. He thought about asking Master Fu more about Master Jiguang and the meaning of reincarnation. He thought constantly for the remainder of the day, until he finally fell asleep, as Monk Jiguang, in his little room in Wang Ling Temple. He was now nearly eleven years old.

Jiguang waited patiently for the next new moon and his lesson with Master Fu. On the day it arrived, he completed his utility duties, attended morning meditation, and exercised vigorously during his Tai Chi. Now he sat silently during his quiet time in Master Fu's hall, waiting for the master to arrive. Master Fu appeared on his cushioned podium.

"Welcome Jiguang, I am pleased to hear you are progressing well with your lessons. I have also been observing you these past moons and I am pleased your naming ceremony concluded successfully, despite the unexpected absence of Hui. However, before today's lesson commences, do you have a question, Jiguang"?

"How does reincarnation happen, Master Fu?" asked Jiguang.

"I have previously explained briefly, so I will elaborate a little more. Within your true self, your spirit, there is an eternal point of consciousness that lives within Chi and the universal midst of constant change. Within your life self, lives your subconscious, an extension to your consciousness that travels through lifetime after lifetime, experiences change after change, but remains essentially you, your life self, with all your quirks, your gifts, and lessons you have learned and stored within your conscious. It is a life of eternity, through many incarnations, and with many more to come. How do we know this? Through observations of nature and the cycles of the universe, everywhere you look everything is recycled and transformed. Nothing is wasted. Your subconscious is part of nature, not apart from it, and goes through the cycles of life and death, returning to your eternal conscious after each lifetime. There within your conscious and the universal energy force of Chi, celestial spirits plan your future and your subconscious gathers the wisdom for your next rebirth experience. It is this cosmic cycle that presents you with life after life."

Master Fu paused. "Let us contemplate this for one moment Jiguang," said Master Fu, sitting still in meditation.

"From my observation and for today's lesson, I will provide general teachings to help you progress forward, Jiguang," began Master Fu, breaking the silence. "I notice that you are becoming proficient with your calligraphy, and you look to be enjoying meditation. However, you should understand that Tai Chi also plays an important aspect towards your progress. Tai Chi is not only development for your body, but also your mind. The physical movement of your body combined with the controlled use of your breath brings about balance and increases your energy flow of Chi. This will help you clear your mind during meditation and assist with walking the five hundred steps. Something you are struggling with I believe."

Master Fu paused again and looked at Jiguang as if waiting for an answer.

"Yes, Master Fu," responded Jiguang.

"Within meditation Jiguang, you should focus on Wuji, empty your mind and cultivate emptiness, stillness, a single point of space-time conscious." Began Master Fu. "Harmonise with the energy flow of the cosmic forces of the universe, and the way of the Tao. Eventually, you will be able to journey to the higher realms of consciousness and enlightenment. Through the daily practice of mindfulness, contemplation, concentration, and controlled breathing, applied during both your meditation and throughout your day's activities, all will help you achieve enlightenment. Living the way of the Tao is the true way of life," said Master Fu. "The word you should contemplate, Jiguang, is 'application'. Do you understand these explanations?"

"Yes Master Fu," replied Jiguang.

"Then that will conclude today's lesson."

Jiguang remained in the silence of Master Fu's smoky hall and thought about the word 'application', as he contemplated his lesson. He was slowly beginning to realise that each of the daily activities he was performing was not just separate actions, but that each action complimented other actions. He began to see how his lessons were slowly coming together and that by applying his thoughts and actions into his daily activities he would gain wisdom. Would this be the wisdom Master Fu was expecting? Jiguang thought. And when will I have learned patience?

Days and moons passed as Jiguang studied and practised the teachings from Master Fu's lessons.

Jiguang stood at the bottom of the steps and prepared himself to walk the steps to wisdom. He calmed his mind, applied rhythm to his breath, and concentrated on the steps before him. He took his first measured step, followed by another equally paced, transferring balance like a Tai Chi move.

He breathed rhythmically maintaining his focus, his mind calm. Steadily, he walked the steps to wisdom. He came to the small plateau and the running water of the waterfall and continued upwards. As he approached a difficult narrow section with several large and high steps, he sensed someone was behind him. Jiguang stopped walking and looked behind. Two monks were gaining on his ascent. He remembered the protocol for faster walkers and stood to one side, allowing the two monks to pass.

He resumed his walk. The next step was high and difficult and he put his hand out against the rock wall to keep his balance. His focus had gone. His legs ached. His steady breath became a pant, and Jiguang continued to climb to the top of the steps. Disheartened, Jiguang went to sit in front of the Gong, to catch his breath and take a rest. He was disappointed. I was going so well, he thought. Next time, next time I will walk the steps.

The next attempt failed similarly, as did the next. Jiguang became frustrated with his attempts at walking the steps

One morning Jiguang was performing his Tai Chi, he was not paying particular attention and letting his mind wander throughout the exercises.

-

Gradually he became calm; his movements flowed, weightless in his steps. His mind was blank, he did not think about what he was doing, he knew. His subconscious future guided his movements, in tune with himself and his surroundings, and he performed his movements effortlessly and correct.

-

The Tai Chi lesson finished and Jiguang made his way to Master Fu's Hall. He sat crossed legged in front of the small altar and began to meditate. The calm feeling from Tai Chi remained with him and he felt full of energy, warm and peaceful.

-

He felt like time was standing still and his thoughts were slow and clear. He felt like he belonged as if he had been here forever.

-

Slowly his thoughts focused, thinking about his Tai Chi lesson and about how he was feeling and what was happening. His attention changed, the calmness lifted and slowly faded and he was in Master Fu's hall waiting for calligraphy to commence.

That evening during mealtime, Jiguang talked about his experience with Li Qiang.

"You are gaining wisdom Jiguang."

Li Qiang's comment lifted Jiguang, encouraging him to try to achieve the experience again, and apply what he has learned when walking the steps.

-

It was a wind-blown morning as Jiguang made his way to meditation. He pulled his robe tight around his body as he walked across the courtyard and stood at the foot of the five hundred steps. He relaxed into a calm conscious awareness, visualised the action he was about to perform and concentrated his thoughts on his rhythmic breath. He proceeded walking the steps to wisdom.

-

He began to feel like he was in a trance, and walked effortlessly, as if in slow motion, and time had no relevance. His mind was clear and calm and his body glowed with the energy of Chi.

- -

With his last stride, he stepped through the paifang archway and onto the large, tiled courtyard in front of the Gong. He had walked the five hundred steps to wisdom. Jiguang quietly smiled.

He kept his achievement to himself. He wanted to practise to make sure he had mastered the task before he said anything to Li Qiang or Master Fu. It would soon be his lesson when he had decided to make his announcement. Jiguang practised walking the steps for the next few days but became suspicious Li Qiang was aware of his achievement. Each time they met at the top of the steps before entering the Gong for meditation, Li Qiang would greet and look at Jiguang with a smiling and inquisitive, questioning expression.

The new moon arrived, Jiguang waited patiently in Master Fu's small smoky elaborately decorated hall for his lesson to commence. During his quiet time, he sat in the middle of the floor before the Master's podium and meditated. He was still in the glow of meditation as Master Fu took his place on his podium. Master Fu waited. The door to the hall opened and closed and Li Qiang entered and sat quietly on the floor behind Jiguang. Slowly Jiguang came out of his meditation.

"Welcome Jiguang, I see you are improving in your meditation," Master Fu began.

"Yes Master Fu," replied Jiguang, his mind slowly returning to the hall, and wondering when it would be possible for him to make his announcement.

"You have developed significantly these past moons."

"Thank you, Master Fu," Jiguang said, wanting to add more.

"Sufficiently so, that I believe you have now gained the wisdom of the five hundred steps, Jiguang."

Jiguang looked flabbergasted. "Yes, Master Fu," was all he could reply. "How do you know?" he slowly added, disappointed he could not surprise the master with his announcement.

"Your aura has been quite illuminated these past days Jiguang. This happens when you apply Tao in your thoughts and actions. Its appearance demonstrates you have achieved one step towards wisdom and enlightenment," answered Master Fu.

Jiguang sat motionless looking at Master Fu, wondering what his aura was.

"Li Qiang noticed your progress some days ago, he has informed me." Master Fu gestured with his hand towards Li Qiang.

Jiguang turned to look at Li Qiang, he smiled, he was right. Somehow, Li Qiang knew he had walked the steps.

"I will make arrangements for you to commence training for ringing the Zhong," continued Master Fu. "These lessons will now become time for you to study the scriptures and progress with your calligraphy. You will attend my lesson every third new moon; I will guide you on your path toward enlightenment, Jiguang. To help with your progress you may now approach The Moon Garden; Li Qiang will guide you there."

"Thank you, Master Fu," said Jiguang, excited by what he was hearing, excited by his achievement, excitedly, but unknowingly, playing with his fingers behind his back.

"Do you understand today's lesson Jiguang?" asked Master Fu."

"What is my aura?" asked Jiguang.

"Your aura is the energy of Chi that flows through and surrounds your body, Jiguang. It is a luminous projection of Chi energy that emanates and radiates around you and becomes prominently illuminated when your mind and body are in balance with the flow of the universal energy and the way of the Tao," replied Master Fu, pausing. "There is something more you wish to ask?"

"Have I learned patience, Master Fu?" ask Jiguang.

"You have displayed patience Jiguang, and you have practised patience, but you must always, throughout life, learn to be patient. Is that all for today?" asked Master Fu.

"Yes, thank you, Master Fu," replied Jiguang.

Master Fu bowed before leaving his smoky hall. Jiguang quickly responded to Master Fu before turning to look at Li Qiang to share his achievement and quiz him about how he had observed his aura.

It was several days before Jiguang walked the steps to wisdom together with Ji Qiang. He was about to turn fifteen and begin his training for ringing the temple Zhong. This made him the youngest monk to achieve this accolade, for which he was very proud.

Together they effortlessly took their last stride off the steps of wisdom and walked through the great ornate paifang arch towards Jiguang's Zhong. There waiting by the bell was the current bell ringer. He smiled and greeted Jiguang with clasped hands and a long bow. Li Qiang departed from the bell and joined the line of monks heading towards the Gong for evening meditation. It was now Jiguang's responsibility to be present to watch the ringing of the bell on every occasion. He waited in anticipation for his first experience of watching the monk strike the bell.

The Zhong was huge, more than twice Jiguang's height and a little wider than his arm span. It was aged, and weathered, a dull grey, adorned with dragon, phoenix, and yin-yang carvings. Its true bronze colour shone through where the large wooden striker made contact with the bell. The great Zhong hung, suspended from the heavy roof timbers of the pavilion, just clear of the floor but possible to crawl under. The pavilion was square, built with hefty, red coloured, pillars at each corner to support the weight of the bell and the green tiled roof.

The moment was approaching, Jiguang watched as the monk took his place holding the support ropes of the long, round striker. The monk drew back the heavy timber and at some predetermined moment, known only to the monk, he swung the striker forward. The great bell boomed and resonated vigorously, out across the courtyard and through the Gong, out across the valley of the Changbai Mountains, and deep into Jiguang's chest. Before the resonance dissipated, the monk struck the bell again. The deep vibrating tone filled Jiguang's head, and rang loud in his ears, drowning out all other sound.

At the third strike of the bell, time stopped. Jiguang's mind became calm and peaceful. His subconscious blurred all around him into slow motion. Space-time accelerated and he raced through time infinity, carried on the deep vibrating tones of the great bell. He was the bell. He was the vibration of consciousness echoing through universal time, and deep in concentration as he crossed the parallel.

Parallel Five

Your Subconscious
Lives With You During Each Lifetime
And Is Subject To The Natural Earthly
Cycles Of Death And Rebirth

It Holds All Relevant Knowledge To
Live And Function And Experience
The Challenges Of Each Rebirth

To Help Or Complicate Each Rebirth
You Are Given Choice

The Closer You Follow The Tao
The Greater Your Access To Your
Conscious And Enlightenment

March

1943
Waltham

Bright flashing ack-ack shells shook and buffeted the Lancaster. The drone and vibration from the four Merlin engines resounded unbearably. With the large bomb doors wide open, it looked like the bottom of the plane's fuselage was missing. The noise was thunderous and the raw, graphic view of Essen burning far below was real and frightening.

"Left a bit Skip," said James, peering into his bombsights.

George was deep in concentration, wrestling with the joystick to hold course, monitoring instruments, and watching his proximity to the other bomb-laden planes around him. His ears were ringing with the noise of war but somehow his mind was clear and calm, focused on his objective to turn left a bit.

"Hold it Skip, hold it."

"Roger," replied George.

"Hold it, hold it," repeated James as he watched the red marker flares far below come steadily into his sights. "Hold it Skip."

James held his thumb hovering over the bomb release button until the red flares were fully in his sights and pressed.

"Bombs away Skip, bombs gone," said James, almost without expression.

George continued with the same flight path, allowing time for the camera to record James' strike on the target.

"Course two-two-five Skip," said Henry through the intercom.

George remained concentrating; the noise of the aircraft and exploding anti-aircraft shells filled his head and the engine's vibration buzzed in his chest.

"Two-two-f-five Skip," repeated Henry

George did not respond, the vibration and shaking of the plane resonated and continued to shudder through him as he fought to maintain control. The roar of engine noise and exploding anti-aircraft shells died away as Charles closed the large bomb-bay doors.

"You alright Skip?" asked Henry.

"Yes, two-two-five coming up," replied George, shaking his head, trying to relieve the aching pain in his neck while focusing his attention towards his compass. "I just kept hearing the sound of a loud bell ringing in my head. God knows where that came from."

George turned the joystick and stirred to two-two-five degree.

"Keep as high as you can Skip, less chance for f-fighters to get above us," said Henry. "We can drop back down once we cross the coast."

"What about flak Henry, keep us away from that," George replied.

"Roger that Skip."

"Keep your eyes peeled everyone, we're not out of the woods yet," George reminded everyone.

"I didn't know we were in the woods," laughed 'W'. "I thought we were..."

"You'll be in the woods in a minute; I'll drop you out of the bomb bay if you don't keep quiet," James interrupted.

"Yes, thank you for that one James," laughed George. "Let's stay vigilant everyone."

"Did you score a hit?" 'W' asked, speaking into his intercom.

"That means you too 'W'," said George.

"Sorry Skip," responded 'W'.

"Course three-zero-zero Skip," said Henry.

George turned to three-zero-zero and so continued the zigzag route Henry plotted round the heavy artillery zones that lay between Blue Hornet and the Dutch coast.

"I can see the coast coming up," said James, excitedly.

"You can drop to fifty f-feet now Skip, and get us off Jerry's radar," replied Henry. "Should be home in about an hour boys."

"That's good to hear, I'm freezing back here," Collins responded.

"A strong cup of tea, that's what I want," Charles contributed.

George followed Henry's course and touched Blue Hornet's wheels down on Waltham's runway 18/36 just over the hour.

Charles cut the four engines and the crew remained in their position, each one in silent reflection and relief of the mission they had just accomplished.

"Let me get to my bed so I can get warm," said Collins, breaking the silence.

"Debriefing first boys," George announced. "And well-done everyone, our first sortie safely under our belt, well done. I think I'll join you for that cup of tea Charles."

As Blue Hornet's weary crew alighted from her under-belly, so they repeated their ritual for each man to kiss his hand and slap the kiss on the side of the bomber's fuselage. A heartfelt gesture of appreciation and thanks, for Blue Hornet's contribution in the raid, and for getting them home safe.

Chatter was subdued as the crew journeyed in the old Crossley truck, back to the locker and drying rooms. Breakfast was quiet and thoughtful until.

"What do you think of Blue Hornet's emblem guys?" Collins asked.

"Hey it's fantastic; I'm pleased it was finished for our first sortie," said 'W'.

"Yeah, I reckon that's what kept Jerry away," James added.

"What do you think Skip?" asked Mr President.

"I like it; I think you have all put some good ideas together. Like you say, James, let's hope its magic keeps Jerry away from us," George replied.

"I like the blue hornet f-flying out of the skull's eye," added Henry.

"Yeah, I like its sting; just like us giving Jerry the big sting," said James, excitedly.

"Hey, what about that Lanc getting hit right next to us? I never saw a plane, or anything did you?" questioned Mr President, looking at Collins.

"No, not a thing, that could easily have been us who bought it," replied Collins. "How you're supposed to see anything in the dark, it's impossible."

"Is that why you've not fired your peashooters yet?" commented 'W'. "They're not there for show you know."

"You need to see something to fire at first," stated Mr President. "I'll work your radio and you see what it's like looking into darkness all night, William Wells. Let's see how you do."

"Well gentlemen, I'm going for some shut-eye, I'll leave you to your chitchat and see you all for lunch," said George, leaving the crew with their chatting.

It was mid-morning when George made his way to the Control tower, and stood next to Denis, leaning against the railings, looking to the southerly horizon of runway 18/36, waiting for signs of returning stragglers.

"Morning Denis, how many?" inquired George.

"Morning George, three," Denis replied sombrely.

George stood still and silent amongst the high echelons of anxious personnel gathered on the control tower balcony, listening to the gentle hum of their muted conversation while staring across the empty Lincolnshire fields.

"How are you managing, getting used to the flying now?" asked Denis, still looking to the distant horizon.

"Yes, just about, there's no easy bit," said George.

"I did warn you it would only get harder."

"I remember, how's the new crew going?" asked George.

"They're young, still learning to some extent, but they're keen to learn."

"We're all young Denis."

"But there's young and young George, some of these crews are almost boys."

Suddenly the conversations hushed, all eyes focused at the end of runway 18/36, and spirits began lifting as a distant buzz of merlin engines echoed far away on an unseen horizon.

Black smoke signalled above the distant treeline. Backfire coughed and spluttered amongst the engine roar. Slowly the plane grew in size; with one wheel down it steadily approached the long strip of concrete runway. Fire tender, ambulance, and rescue vehicles started racing around the taxi track.

The bomber's single wheel released a puff of smoke as it touched the runway. Gradually the opposite wing lowered and began scraping and sparking as it slid along the concrete strip. Slowly the bomber turned and its one landing wheel broke away, hurtling across the soft green turf of the airfield. Black smoke billowed from the burning engine as the Lancaster Bomber skidded, rotating out of control. The plane's huge tail wing caught the soft turf at the edge of the runway, grabbing and spinning the plane in the opposite direction, pulling it further onto the damp and slippery grass.

Approaching the perimeter taxi track at the far side of the airfield the stricken bomber came to rest, and instantly thoughts turned towards the afflicted crew inside. The fire tender and rescue trucks duly arrived, retrieving crew, and dowsing flames.

Relieved chatter irrupted on the control tower viewing platform, as the crew were pulled to safety and stretchered into ambulances.

George made his way to the NAFI for lunch and join his crew.

"Coming to lunch Denis?"

"No, I'll stay here a while longer thanks, there's still a chance for the other two," Denis replied, not taking his eyes from the distant horizon.

"How m-many still to come Skip?" asked Henry, as George placed his meal tray on the dining table and sat down.

"Just Tango and Bravo," George replied sadly and respectfully.

"I think it was Bravo that bought it next to us," said Mr President. "I just caught a glimpse of her fuselage as she lit up."

"That just leaves Tango," reasoned Charles.

"Where's your lady friend Henry? I'm beginning to miss her when she's not around to greet me," asked 'W'.

"Hey, keep dreaming 'W', laughed Mr President.

"She doesn't l-live here," Henry replied.

"You could have fooled me these last few weeks," said Mr President.

"Yeah, so how did you do James, have we got a result yet Skip?" asked 'W'. "I hope we didn't go all that way for nothing."

"No, no result yet," answered George, interrupting his meal in order to speak.

"It's a bulls-eye 'W', don't worry," smiled James.

"But I do worry James; I worry how much beer it's going to cost you every time you miss," replied 'W', sending the crew into ruptures of laughter.

"Ha-ha, my money's on you James, I'd be worrying how much it's going to cost you 'W'," laughed Charles.

"I'm with you on that one Charlie boy," said Collins.

Laughing at the banter, George excused himself from the crew, preferring a walk and fresh air before commencing preparations for that night's sortie. Henry joined George on his way back to his billet room; the two men quietly chatting as they exited the main gate and walked along Cheapside. Henry explaining how he was missing Frances, George talking about his love letter for Jean.

"I thought you had posted your letter," Henry assumed.

"I keep meaning to, but other things keep distracting me," George replied.

"Give it to me; I'll post it for you if you're still worried about sending it."

"Thank you, Henry, but I can post it... when I'm ready."

"Just don't leave it too late, or you'll have Frances to answer to," Henry remarked.

"It's the devil or the deep blue sea then," replied George, thoughtfully.

George continued to All Saints Church after Henry had turned off towards his billet. He sat quietly in thought, becoming familiar with the ambience of the church and its quiet calmness. George looked at his hands lying on his lap, his right-hand resting, cupped in the palm of his left, his thumbs raised and touching at their tips. It felt comfortable and natural, though he wondered why he placed his hands together in such a manner. He slowly relaxed, letting his thoughts drift. He felt calm and comfortable and wanted to stay longer in the calm and quiet ambience of the church, away from the turmoil of war but forced himself to return to the airfield and prepare for the night's operational sortie.

The operations briefing revealed the destination was again, Essen. New targets were announced and allocated for the assault. Henry had new coordinates to plot in order to confuse Jerry of the squadron's intended destination. Blue Hornet had been thoroughly checked over, refuelled, and reloaded with her deadly cargo. The flight to the target and the release of the destructive payload ensued without unwanted incident.

Henry gave out new homebound course directions, flying over German-occupied Holland before dropping altitude and skimming the cold water of the North Sea.

As Blue Hornet homed in on the English coastline, sea mist began reducing visibility and George steadily increased height to keep above the fog.

"How are you fixed for position Henry, fog, and mist is building?" George asked over the intercom.

"It's probably just c-coastal mist," said Henry, not really thinking.

"So is Waltham, Henry," George replied. "Waltham is coastal too, remember."

"Hey, we don't want to be missing Waltham, Henry," added 'W'.

"Yeah, sounds like we need to see some of your 'master of navigation skills' tonight," said Mr President.

"You can always ask James Cook if you need help," added 'W'.

"Keep me out of it boys, I've done my bit tonight," remarked James.

"Alright, let's have some order," said George. "Let him sort us out everyone, we don't want another life lost tonight, do we, Mr President?"

"No Skip, not tonight, not when there are pancakes for breakfast," Mr President replied.

"Keep above the mist Skipper; we're about ten minutes off the coast, heading for the Humber. James, keep an eye out for that tower at Grimsby. What's our height Skip?" asked Henry.

"Two fifty feet,"

"Keep it at that Skipper; let's hope it's just a bit of ground mist. We don't want to miss pancakes, you've made me feel hungry now Mr President," Henry replied.

"Get Waltham on the radio 'W', let them know what's happening, and keep them informed," George instructed.

"Okey-dokey Skipper," 'W' replied.

"I've got the tower Henry, dead ahead," said James, excitedly, as he saw the top of Grimsby's Dock Tower poking above the mist.

"How far is it James?"

"About a mile, but we're closing fast Henry."

"Fly round the tower onto course two-zero-zero Skip. James, see if you can spot that windmill at Waltham, it should be on your port side," instructed Henry.

"Roger, Roger," replied George and James, almost in unison.

"Put the wheels down Charles, we better get ready for every possibility," requested George.

"Let the control tower know we are coming in on runway 24/90 and to keep it clear," said Henry.

"Windmill coming up on the port wing," reported James, looking at the mist swirling around the top dome of the windmill.

"Keep it steady Skip. When I say now, turn as tight as you can onto course one-two-five, and keep your f-fingers crossed," Henry instructed.

"Fingers crossed," repeated Mr President. "Why fingers crossed, Henry?"

"Cos somewhere in front of us should be runway 24/90," Henry replied.

"What do you mean, should be somewhere," shouted 'W'. "You need to . . . "

"Turn to one-two-five now Skip," said Henry, overriding 'W's chatter.

"Roger that," replied George, turning Blue Hornet sharp to port and on to course one-two-five, nervously trusting Henry's navigational judgement.

The crew fell silent as George gradually lost height and flew Blue Hornet towards an invisible runway somewhere in the mist ahead.

"Runway 24/90 is all clear Skipper," said 'W', calmly and clearly.

"Lots of flap Charlie, give me lots of flaps. I daren't go any slower," requested George.

"There it is Skip," James called out, over the intercom as the runway landing lights slowly became visible through the mist. "Left, go left Skip."

"Got it, James, I can see it," said George, feeling relieved, lining Blue Hornet up between the two rows of runway lights. "Prepare for landing everyone."

Cheering and jovial banter erupted from inside Blue Hornet as she touched down and rolled successfully along Waltham's runway 24/90.

"Crikey mate, I'll take it all back Henry, that was brilliant, I ow yah one mate," exclaimed Mr President.

"Woo hoo," screamed 'W'.

"You alright back there Collins, you've been quiet?" asked George.

"I'm alright Skip, just listening to the excitement," replied Collins.

Blue Hornet's crew burst through the NAAFI doors chatting indiscriminately, remarking on Henry's navigational demonstration and their latest operation. Excitedly, they queued at the counter and placed helpings of pancakes on their plate before taking a seat at a long canteen table. Charles and Collins brought mugs of hot tea, placing one in front of each of the crew.

"Hmm, these are tasty," announced Henry. "You know, I only think about religion at Christmas and on P-pancake Day."

"That's nothing to shout about," said Collins.

"N-no, I'm just saying. N-no offence, but you never think about pancakes until Pancake Day," continued Henry.

"Yeah, you're probably right about that, but then I don't relate pancakes with religion," reasoned Charles.

"Well regardless of whether they are religious or not, you have earned your pancakes for this year Henry," said Mr President.

"Amen to that, well done Henry," remarked Charles, lifting his mug of tea in salute and recognition of Henry's achievement.

"Yes, well done Henry," chorused the rest of the crew, each raising their mug of tea.

Following breakfast, George and Henry walked back to their billet together.

"I must admit, that was impressive Henry, how did you work all that out so quick? I mean we would have crashed one way or another if it wasn't for you," said George, praising Henry.

"I cheated a little," Henry confessed.

"Cheated, there wasn't time to cheat."

"Exactly, that's why I had to cheat," replied Henry.

"How, where did you cheat, Henry?"

"In the maps room."

"The maps room, I'm not with you Henry."

"One of the older guys in the maps room said there's a fair bit of sea mist and morning fog around this time of year, so I took some coordinates for the tower at Grimsby and the windmill here in Waltham and lined them up to 24/90 runway," Henry explained.

"Why that runway?"

"It was the easiest," said Henry. "Markers for the other runways were difficult to fly."

"Well, it paid off Henry, we can all thank you for that," George replied.

"Just doing my job Skip," smiled Henry.

"So how are you getting on not seeing Frances so regular?" asked George, changing the subject.

"It's a bit strange after her being here so frequently, but I will tell you later after I've read my letter, we're arranging the wedding day," Henry responded, holding up a small white envelope.

"Oh right, don't let me interrupt, I'll see you later at the briefing," laughed George, heading off for his daily quiet time.

George entered All Saints Church and resumed his sitting position on the end of the pew, briefly noting the habitual position of his hands. He smiled, as he quietly thought of Henry engrossed in reading his letter and thinking of his wedding day. George mentally reminded himself that he should really get round to posting his love letter to Jean. His smile returned as he thought of Henry's navigation confession while appreciating his forward planning and for getting everyone home safe.

-

George suddenly shivered and felt goose-pimply as a precognition of a fish out of water, flapping and gasping for air, flashed through his subconscious thoughts.

-

He began feeling unsettled, remembering he had experienced the same vision previously while flying and during his first meeting with Henry and Frances. He wondered what it meant and thought about his experience with Frances and her singing, becoming confused with his thoughts, wondering if all this was part of his déjà vu moment. Had he been somewhere, had it already happened, was it about to happen, and what does a damn fish mean?

There and Back

George had returned to his room and picked up his letter for Jean from his bedside cabinet, then realised the post box was back in Waltham village, so he returned the envelope back to the cabinet draw before heading to the watch office for the pre-ops briefing.

The target was again Essen in Germany's Ruhr Valley. Preparations for Blue Hornet ran smoothly, the evening meal was typically full of chatter and expectation. Kitting out in the locker room passed without incident and George found himself stood in line with the crew waiting to board his Lancaster Bomber.

He let James move clear of the entrance, then kissed the palm of his right hand and placed the kiss onto Blue Hornet's fuselage before climbing through the entrance hatch. Inside, George stopped as he began climbing to his seat. His breathing became heavy and laboured. In the evening darkness and climbing through the tight squeeze along the tunnel-like fuselage, George felt claustrophobic and trapped, unable to move.

"You alright Skip?" asked Charles, following behind, halfway up the ladder.

George took a deep breath, forced himself to climb into his seat, and opened his canopy window.

"You alright Skip?" Charles repeated, as he pulled down his dickey seat and sat down next to George.

"Yes, just a bit dizzy, climbing too fast I should think," George replied.

Charles started the engines and Blue Hornet reached for the sky. Chatter and banter continued to and from the target, while concentration dominated proceedings over the drop zone.

Upon landing back at Waltham, Charles cut the engines and the crew began to alight the bomber.

George took his turn exiting down the fuselage and sighed in relief when there was no reoccurrence of the claustrophobic sensation. He descended the access ladder, stepped down onto the dispersal pan and applied his ritual kiss to the bomber's fuselage. Following the crew to the waiting Crossley truck, George curiously looked back at Blue Hornet and thought about the occurrence of his claustrophobic sensation. He suddenly became confused, and he began thinking and wondering about the sortie he had just completed, as he could not remember anything about it.

Returning to his room, George lay on his bed trying to remember the sortie he had just returned from and wondered where he had been all that time. He lay listening for Denis to return to his room, hoping he might have an answer.

Footsteps clipped down the corridor and stopped outside his door. George jumped off his bed and opened his door as Denis was entering his room.

"Have you got a minute Denis?"

"Yes, sure," replied Denis, turning to look at George. "You alright, you look worried?"

"Yes, well I think I am," said George. "Can I talk to you about my déjà vu moment?"

"Oh, that again," replied Denis, hoping not to sound too disinterested. "Well, if it has got you this worried you had better come in, though I'm not sure I can be of help."

"Thank you, Denis, just talking will help, I think," said George, stepping into Denis's room.

"So, what has happened?" questioned Denis, closing his door.

"You're not going to believe this, but I have just returned from last night's sortie and I cannot remember anything about it."

"What, none of it?" questioned Denis.

"I can remember getting ready, getting in the plane and taking off. I can remember landing and getting out of the plane, but that is all. I cannot remember anything about the raid," said George, sitting on Denis's chair.

"None of it?" repeated Denis curiously, sitting on the edge of his bed.

"None of it," replied George, fiddling with his fingers. "Oh, and for some reason, I felt claustrophobic getting on board the plane. I felt like I was trapped in a tunnel or something."

"Claustrophobic... in a tunnel," replied Denis, thoughtfully.

"Yes, and that's the second time I've had the sensation."

"Well, what can I say? I mean, what is there to say, George, I'm no expert on this sort of thing."

"No, neither am I," said George, slowly and quietly.

The two men sat in silence for a few moments.

"Well, there you are George, I'm sorry I cannot be more helpful," said Denis, standing up and opening his door.

"No, thank you for listening, it's much appreciated Denis," replied George, getting up off the chair and walking slowly and thoughtfully out of the room.

Operations from RAF Grimsby had become a daily routine of pre-op meetings, flying, debriefing, sleep, preparation, and repeat the same again activities. Relationships became strained as fatigue and stress built amongst the aircrews, with the average life expectancy of flying personnel estimated to be three short months.

George kissed the palm of his hand and placed the kiss on Blue Hornet's fuselage. He paused before climbing through the entrance hatch as an hallucination of Essen burning passed through his mind. He whispered a good luck prayer to put it out of his mind before climbing to his pilot seat.

Due to increasing daylight hours, take off was at twenty-one hundred hours, and Blue Hornet sat waiting for control tower instructions at the end of runway 18/36.

"What was that you said as you got on board, Skip?" Charles inquired, as they sat waiting for instructions.

"Oh, something I've started saying, for good luck I guess," replied George.

"Something about there and back you said," Charles repeated.

"There and back to see how far it is," George completed.

"In the hope, we get back you mean," suggested Charles.

"Something like that I guess," George shrugged.

Clearance from the control tower crackled over the radio and Blue Hornet raced down the runway, disappearing into the darkness.

"Where are we going tonight Skip?" asked Collins.

"Berlin tonight boys," George replied.

"What's the target, Hitler's bunker? I'd love to put a bomb or two on that," said James, excitedly.

"All in good time James," replied George. "Keep your eyes peeled, watch out for fighters you gunners, you're sure going to get a chance to fire your guns tonight."

Conversation was at a minimum on Blue Hornet; with concentration high on observation and look out for the hundred and twenty-nine accompanying Lancaster's flying towards Berlin.

"Get ready with your peashooters, there's lots of radio traffic coming through," said 'W', as Blue Hornet climbed up from sea level and onto radar visibility.

An endless volley of anti-aircraft fire, interspersed with swarms of Luftwaffe fighters bombarded the advancing Lancaster Bombers as they approached Berlin. Exploding ack-ack shells and bright beams of searchlight lit up the night sky. Both fighters and bombers suddenly became visible when they burst into flame before spiralling down into the dark abyss.

Blue Hornet received instruction for their turn to bomb the target, and George lined up on the instructed coordinate. James lay beneath George's seat peering through his sights at the burning city far below.

"Right Skip, turn right a bit," began James, with his direction instructions.

A massive explosion erupted as a Focke-Wolf fighter collided with one of the leading Lancaster's flying ahead and lit up the cockpit of Blue Hornet.

-

Time slowed everything into slow motion. All of a sudden, George was floating above Blue Hornet watching the two stricken planes fall out of the sky. He watched himself through the plane's large canopy flying his Lancaster towards the Berlin target. Unexpectedly pieces of debris began to pepper Blue Hornet, time accelerated, and George was back fighting the controls to turn right a bit.

"Hold it Skip," said James. "Keep it steady Skipper."

George held Blue Hornet on target, blinking his eyes, wondering what had just happened. He heard James shout 'bombs gone' and Henry give him new heading directions.

"Course two-six-zero Skipper."

George waited for the camera and turned to two-six-zero. He began to feel his chest tighten and his breathing became difficult as he began coughing. Through the canopy, he visualised a skeleton laying horizontal, ahead in the darkness.

"That was close," said Charles, checking instruments. "Nothing damaged but I think we have picked up a few holes."

George gave a last big cough and cleared his chest. "Everyone alright, any damage?" he asked through the intercom.

"What was all that banging and shaking Skip?" asked Collins, from the tail end of the plane's fuselage.

"Go back to sleep mate, I'll wake you when we need you," said Mr President.

"Nothing to worry about Collins, just planes crashing," replied George.

"Did we shoot one, or something?" asked Collins.

"That would be a first," 'W' commented. "I think that's another life gone, Mr President."

"Keep vigilant boys, it's still a long way home," said George.

Conversation died as the crew concentrated on their responsibilities.

"What's happening with you and your lady friend, Henry? Oops sorry, I meant fiancé," asked 'W', as Blue Hornet approached the English coast. "Have you got a best man yet?

"Not yet 'W'," Henry replied.

"I'm a natural if you want, but then she would want to marry me seeing as I am 'the' best man anyway," said 'W'.

"I was wondering if you would be best man Skipper," Henry suggested, unexpectedly. "We are planning a May Day wedding if you can all make it?"

"I would be delighted to be best man," George replied. "And you shall have a 'May Queen' bride Henry, by the sound of things."

Hearing the Skip's response, the crew broke into ecstatic cheering and shouting.

"You two gunners can be bridesmaid's seeing as you're not doing anything else," said 'W', laughing loudly through the intercom.

"Waltham coming up Skip, steer zero-one-zero," instructed Henry, smiling.

Upon landing, George retired directly to his bed, exhausted from the raid. Staring into the constant darkness had strained and tired his eyes, the constant drone, and vibration of the planes four Merlin engines and the repeated barrage of exploding ack-ack shells left his ears ringing.

His arms ached; the hours of gripping the joystick while fighting the vibrating thrusts had sapped his energy. His body was spent, and before he could begin thinking of what he had experienced, he fell to sleep.

It was mid-morning when George woke. He had missed breakfast and could hear Denis banging about in his room. George popped across the corridor to Denis's room. The door was slightly ajar; he knocked and pushed the door open.

"Oh, sorry," said George, as he saw the orderly packing Denis' possessions. "Is Flight Lieutenant Holdsworth moving?"

"I'm not sure Sir, I am here just to pack his belongings and clean the room, Sir."

George's heart sank; he thanked the orderly, returned to his room and sat on his chair by the window. "God bless you, Denis," said George knowingly.

It was a good thirty minutes before George moved. He opened the drawer on his bedside cabinet and removed his love letter for Jean. George stopped at the post office, opposite The King's Head, and posted his letter before making his way to All Saints Church. He slowly opened the large wooden door and stepped into the quiet stillness of the church. He walked woozily halfway down the aisle and sat wearily on the end of a pew. His hands tingled and he rubbed and wound his fingers into his dry palms, cupped his right hand into his left palm and rested them on his lap. Slumping back, he relaxed into the awkward structure of the wooden pew and gently blew out an uneasy sigh.

In the subdued ambience of the church, candles flickered on the altar like exploding anti-aircraft shells. George closed his eyes and thought of Denis, then saw the tormenting image of Berlin burning; the blast of ack-ack shells still ringing in his ears. He sat still, and let the tension drain from his tired body.

George slowly sank into the quiet stillness as a Wuji moment washed over him and calmed his subconscious. Universal space-time conscious merged with his subconscious, raised him from his body, and raced him across the parallel.

Parallel Six

Within

Cycles Of The Universe

Cycles Of The Planet Earth

And

The Cycles Of Your Life

Nothing Is Wasted

Rather It Is

Recycled - Transformed

And Renewed

Consciousness

Is

Your Being

Part Of The Universe

March

1645
Rushton

Time slowed, Taiji stirred the Wuji moment, and the
energy of Chi stimulated his subconscious thoughts.
William slowly opened his eyes, his body felt light and
relaxed, and his mind was still and calm.

-

William was sitting halfway down the aisle in the still and quiet
ambience of Rushton St. Peters, his hands resting in his lap, his
right hand cupped comfortably into his left. He felt as if he had
been asleep but then remembered riding his horse and wondered
where he had been.

"William Sire, you are still here," boomed Father Franklin's
voice as he emerged from a small anteroom at the side of the
altar. "The service has long been finished."

"Yes Father," William responded spontaneously, surprised by
the loud echo of Father Franklin's voice resonating through the
empty church and making him jump in his seat.

"Just having a little quiet time Father, though I must admit I feel I have been sleeping too."

"That is easy to do Sire, I notice m-many of m-my congregation nodding their head during my sermons, though you do look to have been deep in thought too, Sire. Is there something I can help you with?" replied Father Franklin as he came closer towards William.

"Nothing particularly Father, I would suspect you have made all necessary arrangements for Lent, it is just two days away now."

"That is not too difficult; arrangements have been prescribed for many years previous William. Shrove Tuesday requires the arranging, even though people are familiar with the merriment and anticipation of the event continuing similarly, as they do each year. I leave such gaiety to Edward. The races take place on his green, n-not in my church."

"Yes, of course, I remember your father doing the same when we were all young boys and Edward would always win the race," responded William, trying to draw on the spirit of their boyhood friendship.

William was disturbed by the hint of harshness in Father Franklin's voice. William has known Matthew (now requesting to be addressed only as Father Franklin) and his older brother Edward from long ago as they grew up together. Matthew, was sent to religious college and William went on to Oxford University together with Edward.

William and Matthew are the same age, while Edward embraces one year seniority. William remembered the joyful times with Matthew before he was ordained and returned home with a touch of resentment. William also wondered what was driving Matthew with his current secretive and elusive manner, questioning his suspicious involvement in magic.

Father Franklin paused, allowing his eyes to sparkle while the hint of a smile began to appear at the corners of his lips, exposing an admission of remembrance.

"That was a long time ago William, things were different then, there was no war or the unrest there is today," answered Father Franklin, relaxing his formality.

"But they were happy times Matthew," replied William, trying to encourage Father Franklin to show further recognition of being Matthew, once upon a time.

"Things are different now William, we were boys then, now we are men with inherent roles and responsible positions within society."

"And participating in manly things, Matthew," William quickly replied, again referring to his suspicion of Father Franklin's involvement with magic.

Pausing thoughtfully before continuing, Father Franklin finally responded to William's comment. "Yes, I'm doing manly things now William."

William noticed the change. The short glimpse of his boyhood friend had disappeared, and the presence of an enigmatic Father Franklin had returned. The two men continued their discussion with their respectful courtesy for each other's position.

"How was the christening Father?" asked William, changing to a more sociable discussion. "It is some time since having a new addition to your flock."

"Yes, and n-nice to see your m-mother attend church too," responded Father Franklin.

"Will you be participating in the races Father, or do you have other manly activities to distract you?" questioned William with a sarcastic smile.

"Come now William, we have both surpassed such frolicking, and of cause, I will be attending. After all, Shrove Tuesday's activities are as much a part of Lent as Ash Wednesday and the lead up to Easter," replied Father Franklin. "One cannot abstain from one's responsibilities William."

"Of course not Father."

"Then I shall see you on the village g-green to watch the activities, William," smiled Father Franklin. "Let us hope the weather will be fine."

"Indeed Father, I bid you good morning," said William as Father Franklin continued his way down the aisle and out of the church.

William remained on his pew, fiddling with his fingers and thinking about Father Franklin. "Either he is careful not to be drawn into my questions or he has no idea as to what I am referring to. Perhaps he is innocent to my accusations, and it is I who is mistaken, but that is not an explanation for the evidence I have collected or the replacement cross he is still wearing,"

Curiosity got the better of William and he was determined to go and investigate his suspicions about Father Franklin and the mysterious lodge. He made his way to the stables, requesting the groom prepare his horse and deliver it to the front of the hall. He summoned his valet to help dress him in his riding breeches and boots before returning for his horse and trotting off round the hall's large circular drive and on towards the hall's main gated entrance.

As he approached the gates, on the left-hand side of the driveway stands Father Franklin's large imposing rectory, nestled back into the trees, away from the drive. Two large bays topped by windowed gables stand either side of the recessed entrance, upper and ground floor windows adorn either side of the matching front door, with similar windows located in the two bays. Two large chimney stacks sit astride the steep black slate tiled roof. The house has its own stable, a vegetable garden, orchard, and staff to cater for all Father Franklin's requirements.

William took a long look at the rectory as he trotted past. "Just what are you up to Matthew?" he whispered.

Turning left out of the hall's grand gateway and again left at the junction to Rushton village, William kept his horse off the furrowed track that followed alongside the estate's high boundary wall and soon arrived at the Triangular Lodge. He dismounted and walked his horse through the gateway, tethering it to the overgrown bushes that surrounded the lodge.

William walked round the lodge looking for clues as to who or how many people had been intruding on the private property. He noticed a large number of horse hoof impressions and footprints in the soft ground that lead in and out of the two entrances, suggesting recent and regular visitors. Reaching the lodge entrance William climbed the steps and pushed open the door.

The old table remained in the centre of the dim ambience of the hexagonal room, but the chair he had used while Mary attended his wounds, had been moved and rested under the central cross and circular patterned window opposite the door. William carefully inspected the floor for new markings of a triangle but found nothing. His heart sank and he slowly exhaled a sigh of disappointment.

-

> "You are hiding, I can feel your presence,
> I know you are here."

-

Something was not right; all the fresh hoof tracks suggest people had been and there was a strange smell in the air. William rushed quickly down the spiral stairway to the basement. He abruptly stopped on the bottom step. He held onto the handrail calved into the stone blocks of the stairway to catch himself, and his heart suddenly started thumping in his chest. Chickens were hanging from the hooks in the ceiling's timber beams and there in the centre of the floor was another triangle, stained with the blood dripping from the beaks of the up-turned chickens. This time the triangle was complete; there had been no attempt to scuff it out.

William gasped and held his breath, his heart still raced in his chest and he felt nervous and excited about finding another triangular sign, but he was anxious about the blood and the chickens. This he did not understand.

His hands felt cold and dry and he began rubbing and twisting them together as he remained standing on the bottom step of the stairway. He watched his hot breath mist and drift into the still ambience of the cool basement. He felt the coldness of the room, wondering what he had uncovered. William thought about Father Benedict's explanation of magic and wondered which way the triangle was pointing. Was it up, was it down, how can you tell without further knowledge of what the triangle was used for, other than by being present at the ritual, and what did the chickens and their blood mean?

Feeling nervous about remaining in the basement William returned to his horse. As he stepped out of the lodge and descended the steps, he began looking at the strange markings and writing that decorated the walls of the Triangular Lodge.

Above the door is a carved stone shield bearing his family crest, below which is a Latin inscription: 'Tres Testimonium Dant', which William quickly translated to, 'the number three bears witness', and under that the numbers 5555 are carved into the top of the door lintel.

The upper floor windows that number three on each face of the lodge, are each trefoil shaped, decorated with triangular glass panes in patterns of three. Above these windows are individually carved stones bearing a letter of the alphabet positioned on either side of the window. Walking around the lodge William put the letters together to spell, 'Mentes Tuorum Visita', again translating its meaning to 'visit the minds of thy people'.

William became confused by so much detail covering each side of the lodge. Every window, every gable, almost every surface was covered with numbers or letters that referenced three, symbols that had religious content, Latin phrases with hidden meaning, signs that were indecipherable, and he began thinking about what it all meant. He had seen the mysterious writing, the symbols, and numbers many times before, but this was the first time he had looked for their hidden magical or spiritual meaning.

He wasn't certain if there was magic in Mary's potions. He did not feel anything unusual other than his wounds healed quickly from their application, but the feeling of magic from the triangle and the blood and the coldness of the basement room has to be from the evil practice of sorcery. If Father Franklin is involved in practising magic, then William felt he should inform Father Benedict quickly. Perhaps he is also right about the myths and magic that surrounded the Triangular Lodge.

William collected his horse and walked him one time round the lodge before taking the private pathway across the Rushton Estate.

Approaching the small hamlet of the estate workers cottages William made a detour when he observed Jon the Shepherd under a tree, minding his sheep.

Jon got to his feet as he noticed William coming towards him. "Sire," said Jon, removing his hat in polite respect, holding it two-handed up against his chest.

"Ah Jon, just the man I am looking for."

"Sire," repeated Jon, with a concerned and worried look appearing on his face.

"Nothing to worry about Jon, I am in need of some information, and I am told Jon the Shepherd would be the best man to talk with."

"Sire," Jon again repeated, though now looking a little more relaxed.

"Jon, do you recall any strangers visiting or entering the lodge recently?"

"Na Sire," he thoughtfully replied.

"No one, nothing suspicious?" asked William, pulling at his reins to control his horse's movements and bring it to standing still.

"Na Sire."

"What about a Green-Wood Man, Jon. Have you seen such a man, perhaps lingering by the lodge?" William asked suggestively, wanting to get to the point of his questions.

Jon's face lit up as a smile began to appear. "He is not alive Sire, the Green-Wood Man is spirit, he is everywhere in the forest Sire."

"Spirit you say, like a ghost?" replied William, surprised by Jon's answer, feeling a little foolish to mention the Green-Wood Man.

"Na Sire, he is like God, you cannot see him, but he is there, all around you in the forest to protect and guide you Sire. When you are in the forest and you feel you are not alone, that is when the Green-Wood Man is with you."

"And you cannot see him?" said William, as his body suddenly gave a shiver.

"Na Sire. He is made of the plants of the forest."

"How do you know this if you cannot see him?" William questioned.

"You do not have to see him to know of him Sire, but there is a carving of him above the door of Rushton St. Peter, Sire."

"I do not recall a statue above the church door, Jon."

"Na Sire, not a statue, only his face with leaves and plants surrounding him Sire."

"Oh, that is the Green-Wood Man." William realised. "I have seen the carving many times, but I thought it was just a church decoration."

"Na Sire, the Green-Wood Man represents the cycle of life and death. The carving you have seen above the church door is the time of awakening and renewal, the figure of spring and rebirth. There is another figure for the Wood Man Sire, the figure of death. This figure is carved onto gravestones; it is a skull with vines and roots growing from his eyes and mouth and other openings of the skull. The skull represents death and the vines and roots represent rebirth, Sire. You can see such carvings on gravestones at the Church of Holy Trinity in Rowel and Barford and there is one in All Saints Church in Rushton village Sire."

"You are quite knowledgeable about such things Jon, do you know about triangles and their magic?"

As if spooked by some unfelt force, William's horse became restless as he spoke the words to Jon and it took William some moments to re-settle him.

"Na Sire, the lodge is a triangle building and the church preach of the Holy Trinity and their meaning of Father, Son, and Holy Ghost, but I know nothing of their magic Sire," Jon replied, as he turned his eyes to the floor and began pulling and fiddling with his hat.

William saw that Jon the Shepherd had become uncomfortable with his last question and decided not to ask anything further on this occasion. He was sure Jon did know about such things and did not want him to lose trust.

"Thank you, Jon, you have been most helpful. I will go and inspect the carvings of the Green-Wood Man, now I know who he is and where to find him."

"Thank you, Sire," smiled Jon, exposing his black and missing teeth.

"Perhaps you would keep an eye open for anyone entering the lodge," William requested, pulling and tugging at his reins to control his unusually lively horse.

Aye Sire," Jon replied, placing his hat back on his head as William rode off across the field; parting and scattering the sheep.

Jon remained watching as William turned his horse and rode back towards him. Standing his ground, Jon caught the bridle of William's horse with one hand and placed his other hand over its warm soft nostrils to hold him steady as William brought the horse to a halt right in front of his shepherd.

"Jon, there are chickens hanging in the basement of the lodge."

"Aye Sire, Peter your gamekeeper puts them there to stay fresh Sire."

Annoyed by Jon's knowledge of the fact and his prompt reply and simple explanation; William tugged at the reins, backed up his horse and rode off, scattering Jon's sheep once more across the field.

Shrove Tuesday

It was mid-afternoon when William arrived back at Rushton Hall. He retired to his room to think about what he had uncovered, remaining irritated at Jon the Shepherd's quick response and knowledge of the chickens. However, he was pleased to have learned more about the Green-Wood Man and that he now understood why Mary would sing as loud as she journeyed through the forest. Though, he was quite disturbed not to have progressed further with his understanding and presence of a new triangle. He began to contemplate Father Franklin's involvement in the things he had discovered when a knock on his door was followed by the entry of his valet.

"Lady Josephine requests your presence in the reception room Sire, you have a visitor."

"Then you had better dress me suitably for my guest, I suspect these riding breeches and boots would not look appropriate."

William entered the reception room dressed in matching blue doublet, cape and breeches, red stockings and blue buckled shoes, his long dark hair spilling down over his broad white lace collar.

His mother, wearing a black and gold full-length gown, with her hair bunched up into a mass of curls and her gold slippers protruding from under her gown, was sitting facing William on a long, polished walnut sofa with patterned cushions.

Stepping further into the large reception room, his visitor sat with their back towards him on a duplicate cushioned sofa, separated by a large green and elaborately patterned carpet. William noticed the beautifully styled hair of his visitor, her red embroidered dress bushing out from the edge of the sofa and over the carpet.

As he stepped into the centre of the room, his mother announced...

"William, you have a visitor."

"How nice to see you again Lady Ann," said William with a broad smile.

"And you also, William."

"When did you arrive home? I spoke with your brother Matthew only this morning, he never mentioned you were returning."

"I did not send word of my return; I arrived only a few hours ago."

William stood warming his back from the heat of the fire burning in the large stone carved fireplace between the two sofas.

"Then you shall stay the night and return home tomorrow. I shall have a room prepared and inform the chef, mama will enjoy your company, and I can show you the garden. Spring is around the corner Ann."

"That is kind William, but I think..."

"Nonsense," interrupted William. "You are not expected at home, and besides, now that you are here, I would like to speak with you."

Ann is Father Franklin's sister, four years his junior, and has a soft spot for William. She has her heart set on becoming William's bride, though realises William would be a fine catch and that her dowry would not match that of a far wealthier bride that may be attractive to William. She hopefully relies on the bond of their childhood friendship and her youthful complexion to play in her favour when William is ready to choose a bride. She also knows William would not be persuaded or driven by wealth and position and that she holds his trust to confide in her when he has problems to resolve.

"Mama, do excuse us while I show Ann the garden before it turns dark."

William escorted Ann into the garden, engaged in polite conversation as they walked the manicured lawns that run between the exotic flowerbeds. He guided her towards the circular mound and climbed the spiral pathway observing the early buds forming on the cherry trees. At the top of the mound, William invited Ann to sit on his favourite seat and enjoy the spectacular view of the gardens and the estate's fields beyond.

"This is wonderful William, but I suspect not the only reason you have brought me here."

"How well you know me, Ann. How was your visit to Stamford by the way?" asked William, being courteous.

"Pleasurable and so busy for the time of year, but that is not why you have brought me to the top of this hill William."

"No, though I am pleased you have returned Ann... I need your help," confessed William, quickly changing the subject.

"My help, whatever for William?" exclaimed Ann.

"How well do you know your brother, Ann?"

"Which one, I have two?" she replied with a slight giggle.

"Sorry, I mean Matthew, how well do you know him?"

"Why is there a problem?" quizzed Ann.

"I'm not sure, he is acting strange. I know he can be stubborn and awkward, but this is something quite different, I've not seen him behaving like this before," William explained.

"Different... in what way?" asked Ann.

"Secretive."

"That is nothing different William, Matthew has always been secretive," replied Ann.

"He seems to be acting a little strange from what I have seen and I cannot work him out at the moment," William continued.

"Sometimes I think he does strange things because he is jealous," said Ann

"Jealous," gasped William. "Of who?"

"You... and Edward."

"What has he got to be jealous about, we all grew up friends together. Hmm, though that is a coincidence, we talked about that only this morning and I wondered why his words seemed so harsh."

"I do not think William, I know. He has been jealous ever since he went to religious college and you and Edward went to Oxford. Why do you think he only wants to be addressed as Father Franklin?" Ann urged.

"Now you mention it, this morning he was reluctant to discuss or reference our younger days," stated William, thoughtfully.

"There you are, he has pushed out of his mind any reference to ever being Matthew, even within the family too I should add.

He has become worse since father died and Edward took over the manor and he is angry about what you will inherit one day William," explained Ann.

"But that was Edward's inheritance, he did not choose to be firstborn, and I only inherit Rushton Hall because my older brother has died. How can he be jealous of that, he has a good position in Rushton St. Peter, and he is well respected? I don't understand him," said William.

"What makes you think he is being secretive, and what about?" asked Ann.

"I cannot tell you at the moment, Ann, please don't ask more, it is just my assumption at the moment, and I don't want to say anything in case I'm wrong. I know I can count on you not to say anything to your brother," pleaded William.

"Well, I don't know what I can say, William, you haven't really said anything that we don't already know," smiled Ann.

"Come; let us return to mother before it is dark. I will tell chef he can serve dinner," said William, smiling back at Ann.

A blustery Tuesday afternoon soon came round and villagers and folk began gathering on Rushton's village green for the Shrove Tuesday pancake races and feast. The green is part of a livestock field for cattle and sheep, situated by the side of All Saints Church and in front of The Lion village pub. It also looks across towards the grand gates of Rushton Hall with its stylish gamekeeper and gatekeeper's cottages standing on either side.

It is an occasion for the villagers to come together and chatter about whom, what and when. It is an opportunity for Miriam and Michael to parade their baby. It is a time of frivolity and gaiety and enjoyment, and it was a time for Mary to gossip and chat with William without drawing attention or suspicion.

William arrived at the front of The Lion in a covered horse-drawn carriage along with his mother and greeted by Edward and his sister Ann. Village folk armed with an array of burnt black frying pans and skillets were gathering on the village green, looking towards Edward in anticipation of the races commencing.

"Have you seen Matthew?" asked Edward, a little harshly. "I told him the races should begin by three-o-clock and he has to give his blessing before we can begin."

"It is not like Father Franklin to be late," replied William.

"Here he comes now," said Ann, excitedly, looking across the field towards Rushton Hall's gates.

All eyes looked towards Father Franklin exiting the gates and scampering along the short-cut pathway etched across the field towards The Lion and the waiting villagers. His ecclesiastic robes flapped wildly in the stiff breeze, scattering the cattle and pregnant sheep to the corner of the field behind All Saints Church. He was a little out of breath by the time he reached Edward.

"Sorry I am late Edward," said Father Franklin, his face flushed and his breath panting quite strongly.

Without hesitating further Father Franklin quickly took to the high ground, standing on the steps of The Lion public house. He took a deep breath and began delivering his blessing. Unfortunately, his voice and his prayers for the Shrove Tuesday pancake races were mostly blown away in the opposite direction and unheard by the attentive congregation.

"There, that's that done, now we can begin Sire," sighed Father Franklin, while smiling at William and his mother Josephine. "I note you have not been attending church regularly these past weeks Lady Josephine," he continued while retaining his smile.

-

The premonition of a fish out of water flapping and gasping for air flashed through William's mind as Father Franklin spoke.

-

"I have been at Glendon Hall, visiting my sister Father. Rushton is so quiet when Lord Rockingham is away," replied Lady Josephine with the sharpness her husband would have been proud of returning in parliament, and while returning her smile.

While the villagers mingled and began to gather in the field for the start of the races, Mary took an opportunity to talk with William about his injuries and their healing. She also asked if he had learned anything further about Father Franklin. William kept a polite smile on his face and thought about his fish premonition as Mary chatted away, knowing he had no control of her exuberance.

"Oh look, there are Miriam and Michael with their baby, excuse me, Sire," Mary concluded dashing off to swoon over the baby, leaving William relieved.

As Mary departed William's company, the races commenced, and the excitement and enjoyment of the villagers grew with each passing race. Between each event, the inquisitive cattle would venture towards and onto the racecourse before trotting back to safety as the noise and excitement resumed during the next race.

"What did Mary want?" Ann enquired casually as Mary departed.

"Just enquiring about my injuries," William replied.

"Why would she enquire as to your injuries?" Ann asked, having overheard their conversation.

"I will explain later; this is not the place Ann," smiled William, returning his attention to the races.

"What injuries?" Ann whispered into William's ear as she leaned forward.

"Please not here Ann, not now."

William watched the racing and let the thoughts of his fish premonition go as he became engrossed in the final race.

As the finish line approached, a young girl came alongside the leading boy, distracting his attention. He glanced over towards the girl, failed to notice the fresh cowpat, slipped and spilt his pancake from his pan as he fell over the finish line in second place. Most of the cheering spectators saw the funny side of the boy's misfortune, and even Father Franklin allowed himself to smile.

It was during the next race that William glanced over towards Rushton Hall, noticed Father Franklin's two burley accomplishers exiting the hall's gates, and proceed toward the junction for Rushton Village. Once there they turned towards the Triangular Lodge and galloped off out of sight. William turned to look at Father Franklin who immediately turned his head away from William before they made eye contact, but each knew one had seen the other observing the two departing riders.

As the races came to an end, William and his mother made their departure from the festival while the village folk began to gather at The Lion to enjoy the pancakes and beer before commencing their commitment to fasting for the coming period of Lent.

The following day, Ash Wednesday was a day of prayer and the commencing of fasting. William continually watched Father Franklin during the church services, but he did not look in William's direction. The reverend also made himself quite scarce throughout the day and William determined to confront the reverend as soon as he was able.

The following morning, William visited the lodge to see if the two riders who left Father Franklin's home during the pancake races had also visited the lodge. There was no indication of visitors in the grounds surrounding the lodge, however, the chickens hanging in the basement and the blood and triangle on the floor had gone. William also checked the upper floor and found nothing suspicious. He returned to the mid-level entrance floor and sat in the chair contemplating the events that had been unfolding, wondering what was true and real, and what he was not sure about. William decided to visit Jon the Shephard and question him again, only this time a little stronger.

He found Jon sitting under the same tree eating an apple, slicing off chunks with a grubby looking knife. William remained in his saddle while Jon got to his feet and removed his hat.

"Sire," said Jon, looking up at William astride his horse.

"Jon, you were helpful with my questions the other day," began William, hoping to make Jon feel comfortable with his praise.

"Kindly Sire," smiled Jon in reply.

"However, I believe you know more than you will admit too," continued William, looking down from his horse, feeling he was in a powerful and dominant position that commanded respect.

"Sire."

"Jon, I am told you are a teller, able to understand the mystery of magic," William insinuated.

"Na Sire," Jon quickly replied, a look of astonishment appearing on his face.

"I believe you are able to tell fortunes, heal, and perform magic," William added sternly.

"Na Sire," said Jon shaking his head.

"Jon, I have seen the charm you gave to Mary. I am not here to ridicule you, I am here for your help," William informed Jon, sympathetically.

"Sire," replied Jon, gradually relaxing as he interpreted William's comment.

"What do you know of the things taking place in the lodge?"

"Father Franklin meets there with two other men Sire, and Peter keeps game there to keep it fresh, the basement is always cold Sire," Jon replied quietly and nervously.

"Never mind Peter and his game Jon, do you know these other men?"

"Na Sire."

"Do you know what they do at these meetings?"

"Na Sire, it is not my place."

"What about the triangles that appear on the floor Jon, what do you know of this?" William asked slowly. "Do they appear at Father Franklin's meeting?"

"Yeah Sire, after they have gone the sign is there."

"What do they mean, Jon, what do the signs mean?" asked William, believing he was getting somewhere at last.

"I know not Sire, the triangle has many meanings, and you must be there to know what the sign was used for."

"Is it for magic, is the sign used for magic?" William asked, feeling his disappointment returning.

"It is possible Sire," Jon simply replied.

"You mean you do not know, or you are not sure?" William exasperated.

"It is a triangle scratched in the floor Sire. All I can tell you is that this sign is sometimes used in magic," Jon explained.

"Thank you, Jon, you have been most helpful. Please watch the lodge for me and inform me if Father Franklin and his men return." William requested, realising there was no further point to continue with his questions and rode back to Rushton Hall.

The Doll

It was several more days before William and Father Franklin's paths crossed; quite accidentally as together, they both opened the door of Saint Peters Church, one from either side.

"W-William," exclaimed Father Franklin.

"Reverend," cried William, simultaneously.

"G-good day to you Sire," stammered Father Franklin.

"And to you Father," gasped William.

There was a short pause while each man gathered his composure.

"How did you enjoy the races Father?" asked William, spontaneously.

"Quite enjoyable thank you, I think everyone enjoys Pancake Day William, it is a pleasurable activity to have on the calendar, don't you think?"

"Yes, very enjoyable, though it was not like you to arrive late Father," stated William, putting Father Franklin on the spot.

"No, I was a little distracted from the time William, it was unfortunate."

"Did you notice the rider leaving the hall? I was surprised, as I was not expecting visitors," questioned William, keeping to his point of conversation and causing Father Franklin to become uncomfortable.

"N-no, I don't believe I did," Father Franklin replied, struggling for words, avoiding eye contact with William.

"Yes, he left during one of the races, as if using the race as a distraction from being seen," William suggested.

"Well I c-can't comment William, as I say, I did not s-see the riders."

"I saw only one rider Father, there was another?" asked William, pretending to look surprised.

"I'm s-sorry, I thought you s-said two riders," the reverend awkwardly replied.

William noticed Father Franklin becoming uncomfortable and his stammer more pronounced.

"Perhaps the rider, or riders as you say, was the reason for your delay in attending the festival Father?" reasoned William.

"I am not sure what you are s-saying William. Are you suggesting I knew about these riders?" said Father Franklin, his voice becoming sharp.

"It is strange that you arrive late to the festival and two riders, as you keep referring, are seen leaving the grounds of Rushton Hall shortly after you arrive at the races. Very coincidental wouldn't you say, Father?"

"I think you have lost your m-mind Sire," Father Franklin quickly replied.

"I think you have seen these riders before and you have some association with them Father. My gatekeeper has confirmed two riders did indeed visit the rectory, and you have been seen together with these men trespassing at the lodge Father."

"I have no comment on who may or may not have visited my house, nor am I restricted to whom I choose to meet. I bid you good day Sire," snapped Father Franklin as he departed quickly across the church's patio.

"What do you know about magic and triangles Matthew?" William called after Father Franklin as he marched away.

William watched Father Franklin disappear along the drive and casually looked up at the carving above the pinnacle of the arched church door. It was not a sinister-looking carving more a friendly, inviting, and reassuring face surrounded by leaves emanating from the eyes, nose, and mouth. Despite the tension of the uncomfortable conversation William had just experienced, he felt strangely calm and comfortable looking up at the appealing face of the Green-Wood Man.

-

Several days later, agitated from wrestling with his thoughts, William rode to Rowell to speak with Father Benedict again. Sitting once more in the worn and comfortable leather chair opposite Father Benedict, William was more relaxed and less anxious on this occasion. He was not so desperate to hear Father Benedict's answers to his questions, or impatient in presenting his next question and felt a little more knowledgeable to talk about magic and sorcery. William divulged his findings and understanding of triangles and their use in magic. He included detail of his discovery of the Green-Wood Man, knowing it was not relevant to the question of magic, but for some reason, he remained silent about Mary's possession of a magic charm.

"Well, you have been busy William, but what is this about, who is behind the magic, and for what purpose?" asked Father Benedict? "Sorcery and magic are not performed without purpose or reason William."

"I am not sure of purpose or reason Father, all I know is what I have seen and explained."

"Have you learned who is behind the magic?" Father Benedict requested.

William paused before answering. "I believe it is Father Franklin," he replied.

Father Benedict remained silent, his posture stiffened and his face flushed.

"That is a serious accusation William," Father Benedict answered eventually. "What proof of this do you possess to make such a statement?"

"I have seen it, Father," William replied confidently.

"You have witnessed Father Franklin performing magic?" enquired Father Benedict, looking quite surprised.

"I have not seen him performing magic Father, but I have seen the signs after he and his accomplices have left the lodge," William stated.

"That is insufficient proof to accuse someone of sorcery William, especially someone in the position of Father Franklin," replied Father Benedict, quite angrily. "For what reason would he be involved in sorcery Sire?"

"I am not sure Father, he has two accomplices, perhaps they are the ones who are the sorcerers. I have seen them together on two occasions at the lodge, and again I saw them leaving the hall on Shrove Tuesday during our pancake racing celebrations.

Perhaps Father Franklin is not performing the magic Father, but he is involved," William answered confidently.

"Have you spoken with anyone else about your suspicions William?"

"No Father," William answered, again holding back his conversations with Jon the Shepherd.

"Then leave it with me and I shall make some enquiries," Father Benedict casually requested. "And be patient William, one must be cautious when discussing such delicate matters."

"Very well Father," William replied.

Father Benedict continued with a few pleasantries of conversation before William bid him farewell and made his way back to Rushton Hall. As he rode homeward, he felt dejected about Father Benedict's response to his discovery and sensed a lack of surprise or genuine support from the reverend. William was in no particular hurry to return to Rushton Hall and he let his horse walk steadily homeward while he contemplated his conversation with Father Benedict. William let his horse wander along through the forest to avoid confrontation with possible cavalry patrols. He was aware the country is at civil war and cavalry activity within Northamptonshire is steadily building, and he did not want to attract their attention.

William suddenly noticed his horse's ears begin twitching and turning. He also heard the sound of many horses cantering in the distance and guided his horse into a nearby thicket. William dismounted to be less conspicuous, he stood holding the reins and bridle to keep his horse still and quiet. Gradually the sound of horses disappeared and William felt strangely alone.

The sound of the forest suddenly fell quiet and motionless. William stood still listening to the silence. He slowly looked around at the tall trees and the rays of sunlight streaming through the bare leafless branches like sparkling raindrops.

-

Time stopped as a warm sensation passed over him and raised the hairs of his neck and a gentle breeze whispered through the forest.

-

William thought of the Green-Wood Man and the moment was gone. He looked around through the trees holding the reins of his horse. There was no one there and he wandered about the sensation he had just experienced. He was not worried or nervous about what had just happened, in fact, he felt calm and composed, similar to the feeling he felt while looking at his carving above the door at Rushton St. Peters.

Rather than return to Rushton Hall, William decided to go to All Saints Church and find the gravestone bearing the skull of death of the Green-Wood Man. He was suddenly interested to see how it looked in comparison to the friendly face of spring and rebirth.

As he crossed the narrow bridge spanning the Ise River, William noticed Mary through the trees, collecting water from the holy spring, an ancient sacred spring having nine outlets, situated amongst the trees in the grounds of Rushton Hall. The fresh spring water, used for christenings, healing, occasionally for ceremonial events, and drinking, is under the control of Father Franklin.

William made a detour to investigate why Mary was collecting holy water and she froze to the spot when she saw William appear before her.

"What are you doing Mary?" William asked sternly. "You know taking holy water is forbidden."

"It is for Miriam's baby Sire, she is sick," Mary sheepishly replied.

"Does Father Franklin know of you taking the water?" asked William sympathetically.

"No Sire."

"Then let this be the last time Mary, now be gone with you," William replied with the hint of a smile.

William watched Mary disappear through the trees along the bank of the river before returning to his initial intention and rode off to All Saints Church.

After some searching, William found the gravestone containing the carving of the Green-Wood Man's skull. It was as Jon the Shepherd had described, with vine leaves surrounded the skull, their roots protruding through the empty eye sockets and its open mouth that displayed two rows of even teeth.

"So, this is the mask of death," whispered William.

"It is evil," added Lady Ann, startling William as she stood by his side.

"How long have you been there?" William gasped.

"Long enough to know you are in deep thought about something William."

"This is the representation of death and rebirth Ann," replied William, pointing to the carving on the gravestone.

"Whatever are you talking about William?" Ann replied. "I don't know about Matthew acting strange, but at the moment you are most certainly strange."

"Sorry Ann, I have startled you, let me take you out of here and we can walk a while."

"You promised to tell me about Mary at the races and her interest in Matthew," requested Ann.

William began explaining his story and Lady Ann listened in silence.

"You let this woman apply potions to your body?" Ann stated, slowly and thoughtfully.

"I was in pain Ann; Mary works in the garden and is knowledgeable about plant's healing abilities. She is not a stranger to me Ann, she has lived on the estate all her life," William explained.

"Witches perform healing as you have described William," Ann suggested.

"Mary is not a witch Ann, I would know of such a thing and she would not be living on this estate if that were true," replied William, quite surprised by Ann's comment.

"Well, I find it strange that you would allow such a thing, William."

"I did question her about using the potions and she was quite disturbed about the thought that her actions could be associated with magic," said William.

"Magic," exclaimed Ann, startled at William's use of the word. "What are you saying, William?"

"Ann, there was no magic, my wounds are healed, and I am fine," William replied. "I thought you wanted to know about your brother?"

"What about him?" said Ann.

"I think he and his two associates are performing magic in the lodge," stated William. "That is why I have been to Rowell, to speak with Father Benedict."

"That is absurd William, you said before that Matthew was acting strange and being secretive, is this why you think my brother has been acting secretive?" Ann questioned.

"Yes," replied William.

"Well, I have seen nothing to suggest he is being secretive or that he is performing magic, as you say," said Ann, retaliating a little defensively.

"You have just returned home Ann, these things have occurred while you were away," William stated.

"Then I will be more observant and let you know if I come across anything suspicious," Ann replied, feeling a little unsettled by the conversation.

"Thank you, Ann that would be most helpful," said William reassuringly, collecting his horse and walking Lady Ann back to Rushton's Manor House.

Several mornings later, William's valet informed him that Jon the Shepherd was at the door wishing to speak with William.

"What does he want?" William asked.

"He would not say, just that he wanted to speak with you Sire."

William wondered what Jon may have to say and made his way to the door.

"Good morning Jon, how can I help you?" William said as he greeted Jon.

"You must come, Sire, there is something very bad," Jon replied hesitantly.

"What is it?" William questioned.

"The lodge Sire, you must come and see Sire."

Guessing what Jon was talking about, he made a casual look round to ensure no one could hear before he spoke.

"There is another sign?" asked William, whispering loudly.

"You must come and see Sire," Jon replied.

"Very well, I shall meet you at the lodge."

When William arrived at the lodge, there was no one there. He looked around the grounds but could not find Jon. Entering the lodge, he called Jon's name but there was no reply. William decided to look in the basement, as that is where the last triangle was found.

As he descended the spiral stairway William focused his eyes downward, as far down the stairway as he could see, hoping to see the basement floor and what he may find, before reaching the bottom of the stairway. Slowly, step by step, the floor came into view and William anxiously gripped the stone handrail, not knowing what he was likely to see. With just a couple of steps to go...

The entrance door banged open. "Sire," called Jon the Shepherd.

Startled, William took another step and the edge of another triangle became visible on the basement floor.

"I'm down here Jon," William replied, calming his nerves.

Stepping onto the basement floor, William could clearly see the triangle scrapped into the dry dust. Only this time placed in the centre of the triangle was a small doll figure. William took an alarming step backwards while looking at the straw doll. Jon the Shepherd came quickly down the stairway and entered the basement.

"What does it mean Jon?" William enquired instantly, unable to take his eyes off the doll lying inside the triangle.

"It is magic Sire," Jon replied. "The doll is there to harm someone."

"How can that happen?" asked William, his anxiety returning and growing.

"Look, there is a pin stuck into the doll. This is to cause pain and suffering, perhaps even death, Sire," said Jon thoughtfully.

"Oh, in the name of God, I did not see that," remarked William, taking another step back from the doll and triangle. "Who is it for, what harm can it cause?"

"Only the person who performed the magic and cast the spell knows that Sire," Jon replied.

"Let me out of here," said William, pushing past Jon and hastily climbing the stairway. "Do something Jon; get rid of it, use your magic on it before someone dies."

Arriving back at the hall, William was still shaken by what he had seen and sent word inviting Lady Ann for dinner.

Upon her arrival, William was reminded of her beauty. Her long black hair hung down like ribbons resting on her bare shoulders. Her green silk gown rippled and sparkled, enhanced by the twisted green and yellow piping running across her shoulders, and round the gown's hemline. Her hands covered in delicate yellow lace gloves protruded the cuffed frills of matching lace.

"Delightfully radiant," William expressed, standing and pausing to feast his eyes on her beauty as Lady Ann entered the grand sitting room.

"Thank you, William," Ann replied, with a smile and slight curtsey. "You wish to speak with me."

"First refreshment Ann, perhaps cider? It will go well, I have selected pork for diner," offered William as a choice.

"Cider will be fine," Ann confirmed.

William went on with polite conversation about her recent visit to Grantham and pancake racing before gradually commencing talking about the magic he had uncovered earlier in the day. He excused the unsavoury topic of discussion explaining he had no one else to whom he could confide and determine how to proceed. William also mentioned his meeting with Mary collecting holy spring water for Miriam's sick baby. To which Ann became a little concerned, referencing Mary's association with herbs and the potions she had applied to William. She also spoke of the growing talk of witchcraft that was beginning to spread amongst the village folk.

After exhausting their conversation, it was gone nine-o-clock in the evening when William requested Ann's carriage.

During the following days, William noticed an anxious atmosphere within the staff of Rushton Hall and amongst the folk of Rushton village. Following prayer one morning, Ann requested William to stay behind after the service as she had some information for him.

Once the church became empty, William left his seat, moving next to Ann.

"Good morning Ann," greeted William. "You have something to tell me?"

"William, good morning, I have spoken with Matthew; he has heard talk of magic taking place in the parish and he believes Mary is behind the gossip," Ann whispered.

"So, that is what folk are anxious about? I have noticed it myself. How can he say such a thing, when it is I who has seen him and the signs of magic at the lodge?" William responded.

"Yes, talk began the day the magic was discovered. Matthew knows Mary has knowledge of the plants and herbs and that she has healed folk in the past. He has also seen her collecting holy water recently," Ann said.

"How has this come to be general knowledge? Only you, myself and Jon the Shepherd know of the magic that has happened," questioned William.

"Perhaps Jon has spoken of it and now it has become common gossip?" Ann suggested. "You know how these things spread William, and magic will surely attract everyone's attention."

"And what of Mary, is the talk of her too?"

"No, that is just Matthew's suspicious comment," Ann replied.

"What more has he said?" asked William.

"Nothing, it was just that one comment he made, that is all," said Ann. "Folk are talking only of the witchcraft and magic, you have uncovered William."

"Now that folk think that magic has taken place it will spread and grow and fear and worry will soon be raging within the parish, I have to do something Ann," said William thoughtfully.

"What can you do William?" Ann questioned.

"I will write to my father,"

"That will take time William," Ann responded.

"Then I shall ask Father Benedict," William decided.

William thanked Ann for sharing her information and immediately made his way to Rowell, where he found Father Benedict busy in the Church of Holy Trinity, though he was reluctant to go to his rectory to speak in private.

William became disturbed when the reverend made little response to the news of another, more sinister sign of magic appearing in the triangle lodge and that the use of magic was being spoken about within Rushton Hall and village. William got the impression that Father Benedict did not take his visit seriously and his mind was on other more urgent matters.

"William Sire, I am trying my best to establish what is taking place at the Triangular Lodge. You must be patient Sire, these things take time my son, please rest assured I will contact you the moment I have news," Father Benedict informed William, though not convincingly.

William politely thanked the reverend and returned to Rushton Hall.

During the following Sunday service, William was suddenly surprised and paid particular attention to Father Franklin when he began addressing the current talk of witchcraft in his sermon.

"This, my brothers and sisters, brings me to the present gossip of witchcraft within this parish. Nevertheless, let us first understand, witches and witchcraft have always been accepted within the rural communities across this land, along with cunning folk. However, there are two kinds of witches, benign witches like healers and midwives, and wise women who we tolerate out of necessity. Then there are hags and sorcerers that practice darker more sinister magic.

Now, for those of you, who are guilty of talking and gossiping about such an evil and dark practice, puts himself and the rest of this community at risk. Moreover, no matter how devout you may be, consorting with evil puts you within the grip of the devil and the parish at risk of abandonment by God.

However, let me reassure you, Father Benedict of Rowell and Sire William Rockingham, guided by the blessing of God, are investigating this distasteful talk and gossip of dark magic."

William was startled at the mention of his name and instantly wondered how Father Franklin knew of Father Benedict's involvement.

On the way out of the church, William came across Mary heading towards the herb and vegetable gardens, still singing the last hymn of the service.

"Mary, did you listen to Father Franklin's sermon?" William asked hastily.

"Yes, Sire,"

"Then I suggest you stop any healing or use of plants you may be performing until this talk of magic has passed. You do not want to raise suspicion upon yourself, and that includes collecting holy water too Mary," said William. "One moment, you said you were collecting holy water for Miriam's baby, are you applying potions too?"

"Just one Sire, for the babe's temperature. I have Jon the Shepherd's charm inside a lavender bag, tucked in the blanket to keep her safe and calm Sire," Mary replied.

"Mary, it is important that you stop what you are doing, and remove that charm at once," William said, quite startled by Mary's comment.

"But the baby Sire."

"For your own good Mary, stop, and remember our little secret too, I do not want to hear talk about that Mary, do you understand?"

"Yes Sire," smiled Mary.

William watched with an unsettled feeling building inside as Mary went on her way, resuming her singing of the church hymn.

William was alarmed at breakfast the following morning when his mother announced...

"I shall spend Holy Week at Glendon Hall William; I do not like this talk of witchcraft, and now I am informed Miriam's baby has died. Such a shame, it seems like only yesterday I was at the child's christening."

"How do you know this Mama?" William responded with a look of amazed realisation on his face.

"You are not the only one who knows what is happening on this estate William. My chambermaids are aware of all such gossip," smiled Lady Josephine.

William's stomach churned and he shuddered at the news, he instantly thought of Mary, and her placing Jon the Shepherd's magic charm in the baby's bedding.

"Are you alright William, you have gone quite pale?" Lady Josephine asked.

"Yes, thank you, Mama, I think someone has just walked over my grave."

"How can you say such a thing, that is witches talk," replied Josephine.

"Everything is witches talk and magic at the moment," William exasperated, leaving the table and walking out of the breakfast room.

"William stop, you are disturbing me," requested Lady Josephine.

On his way to church, William detoured to the vegetable garden in the hope of finding Mary.

"Oh Sire," exclaimed Mary, as she saw William approaching. "The charm, it has gone Sire."

"What about your potions?" asked William, quite sternly, again feeling quite sick inside. "Did you remove your potions, Mary?"

"Yes Sire," Mary replied, upset and approaching tears.

"Then you can do no more, other than keep quiet and be careful what you do and say Mary," said William, turning and walking back toward the church.

"Yes Sire," repeated Mary, wiping her eyes and watching William walk away.

Father Franklin walked round the corner of Rushton St Peters church just as William approached the door.

"Good morning Sire," greeted Father Franklin, smiling at William, showing no bitterness regarding their last encounter at the church door.

"Good morning Father," William responded, politely, forcing a smile.

"Will Lady Josephine be attending church this m-morning," asked the reverend?

"She is returning to Glendon for Holy Week Father," said William, keeping his answer short, then quickly changing the subject. "Have you heard the unfortunate news, Miriam and Michael's baby has died Father?"

"No Sire, I have not heard. Thank you for informing me, though now I am not prepared with m-my service," replied Father Franklin, becoming thoughtful about William's news and forgetting his question regarding his mother. "I shall have to think of something to include, thank you, William."

Father Franklin's service ran smoothly. Though he focused his sermon on the current talk and suspicions of magic, he managed to include the unfortunate death of Miriam and Michael's baby while reassuring the congregation there was not a connection between the death and the magic.

William tried to read between the lines, wondering how he could be so charming and thoughtful on the surface, yet secretly consort with the devil.

"I do not understand your brother, Ann," said William; sitting next to her once the church had emptied. "He is so charming when he wants to be, just like the Matthew I remember. Where does his bitterness come from Ann?"

"I told you, William, he is jealous, and now after your confrontation, he has become angry. He had a discussion with Edward after the pancake races the other day about you inheriting Rushton Hall one day. He said to Edward that you do not deserve it, that he himself would be a better master of the hall. Then they had a big argument about the two riders who left your estate."

"Did he say who they were," asked William?

"No, he refused to say, he claims he knows nothing about them or who they are," Ann replied.

"But he does know, I have seen them with him and I have seen the magic signs," said William.

"I do not think he is aware of that William," Ann stated.

"Ann, do excuse me, my mother is leaving for Glendon Hall, I would like to see her before she leaves," requested William, politely.

"Of course William," Ann replied.

-

Several days later William found himself back in Rushton St. Peters church for Miriam and Michael's baby's funeral. He was curious as to what might be said regarding reference to the baby's death and the rumour of witchcraft and magic circulating Rushton Hall and village.

Later in the evening, William climbed the spiral pathway of his garden dome for some quiet time to contemplate the last few days' activities and determine what he should do about Father Franklin and his magic.

William sat quietly on his favourite white semi-circular seat on the top of the dome overlooking his garden. He looked at the opening buds on the cherry trees and the vast expanse of the pale blue sky, becoming lost in his thoughts.

-

William listened to the dull ring tone of the death knell, chiming for Miriam's baby. Slowly his subconscious thoughts melted into universal conscious, as the energy of Chi and universal space-time accelerated him across the parallel.

Parallel Seven

There Is Only One Time

It Is The Present

A Fractional Moment

Universally Parallel

Memory Provides The Greater Part

Of That Which You Call Time, But Is

Limited To Recording History

Live By The Tao To

Raise Your Vibration And

Cross The Parallel Of Time

Realise The Knowledge And

Experience Of Your Conscious

And The Wisdom Of The Universe

500.BC

Changbai

Jiguang was just waking as he crossed into the parallel. His subconscious thoughts were racing through his mind and his body was restless and fidgety as he lay on his bamboo mattress in his quaint room in Wang Ling Temple. He was dreamily conscious of faint chimes of a distant bell. The room was dark; he rolled over and pulled a warm thick blanket around his shoulders while the ringing of the distant bell echoed in his head. Jiguang remained snuggled under his blanket. The bell tolled louder and he sat up instantly.

'Morning prayer, I'm late!' He jumped off his bamboo mattress and quickly dressed. It was not until he was halfway across the courtyard he realised that the temple bell was silent and it was not time for morning meditation. He stood still in the courtyard and looked around.

The sky was clear; the moon was high and cast soft shadows across the tiled courtyard. Master Fu's hall was in complete shadow of the mountain, while the moon reflected a pale green hue from the roofs of the three other halls round the courtyard.

The air was still and crisp. The waterfall spattered and splashed as Jiguang made his way to the pool.

He dipped his hand into the cool water, formed it into a cup, then sipped slowly, and shivered as the cool water ran down and under his chin. He wiped his wet hand across his face to wake himself.

Jiguang sat on the wall of the pool and wondered what the bell was that he heard in his sleep if it was not the temple Zhong? He sat for a while and contemplated his experience. Today is the day he is to be promoted and made responsible for ringing the temple bell that calls everyone to prayer and he decided that was the reason for the bell waking him from his sleep.

Time passed slowly and Jiguang walked the steps of wisdom to the first plateau. He sat by the stream, looked out towards the dark shadows of the western foothills of the Changbai Mountains, and listened to the rippling water making its way to the waterfall.

Jiguang made his way to his bell. He stood next to the large wooden striker and held onto the support rope as he looked at the large phoenix carved into the surface of the bell. Jiguang suddenly felt anxious. He had witnessed the ringing of the Zhong twice a day, almost since the day he arrived at the temple, and Master Fu had informed him of this day and his future duty. Now he would watch one more time, the striking of the bell to call the monks to their morning meditation before it became his responsibility.

Standing next to the bell Jiguang thought about the deep booming sound it made, how it resonated across the courtyard, and in his ears. He determined this was not the sound of the bell that woke him from his sleep. That was a lower-toned ring, a shorter, duller ring, more like a bong from a smaller bell than the boom from his huge temple Zhong.

Jiguang became more anxious throughout the day. The time arrived and Jiguang walked the five hundred steps. He crossed the courtyard in front of the gong and took his position beside the bell's large, heavy wooden striker.

The monk who had previously rung the bell came and stood by Jiguang's side; he smiled and bowed slowly towards Jiguang. Jiguang bowed in return and smiled back. He was pleased the monk was there and took confidence from his presence and his smile. Jiguang watched the monks file across the courtyard and enter the gong. He watched the monk standing by the entrance to the great hall, prepared himself, and waited for his signal. Jiguang's palms were sweaty and his body nervously tremored in anticipation. The monk at the doorway nodded his head, and Jiguang cautiously looked at the monk standing by him. The monk nodded his head knowingly and Jiguang pulled back the striker. His heart was beating heavily as he counted three and let the striker swing forward.

The great bell boomed and Jiguang caught the striker support ropes to prevent it striking the bell a second time. He listened to the vibration and prepared for the second ring. Jiguang looked at the monk by his side and received the approving nod of his head.

He let the striker swing towards the bell and the second boom resounded. On the third strike, Jiguang pictured the masters taking their places at the front of the great hall. He watched for the nod of approval and struck the Zhong a fourth time. On the fifth ring, Jiguang pictured the high master taking his position on his raised podium. The last ring boomed and as the vibration died away Jiguang's face lit up with a smile of achievement.

Jiguang was relieved and stood smiling as he watched the monk in the opposite pavilion beat a repetitive rhythm on the large temple drum.

Following the bell ringing, Ji Qiang led Jiguang to The Moon Garden. They crossed the courtyard, passed between the two dragons guarding the wisdom gateway, and began walking the steep steps. A flash thought of Hui entered his memory as he passed the first plateau with the stream and the old cherry tree. He continued upwards, towards the magnificent paifang entrance to the gong. Jiguang thought about his naming ceremony and wondered why Hui might have run away as he progressed upwards towards The Moon Garden. The steps were now steeper and narrower as step by step they walked higher. Jiguang maintained his focus and applied the wisdom he had learned in mastering the five hundred steps. Soon they arrived at a third plateau, surrounded by a high red painted wall, tiled along the top with sloping green ceramic roof tiles.

The steps levelled out onto a worn dusty pathway that continued towards a large circular hole in the red-painted wall. Ji Qiang explained the hole was the moon gate, the entrance to The Moon Garden, a place where it was possible to enjoy and be at one with nature and seek the wisdom of enlightenment. Jiguang passed through the large round opening and entered a lush manicured garden. Inside, the pathway, trimmed and shaped, led to a two-story pagoda, perched on a small mound, by a large drooping willow tree, and overlooking the distant eastern heights of the Changbai Mountains. Grand fir and cypress trees, like large strangely shaped bonsais stood between neatly clipped plants and shrubs decorating the serene, majestic garden. Peach and cherry trees, positioned for their springtime show of blossom, lined the finely gravelled pathway as it continued, and wound its way through the garden to a small oval-shaped rock pond, fed by the endless flow of mountain water, that was destined for the waterfall. Beyond the pond, the gravelled pathway ended at a simple stone seat, decorated with carvings of a dragon and a phoenix, the balance of yin-yang.

"This is the Moon Seat," said Ji Qiang.

Jiguang cautiously made his way to sit on the Moon Seat; situated at the cliff's very edge, on a small outcrop of rock that provided an uninterrupted, and panoramic view of the universe.

"Here you can meditate amongst the stars and the universe," Ji Qiang continued, before excusing himself and leaving Jiguang alone sitting on the moon seat.

Jiguang became captivated by the beauty and tranquillity of the garden, regularly spending time tending the plants and meditating on the moon seat between his lessons and responsibilities to ring the great Zhong and wash the dishes.

Master Fu's lessons, now not so regular became more in-depth, requiring more time reading and learning scriptures, more time in thought and meditation to understand the wisdom of his teaching. Jiguang's calligraphy had not reached the standard required to commence writing, though his meditation and Tai Chi continued to impress the Master and it was soon time for his next lesson.

Jiguang sat crossed legs in the lotus position, waiting patiently for Master Fu.

"Jiguang, time has passed since our last lesson," said Master Fu as he appeared on his cushioned podium. "Though I am told you are progressing,"

"Thank you, Master Fu."

"Let us begin with a question you may have Jiguang."

"How can I understand rebirth and my existence, Master Fu?" Jiguang asked after a moment's thought.

Master Fu also paused before answering.

"Your existence, your form, Jiguang, is three separate elements created in accordance with the universal blueprint for all things in existence, as determined by the natural order of the universe, and the way of the Tao. The physical part of you, the body you are living in now, is created from the universal blueprint for life on this planet and is subject to the natural life, death, and rebirth cycle of this environment, the present parallel. Nothing in the universe is ever wasted Jiguang, rather it is transformed, recycled and renewed. Part of rebirth, part of your existence, there lives your true self, your subconscious, that spiritual part of you which is also part of the present moment of time, the present parallel. Your subconscious holds all relevant knowledge you will require to live, function and experience the challenges of each rebirth you encounter. Each re-birth has its time in universal consciousness for it to exist, within a predetermined life span that is sufficient for the achievement of its purpose. Each re-birth has a purpose, a reason for its existence. It is for your subconscious element of each re-birth, to find and experience that purpose. In order for your subconscious to gain wisdom and progress towards enlightenment, and live the purpose of the experience, the requirement for transformation, renewal, and rebirth is part of the cycle of life for our worldly existence. Now I come to the spiritual part of you Jiguang, your conscious, that which contains all knowledge of all things about your lives and re-births of past, present, and future. Your conscious lives within universal space-time consciousness, the first parallel. By living the way of the Tao, and through the practice of meditation, you are able to access the wisdom of your conscious and gain enlightenment. Wisdom Jiguang, wisdom, is the application of knowledge and the foundation of enlightenment. You should understand, as part of life's cycle, at the end of each re-birth your subconscious returns to your conscious and the realm of universal enlightenment. It is also possible that through meditation and at times of stress you can transgress the element of time and relive time past experiences. Let me demonstrate which is the physical, earthly part of you and which is spiritual, Jiguang."

Jiguang sat comfortably, relaxing in his lotus position with his eyes closed. He focused on his breathing, the rhythmic and steady movement of his chest and breathing. He concentrated on what he was seeing with his eyes closed, apart from nothing physical, he was seeing colours, sometimes a single colour and then changing colours.

"Concentrate on your breath, relax, and allow your mind to empty, think of nothing other than your breath." Master Fu's voice trickled into Jiguang's thoughts. "Now without relating to physical or mental stimulants of your surroundings, and with your mind empty, ask yourself where you are. Are you inside your head, attached to your body, or are you thought, floating in time consciousness, wondering where you are? Within this stillness of nothing visible and nothing physical, where are you? Think about, how big are you, how small are you? Remain silent and still, do not move, you can feel nothing but you still have thought.

Your thought is still present, but where is it, where does it exist, you cannot see or feel it, as it is not physical, yet thought remains. Now, while you are peaceful and relaxed try to touch yourself from inside yourself, physically push outward from inside your body, and feel the boundary of your physicality. If you are truly just a physical manifestation of this world, touching yourself from within your body should be possible, but if you are your true self, your subconscious thoughts, your universal conscious, you are not bound by the limits of a physical re-birth, but free to cross the parallel of time."

After a long quiet pause, Master Fu spoke again. "I believe there is much wisdom to be gained from contemplating the understanding of this lesson Jiguang. I believe you should meditate on the knowledge contained in the teaching of this lesson. Do you understand my request?"

Yes, Master Fu.

"Then that concludes today's lesson."

"Thank you, Master Fu," replied Jiguang, clasping his hands together and bowing as the master vacated his podium.

Jiguang followed Master Fu's request to meditate on the knowledge he had given in his answer and spent many hours contemplating on the moon seat and staring into the universe. He paid equal attention to his other lessons and responsibilities of domestic chores and ringing the Zhong that called everyone to prayer and meditation. Such was the commitment that he placed in achieving his tasks that time passed quickly and time for his next lesson with Master Fu soon came to fruition.

Jiguang entered Master Fu's peaceful and elaborate hall for his quiet time and lesson of wisdom. He sat patiently crossed legs in front of the master's podium, twiddling his fingers, unaware that Master Fu was watching.

"You still play with your fingers Jiguang," said Master Fu, surprising Jiguang.

"Yes, Master Fu."

"Have you understood the knowledge of your last lesson, Jiguang?"

"Yes, Master Fu."

"And do you have a question for your lesson today?"

"Yes Master Fu, how can I understand the passing of Time?" asked Jiguang.

"There is only one time Jiguang, and it has two parallels. The first parallel is universal time, and I will come to it in one moment. the present parallel, true space-time, time of the physical world is a fourth dimension. The time of the present moment, a finite point of consciousness that is present within the universe. True space-time is the conscious manifesting existence of life and the events of life, for all things in creation. It is the moment of universal consciousness when all lifeforms exist, rocks, rivers, mountains, trees, stars, the universe, plants, animals, and you. It is the creation of all things in the universe, held together by universal time, and the energy of Chi, in the order of the Tao. Time and consciousness, are eternal and exist side-by-side; time manifests consciousness, which in turn manifests time, a perpetual motion where one cannot exist without the other."

Jiguang sat listening to Master Fu, trying his best to understand this lesson.

"Time is a perception, measured by your thoughts and your memory. If you look at the stars, the light you see has taken hundreds, and thousands of years to reach that moment in time when you observe the light. You are not looking at the light of the moment; you are looking at the light from the history of existence. Time is measured by your memory of a collection of historical events, the passing of the four seasons, the waxing and waning of the moon, the counting of days, the passing of each moment. Your memory holds your history of time past, anxiety precedes your future time to come and only the present moment exists. Do you understand so far, Jiguang?"

"Yes Master Fu," replied Jiguang, concentrating hard on Master Fu's words.

"The perception of time is relative; as such, that time is different in different places. Mid-day here in Guan Ling Temple is not the same time as mid-day in Peking. Time, in this case, is determined by the time it takes the sun to travel from mid-day here in Guan Ling to mid-day in Peking. However, in both places, time is relative, and parallel to its relationship with the present moment of universal time. The order of time is such that time can pass more quickly or more slowly from one place to another. Relatively, while your feet are stuck in the history of your past, your head lives in the mystery of your future. Likewise, your thoughts and your conscious are relative to the moment of time, and therefore, through enlightenment and your subconscious memory you are able to relive the events of your past, within the present parallel moment of space-time conscious."

Jiguang was beginning to understand the depth of the question he had asked Master Fu.

"If you were to look for time Jiguang, you may see it as the point at which a beautiful rainbow touches the ground, but if you were to go to look for that point, it would not be there, even though you had experienced its presence. Time of the first parallel Jiguang, is the fifth dimension, the Wuji of universal time, the spiritual time of universal enlightenment and of the Tao. A time that is not limited to the moment of the present, but lasts for all time, infinite in its existence, minute in its presence, it is the time for all time, and the existence of all things. Does that explain your question Jiguang?"

"Thank you, Master Fu," Jiguang answered.

"Then that concludes today's Lesson," said Master Fu, with a smile.

"Thank you, Master Fu," Jiguang replied, clasping his hands together and bowing politely as Master Fu vacated his podium.

Before Jiguang's next lesson, conflict broke out amongst the tribes of the Dongyi Province. Fierce fighting spread throughout the region and was soon active in the foothills of the Changbai Mountains. Within weeks tribesmen were burning, killing, and destroying their way through the village below Wang Ling Temple. Many of the warriors were already at the temple gate, laying their torches at the last defence. The temple's inner courtyard roared with the sound of silence, deserted of any living presence. Only the fluttering flags above the burning gateway moved. One lone monk rang Jiguang's Zhong, hanging in the deserted courtyard of the gong. It boomed loudly and echoed throughout the heights and valleys of the Changbai Mountains. The closed doors of the great gong contained the rhythmic murmuring sound of monks chanting their ancient scriptures.

Jiguang sat alone on the moon seat, it was only time before the marauding tribesmen would reach him. He cupped his right hand with his left, thumbs touching at their tips, resting them in his lap.

-

He looked out into the universe, into the vast consciousness of time, his body resonating, his aura glowing. Jiguang's subconscious thoughts fused with his everlasting conscious and drifted into the enlightenment of universal space-time conscious. He was gone; his spiritual conscious had crossed to the parallel of enlightenment before the sword severed his head from his body.

Parallel Eight

Your Existence

Your Conscious

Lives Only In The

Everlasting

Universal Conscious

Of The

Present Moment Of Time

Without Which

There Is No Future

There Is No Past

There Is Nothing

April
1645
Rushton

In that same parallel moment of universal time, William was contemplating on his semi-circular seat on the top of his garden dome. He cupped his right hand with his left, resting them in his lap. He raised his eyes and looked out into the sky, into the heavens and into the universe. A warm glowing sensation vibrated through his body and a sudden sharp sting pained his neck, as he wondered how many people had looked up to the heavens and marvelled. A sudden premonition of a fish out of water flapping and gasping for breath flashed through his mind and washed away his peaceful tranquil moment.

Confused he let the thought go and focused his attention back towards the growing talk of witchcraft spreading through Rushton Hall and the local village folk. Rubbing the pain in his neck, William made his way to Rushton St. Peters church for prayer, and to listen to Father Franklin's sermon.

Throughout his delivery, Father Franklin called for calm during such a stressful time and prayed for the protection of Christ against evil. He bade the congregation not to gravitate towards suspicion or superstition, explaining the death of Miriam and Michael's baby was of natural causes and not that of magic. He mentioned the good that witches contribute to the community during folk's sickness and childbirth, and they should not be persecuted in unsettled times. However, William became disturbed when Father Franklin revealed that Mary had helped care for the dead baby, using potions and holy water, thus planting a seed of suspicion into the minds of the gathered parishioners.

Following the church service, William became curious and decided to visit the Triangular Lodge, asking Lady Ann if she would care to visit also.

William arranged a carriage and they travelled together to the lodge. He explained to Lady Ann that perhaps now; after the death of Miriam's baby that he was curious to see if the activity of witchcraft and sorcery had gone away.

"It is a long time since I visited the lodge, William. I remember, as children, we would play and have picnics there all together, Matthew, Edward, mama and father. They were such happy occasions," said Ann, thoughtfully reminiscing.

"You have a long memory Ann," William replied, smiling. "I had forgotten."

The carriage stopped at the lodge gate and William helped Lady Ann alight. He could hear the buzz of excited talking coming from the grounds of the lodge and as they passed through the gate. William saw the crowd of village menfolk gathered by the door to the lodge.

"What is going on?" demanded William, in a loud commanding voice.

A hush slowly passed amongst the crowd as they saw William and Lady Ann standing before them.

"Tis witchcraft Sire," called a voice.

"Then why are you gathered here?" requested William.

"Jon the Shepherd is inside speaking some words to remove the spell Sire," came another voice from the crowd.

"Tis witchcraft Sire, it is still amongst us," called another.

"Tis Mary, Sire, she killed the poor babe with her magic."

"She be a witch Sire," continued the shouting, becoming uncontrollable.

"Stop this talk, stop it I say, go back to work, go home and pray to God that Jon the Shepherd can put a stop to this magic," shouted William loud and stern, for everyone to hear while, avoiding repeating Mary's name. "Go, and I shall speak with Jon and Father Franklin about this."

Slowly the crowd began leaving, taking the pathway across the estate. Lady Ann was standing cautiously behind William, watching, and listening curiously as the crowd of village folk became angry, agitated by their own shouting and calling.

As the crowd began to disperse, Ann started walking round the lodge looking at the display of mysterious symbols and lettering.

"I never really took notice of the carving and decoration when I was younger," Ann stated. "Now it looks sinister and mysterious, I can see a resemblance to its connection with sorcery and witchcraft, and a religious connotation too. I can see why it would be a place for witchcraft too..."

Suddenly the lodge door opened, startling Ann and causing her to stop speaking as Jon the Shepherd stepped out of the building.

"Sire," said Jon, a little shocked to see William and Lady Ann.

"What did you find?" asked William, as Jon came down the steps.

"Just a triangle Sire," replied Jon the Shepherd. "I have said some words and scuffed out the sign Sire."

"Can I see?" said Lady Ann, excited by the thought of seeing magic while surprising William and Jon the Shepherd at the same time.

"Let me check inside before you enter Ann, I do not want you to be alarmed should there be anything inside," William suggested.

"No, I want to see for myself," Ann insisted.

"There is nothing Sire," said Jon, reassuringly.

Ann's assertion surprised William and he conceded to allow her to enter the lodge first. She pushed open the large wooden door and stepped inside.

"Oh William, look," Ann said loudly, with a little nervousness appearing in her voice. "There is something on the floor."

William looked past Lady Ann standing motionless and staring at the scuffed out scratchings of a triangle in the centre of the dusty floor.

"What does it mean?" asked Lady Ann. "And what is that smell?"

William excused himself and descended the spiral stairway to the basement. Hanging from the beams were a brace of pheasant and a rabbit.

"It is just game Peter keeps here, nothing to worry about," said William, as he returned to Lady Ann.

"Should I worry about this?" asked Ann, looking down at the remains of the triangle.

"That was the magical sign I have seen several times and enquired about, Ann," William replied. "It looks like the witchcraft has not gone away, and I am not sure if you should worry or not. I will talk with Jon the Shepherd about when this sign appeared and then I shall confront your brother."

"My brother, how can you think my brother has anything to do with this?" questioned Ann, defending Father Franklin.

"I have seen Matthew and his two accomplices here at the lodge several times, and each time a new triangle has appeared. Jon the Shepherd has also seen them, long before I discovered the signs, Ann. The last sign had a doll placed in the centre of the triangle and Jon the Shepherd said it was there to cause harm. Now Miriam's baby has died," continued William. "You have told me yourself Matthew has denied knowing the two riders and argued with Edward, what more proof do I need before I confront him?"

"I see what you mean William, you are right, something has to be done," replied Lady Ann. "I want to leave now; I am beginning to feel frightened."

William returned Lady Ann home to Rushton's Manor House before looking for Father Franklin. Unsuccessful in his search he sent a request inviting the reverend to dinner that evening.

Father Franklin arrived in good spirit, smiling and shaking William's hand.

"Wine or cider, Father?" asked William, hoping to keep the meeting cordial.

"Wine, thank you," replied Father Franklin.

William allowed the conversation to remain as casual chatter during reception and partly through dinner. Towards the end of their feast, the conversation gradually turned towards the talk of witchcraft now dominating discussion and temperament throughout the parish.

Father Franklin's tongue, sufficiently loosened by the wine, enquired upon the reason for his dinner invitation.

"I am curious as to your connection with the two riders who keep appearing within the parish and the practice of witchcraft being performed in the Triangular Lodge Father," William asked, coming straight to the point.

"William, as you have broached this s-subject previously, I can only repeat I have no connection or as-association with whom you are referring. As for my as-association with m-magic and w-witchcraft taking place at the lodge, how can you make such a suggestion Sire? I am your parish priest William." Father Franklin replied, just about holding his stammer under control.

"Matthew, I have seen you with these men, together at the lodge, and I have seen the magical signs you leave behind after performing your rituals," reasoned William.

"You are m-mistaken Sire," said Father Franklin, bluntly.

"Matthew, it is I William, your friend. Are you beholden or possessed by these men Matthew, do you understand what is happening within your parish? Today a new sign has appeared in the lodge, what do you know of this Matthew?" William reasoned.

Father Franklin remained silent and drank his wine. "Why should I know of such a thing appearing in your lodge William?"

"Matthew, this morning you said there is no connection between Miriam's baby dying and the suggestion of witchcraft. You also said witches are useful and welcome, then pointed out that Mary, who we know is a healer within this parish, cared for Miriam's baby, applying potions and holy water. That was incriminating Matthew, why would you make such a statement if it were not to point a finger?" William continued.

"Please Sire, my n-name is Father Franklin and I can make n-no comment towards your accusations Sire," Matthew replied.

William could see Matthew had drunk too much wine and Father Franklin was becoming more dominant in Matthew's conversation. Realising he would not gain a resolve to the reason of magic and witchcraft, William changed the subject and chatted politely until Father Franklin departed with a pronounced stammer, a slur and a stagger.

Mary

During the following days, William noticed that panic and worry was spreading throughout the parish, and folk were becoming restless with the increasing speculation about witchcraft and magic. They were gathering in little groups with Mary's name and her use of plants and potions echoing within their rumour and gossip; fuelled by the reference and comments made by Father Franklin in his sermon.

William could not stand by and allow the gossip to escalate; fearing that talk about Mary would intensify, he made a desperate journey to speak one more time with Father Benedict. On his way, William became apprehensive about meeting with Father Benedict. Easter had come and gone since he first came to Father Benedict for help and he felt nothing had been done to determine or resolve the practice of witchcraft taking place in Rushton Parish.

As William rode into Rowell's market square, his heart skipped a beat, when he spotted Father Franklin's two henchmen by The King's Head Inn, still mounted on their horses.

William quickly hid behind the market house and dismounted from his horse to be less noticeable. He found a safe spot from where he could spy on the henchmen, and coincidently, Father Benedict.

While concentrating on the two horsemen, William suddenly saw Father Benedict leave the rectory. He watched the reverend cross the road heading toward the two henchmen and began holding a conversation with them. William watched intently, unconsciously twiddling his fingers together with his horse's reins. He kept watching as Father Benedict quickly returned to his rectory and the two horsemen rode off towards the Market Harborough coach road.

William's head was full of thoughts; realising Father Benedict was also in some way connected with Father Franklin's two henchmen. Perhaps this was the reason Father Benedict appeared non-committal towards William and his questions of magic and witchcraft. He steadily made his way home deep in thought and became distracted as he approached the narrow bridge spanning the Ise River, not far from Rushton Hall's main gates.

An agitated crowd had gathered on the bridge, more folk were down on the banks of the river, and a body screaming loudly was dangling over the side of the bridge wall.

-

William's universal space-time consciousness stopped while a déjà vu moment passed over him.
A slow-motion vision of a fish out of water, flapping, and gasping for air passed before him as the body suspended from the bridge was lowered, screaming, and yelling, into the cold flow of water passing under the bridge. William

had seen all this before and walked his horse steadily
forward as he gradually realised the horror of the activity
being performed before him.

-

"Drown the witch," shouted a voice from the crowd as William's
universal space-time accelerated him back to the present
moment.

Jeering and shouting erupted as the body entered the Ise water.
Returning to his senses, William spurred his horse forward,
gripped by the evil of the event he witnessed. He watched the
tied and bound body sink into the cold water, wriggling and
gasping for air as it sank, deeper and deeper.

William rode his horse into the crowd on the bridge.

"Stop this I say," William shouted at the hysterical and frenzied
mob.

William saw Father Franklin standing on the opposite bank,
dressed in his ecclesiastic robes, holding a cross to his lips and
clutching a bible.

"Stop this Matthew," William screamed.

It was too late, the wriggling and splashing of the water had
ceased, and the frantic mob fell silent, bowing their heads,
looking solemnly into the steady flow of the cold Ise water.

Silent moments of an anti-climax passed before the shameful
village flock dragged the body from the river. William trembled,
he felt sick and weak as he recognised Mary's body lying limp
and wet in front of Father Franklin.

"Let us thank the Lord for his guidance and protection over
evil. Let us also pray for Mary, that her sins may be forgiven,"
said Father Franklin, as he opened his bible.

William wanted to go down on the riverbank to confront Father Franklin and condemn him in front of his frenzied flock of village folk for allowing, and possibly promoting, this illegal and shameful mob murder of an innocent member of the parish community. Instead, he whispered a prayer for Mary as he wearily continued home to Rushton Hall.

Arriving home, William retired to the library for a jug of cider to calm himself. He was surprised and relieved when he entered the room and saw his mother and father. William greeted and welcomed his father and wearily began explaining the murder he had just witnessed. Lord Rockingham was distraught and angered by William's revelation and questioned him further about the discovery of witchcraft and magic taking place in the Triangular Lodge. William explained all, including his discovery of Father Benedick's association with Father Franklin's two henchmen. Upon William's detailed conclusion, Lord Rockingham sent for Father Franklin, demanding his immediate attendance.

While waiting for Father Franklin, Lady Ann arrived at Rushton Hall, startled by the news of Mary's shameful murder and wanting to discuss the fact with William.

"Oh, Lord Rockingham, greetings Sire, I was not aware of your presence," said Lady Ann as she entered the library, performing a polite curtsy.

"No, though I believe it is quite a timely arrival Lady Ann," Lord Rockingham replied, with a nod of his head. "And so nice to see you again,"

Upon Father Franklin's entrance, Lord Rockingham, quite annoyed by the revelations described by William, dispensed with pleasantries and began questioning him on the facts William had previously provided.

"It is with respect Sire, that I believe the facts and evidence, upon which you have spoken, point toward William Sire, not I," Father Franklin replied.

Lord Rockingham was not amused by Father Franklin's accusation.

"How can you deduce such a claim, what evidence do you have, what proof do you have to substantiate such a remark," Lord Rockingham responded.

"Sire, all the claims of witchcraft and discoveries of magical signs have been made by your son William, Sire. His accusation that I am the instigator and practitioner of magic are unsubstantiated Sire. It is unfortunate that today's spontaneous and unthinkable drowning carried out by frightened village folk occurred because Mary was William's accomplice, a witch Sire. And I have physical evidence to support these facts," said Father Franklin.

Lord Rockingham and William, Lady Josephine and Lady Ann were shocked by Father Franklin's assumption and remained silent, each looking from one to the other, lost for words.

"Where is this evidence, this proof you claim to hold?" asked Lord Rockingham.

"If you would permit me, Sire, I shall bring it," Father Franklin requested.

For a few moments after Father Franklin's departure, the library remained silent as each person gathered his or her comprehension of Father Franklin's remarks. William excused himself from the room avoiding the flurry of questions that came forthwith and returned to his private rooms.

Father Franklin returned to the library carrying a crumpled hessian sack, shortly after William had returned. William looked in astonishment at the old brown sack as Father Franklin made his way into the room. Lord Rockingham looked bemused at the sack too before resuming his questioning.

"And this is your proof Matthew, an old brown sack?" suggested Lord Rockingham.

"No Sire, not the sack, but its contents," replied Father Franklin.

"Then let us get on with it, show me your proof," requested Lord Rockingham.

Father Franklin first displayed the small lavender bag, explaining its retrieval from the bedding of Miriam's baby. There were uncomfortable gasps from Lady Josephine and Lady Ann when Father Franklin removed the small piece of parchment from the lavender bag, explaining it to be a magic charm and reading the words, 'Sator arepo tenet opera rotas', the words written on Father Franklin's exhibit.

"This is a magic charm used by witches and sorcerers Sire," Father Franklin added. "Mary had been helping care for Miriam's baby and using holy water she collected secretly from the holy spring Sire. I believe this is proof that Mary was indeed a witch Sire."

"And William?" asked Lord Rockingham. "What proof do you have against my son?"

Father Franklin tipped the contents of the hessian sack onto the floor. There were gasps as the blooded polka-dot shirt, torn and punctured leather doublet, and muddy bootleg spilt across the floor.

"I believe these are your belongings, William," said Father Franklin, looking directly at William.

William did not respond, other than to give a small smile.

"Sire, I believe the bloodstains are a result of pricking, a method used for proving if a person is a witch or not Sire by inserting needles into a witches flesh and skin. I cannot think of any other way William's garments would have gained such markings Sire," Father Franklin concluded.

"And this is your proof?" said Lord Rockingham, looking at Father Franklin.

"Yes, Sire."

"What do you have to say of the two elusive horsemen that have been seen on regular occurrences within the parish, including a visit to your rectory?" Lord Rockingham asked.

"They are witch-finders Sire. With the discovery of witchcraft in the parish I sort their help and assistance Sire," Father Franklin volunteered.

"Yet though you were being assisted by these two witch-finders, you took it upon yourself to allow parish folk to take and drown Mary, without trial or confirmation from these witch-finders, that Mary, God rest her soul, was actually a witch," Lord Rockingham responded,

"The village folk took it upon themselves to drown Mary, Sire. I was there only..."

"You were there Matthew," interrupted Lord Rockingham. "That is sufficient."

Lord Rockingham paused to comprehend Father Franklin's allegations.

"What do you have to say, William, these are strong accusations? However, they are not proven fact and can be explained," Lord Rockingham continued, looking at his son.

William looked at Father Franklin and watched his face closely; he held his clenched hand up to Father Franklin's face. Without saying a word, William let the wood and silver cross and necklace he had found at the Triangular Lodge fall from his hand and dangle in front of Father Franklin.

Lady Ann gave a quiet and muffled gasp of recognition while William watched Father Franklin's eyes dilate and his eyebrows slightly rise. "Do you recognise this?" William asked, still looking closely into Father Franklin's face.

"Should I?" replied Father Franklin. "I have never seen it before in my life."

"Like you have never known Mary to be your half-sister, Matthew Franklin," said Lady Josephine quietly and sternly.

Lady Ann gasped again, only this time louder and shocked with disbelief.

William watched as life drain from Matthew Franklin's face as he listened to Lady Josephine's revelation.

Again, the library fell silent with thoughts of wonder and surprise, shock and disbelief, horror and anger, filling the room with an uncomfortable presence.

"I do not believe there is certainty or any positive proof to any of these accusations, or magical proceedings other than an innocent baby, and Mary, your half-sister, have lost their life. I would suggest you go home Matthew and contemplate today's events and your future. I believe today's proceedings will put an end to this talk of magic and witchcraft and we shall hear no more about it," concluded Lord Rockingham.

Matthew hastily left the library, Lord and Lady Rockingham commenced a private conversation, while Lady Ann stood up from her seat and with eyes fixed on William, she quickly stood before him.

"Did you know Mary was my sister?" she inquired politely, with a whispered voice.

"Your half-sister, yes," corrected William, before his truthful admission.

"Why have you not told me, why did you not do something? You let Matthew murder his own sister," said Lady Ann, becoming emotional.

"I was under oath never to reveal that fact, and with that knowledge, I have always cared for Mary," replied William. "It is your brother who has wronged Lady Ann, not I."

Torn between family support for her brother and the affection she held for William, Lady Ann excused herself, confused and tearful she left the library.

Roundhead Cavalry

During the next few days, the temperament of the local folk and atmosphere around Rushton Hall and its neighbouring village began to lift as the talk of witchcraft and Mary's drowning gradually diminished. May Day and the celebration of spring and the coming of summer was approaching, lifting folk's enthusiasm as they chatted and gossiped in excitement about the coming festivity.

Father Franklin, under the instruction of Lord Rockingham, was preparing a small funeral service for his half-sister, Mary, when he suddenly rushed from the church towards Rushton Hall. William, returning to the hall, watched Father Franklin from his carriage window, hurrying across the large circular lawn towards the hall's main doorway. William alighted from his carriage at the hall's entrance as Father Franklin rushed up, slightly out of breath and in a loud fearful voice declared, "Mary's body has gone Sire!"

Together, William and Father Franklin dashed through the hall's entrance door in search of Lord Rockingham. Bursting into the library, together they stated, "Mary's body has gone, disappeared, Sire," startling Lord Rockingham in the process.

"Stop, gentlemen stop, whatever is the meaning of this hasty interruption?"

"Mary's body has vanished Sire," repeated Father Franklin, more calmly, yet still panting out of breath.

"What shall we do Father?" added William.

"Well, at the moment I am not sure, vanished you say," said Lord Rockingham, repeating Father Franklin's word while looking at him.

"Yes, Sire."

"And when did she vanish?" asked Lord Rockingham.

"I am not sure Sire, one moment she was there, the next she had gone," answered Father Franklin.

"As quick as that," Lord Rockingham replied.

"No Sire, I mean I am not sure, I do not know when the body disappeared Sire," said Father Franklin.

"Nothing to do with magic?" suggested Lord Rockingham, looking at William and Father Franklin, one to the other.

Neither man replied to Lord Rockingham's comment, unsure of its intention.

"Then leave it with me, I shall visit my friend Father Benedict, perhaps he can be helpful in such circumstances," said Lord Rockingham, thoughtfully. "Matthew, do not continue with the funeral preparations, we have nothing to bury at the moment and try not to let the knowledge of Mary's body vanishing spread around the parish. I do not want the gossip of magic resurrecting.

-

As the days' passed, talk of Mary's murder gradually gave way to the anticipation of the annual celebration of May Day, and the gathering of wood for the bonfire gathered pace. The bonfire was built on the village green, in front of The Lion public alehouse in readiness for the festivities. A four-posted marquee with raised platform erected on the green, adjacent to The Lion and opposite the growing pile of firewood, awaited Rushton's dignitaries.

For country folk, May Day is a celebration of spring and the arrival of summer, a transition from the old to the new, from winter to the season of summer, celebrated throughout the land.

It was early on the eve before May Day when trumpet and drum hailed the arrival of Rushton's dignitaries, waving politely and taking their place under the marquee. Refreshment was served from The Lion, along with the lighting of the bonfire.

The representation of the bonfire is believed to counteract evil spells towards livestock and the newly planted crops. All hearth fires and candles in the parish homes were extinguished, with only the bonfire remained alight in the belief that incantations spoken by tellers and cunning folk, and ritual dancing round the fire would dispel the evil of witchcraft and sorcery, was burned in the flames of the fire. Before the bonfire burned itself out, village folk retrieved the holy embers and ashes from the fire, rushing away to relight and purify their home fires, saving the ashes to scatter on their new sprouting crops in the hope to yield a good harvest.

Cakes and pies prepared for the celebration were consumed with large volumes of ale at The Lion before the parish young folk dispersed into the forest for a night of romance. The following morning the weary youths returned with garlands of flowering violets and daisies for decoration, with boughs of newly flowering hawthorn and blackthorn for the crowns of the May Queen and the Green-Wood Man. They also returned with a long tree trunk that was to become the Maypole, decorated with painted spirals, festooned with flowers and ribbons, and mounted vertically on the village green in front of The Lion.

The tree is the largest and most venerable living thing on earth and their lives span many human generations that represent longevity. They also represent life's preservation and renewal with their new foliage returning each spring.

On the morning of May Day, the parish women folk rushed to the meadows to partake of the morning dew, applying it to their faces, for its magical healing and cosmetic properties.

The youths who had been out in the forest all night began carrying out the rounds of the village, decorating the outside of folk's houses with flowers, and garlands, while singing songs and blowing horns. This way the entire village, house-by-house in a family-specific manner, came under a divine blessing and protection.

It was during these activities Lady Ann saw Father Franklin's two henchmen leaving through Rushton Hall's main gates as she resumed her seat under the marquee.

As the day wore on, folk gathered around the maypole, and organized ritual took place, where the May Queen defeated the Queen of Winter, before her marriage to the Green-Wood Man, a virile figure covered with fresh green foliage.

Lady Ann seized her moment to sit beside William and apologise for her outburst over Mary. William smiled in return, and suddenly recognised the figure of the Green-Wood Man and realised he had known of the keeper of the forest, the spirit of spring and protector of the cycle of life, for a very long time.

He watched intently as the May Queen and the Green-Wood Man were crowned with rings of flowering blackthorn and hawthorn, followed by a mock sacred marriage, at the base of the maypole, marking the revival of fertility, a symbol with obvious phallic significance.

The celebrations continued into the early evening with dancing and singing around the Maypole as William and his parents returned quite exhausted to Rushton Hall.

The following morning Lord Rockingham announced to William that he and Lady Josephine would leave for Glendon Hall before he returned to London and parliament.

"Your mother will remain with her sister for some time William," informed Lord Rockingham.

While Lord Rockingham prepared to leave Rushton Hall, Jon the Shepherd visited William, requesting him to come to the Triangular Lodge. William did not think he would be away long and could say farewell to his parents upon his return.

William quickly rode to the lodge along the carriage road running alongside the estate wall. He wondered what Jon the Shepherd wanted him to see and hoped it was not another triangle. William rode his horse through the lodge gate, dismounted, and tethered his horse to a dangling tree branch.

"Yes Jon, what have you discovered this time, another triangle?" William asked by way of a greeting.

"Na Sire, come," Jon the Shepherd replied, walking towards the gateway that leads over the estate, beckoning William to follow.

Jon walked through the gate then stood to one side, pointing to the ground, and allowing William access through the gate.

William stood in shock and disbelief looking down at the new gravestone, set back against the tree line that surrounded the lodge. Its inscription was plain and simple, with only one word,

'Mary'.

Carved in the top right-hand corner of the gravestone, was the skull of the Green-Wood Man, with vines and roots protruding from its ears and eyes.

"When did this appear?" asked William, almost in a whisper.

"I saw it just this morning Sire while grazing my new lambs' Sire," Jon replied.

"Then leave it, I cannot deal with it at this time," said William. "At least she can rest peacefully Jon."

"Aye Sire," replied Jon with a toothless smile.

William returned to Rushton Hall to say farewell to his parents, but unfortunately, they had already left for Glendon Hall and Lady Ann awaited him in the reception room.

"Oh William, I must speak with you," said Lady Ann excitedly as William entered the grand room.

"Ann, what is it, you look disturbed?" inquired William.

"William, the other day with Lord Rockingham, I recognised the crucifix you showed to Matthew. It is a family heirloom; father gave it to Matthew after graduating college. It belongs to Matthew William, why would he say he has never seen it before?" said Lady Ann.

"I don't know Ann, Matthew is hiding something," William replied, thoughtfully.

"I know, I believe you should be careful William. The two riders you spoke of, they are not witch-finders William, they are Roundhead Cavalry officers. I saw them during the May Day festival, and they visited Matthew again at the rectory last night. I heard them say something about you being all together here at Rushton Hall and it has to be now," informed Lady Ann.

"What has to be now?" asked William, wearing a puzzled expression.

"I do not know William. He said something about claiming his reward too!"

"Please wait here Ann, I must go to Glendon Hall and speak with my Father, urgently, I believe he may be in danger," said William.

William set off along the coach road alongside the estate wall. He quickly turned off into the woods when he saw Roundhead Cavalry at the gate of the lodge. William walked his horse slowly closer to the lodge until he saw the figure of Father Franklin talking with his two henchmen, now dressed in cavalry uniform. William turned away and went deeper into the forest, still heading for Glendon Hall.

"He is a spy, a Roundhead, Matthew is a Roundhead spy," thought William as he galloped through the forest. "He is helping to capture my father, why, what could he possibly gain, what reward?" William's mind was racing as he charged through the trees. "Reward... his reward is the hall; Father Franklin wants Rushton Hall in return for capturing Lord Rockingham."

Arriving at Glendon Hall, William remained cautious, staying in the forest. He could hear the clatter of hooves and armoured breastplates and realised Roundhead Cavalry had beaten him to the hall. Then peering through the trees, he saw Lord and Lady Rockingham being escorted from the hall.

William panicked and fled back to Rushton Hall.

-

As he rode through the forest, William began to feel calm and protected, as if the trees had closed in around him, hiding him, protecting him. He heard no sound as he galloped along. He subconsciously thought of Mary, singing as she strolled through the woodland, he thought of the mysterious appearance of her gravestone at the lodge, and he thought of the Green-Wood Man, protector of the forest. In no time, he arrived at Rushton Hall and remembered nothing of his journey.

-

William went through the gates of the Triangular Lodge, pausing to look at Mary's gravestone. He whispered a quick 'thank you' and continued across the estate. William arrived at a back entrance close to his rooms. He entered the hall and looked through the inner windows. He could see cavalry across the inner courtyard gathering at the hall's front entrance. As he turned, he saw more cavalry coming across the estate grounds.

Thinking quickly, William opened the door hidden in the wall panelling that leads to the secret priest hole. He grabbed the torch from its holder, running quickly to the kitchen to light the torch, before returning to the secret room and closing the door behind him. The little hideaway had a musty, damp smell and the light from the torch flickered around the narrow walls.

William pushed open an inner door, the entrance to the secret escape tunnel that ran all the way to the Triangular Lodge. William nervously entered the narrow tunnel, closing the door behind him. The roof of the tunnel was not so high and smoke from the torch soon began to make him cough. William progressed forward, stumbling on the uneven floor. He could hear and feel the splash of water at his feet as he felt where to place each step forward. His progress was slow and laboured.

After a while, William came across a small collapse of earth. He thought the tunnel was blocked and that he was trapped. Determined, William held the torch high with one hand and began digging with the other. Eventually, he crawled through the little hole he had created.

Exhausted, William sat on the soil he had dug out of his escape hole and took a rest, breathing heavily, continually coughing, and inhaling the black smoke. His thoughts were angry as they flashed painfully through his mind; Roundheads, Mary's murder, losing Rushton Hall, all at the hands of Father Franklin. He became aware of his eyes stinging and continued coughing in the smoke as he sucked in every breath.

William was tired, he sat watching the flicker of flame from the torch gradually diminish as it burnt up the oxygen in the tunnel. William slumped back against the tunnel wall, struggling to breathe. He sighed as the final flicker of flame went out. Sitting in the darkness, William nervously twiddled with his fingers, as space-time slowed. He let his last gasp of breath slowly exhale as a warm cosmic glow enveloped his subconscious and lifted him to a higher vibration of universal consciousness that carried him across the parallel to a higher cosmic dimension.

Parallel Nine

Your
Sub-Conscious
Is Part Of
Your
Conscious
Which Is Part
Of Universal Conscious

That Which
Is All Knowing
Of
All Things

Past – Present - Future

April
1943
Waltham

George's spiritual subconscious floated effortlessly above the pews in the dark subdued ambience of All Saints Parish Church. Candlelight flickered on the altar, reflecting off the polished silver candelabra, emitting sharp splinters of light onto the church walls and support pillars. George looked down at his lone body slumped in the corner of an uncomfortable pew, gasping deeply for breath. The Taiji moment, stirred the energy of Chi, his spiritual aura glowed around him, space-time slowed his subconscious vibration and raced him across the parallel.

-

George opened his eyes, coughing in the semi-darkness; for a moment, he felt a little claustrophobic and wondered where he was before recognising the inside of Waltham Church. Somehow, he felt strange; slumped in the corner of the pew like a discarded skeleton.

He sat up straight, feeling as if he had been somewhere, and questioned if he had really just been looking down at himself from the high vaulted timbers of the roof above him. He shuddered.

-

George suddenly felt cold, he remembered being out of his body watching two planes collide in front of him. The cold feeling subsided, slowly replaced by a warm comforting glow, he visualised the vivid colours of the exploding aircraft.

-

Denis jumped into his mind, it was Denis, Denis is dead, he had watched his plane collide and fall slowly out of the dark sky, into the depths of the deep black abyss that had surrounded the raiding Lancaster planes. The thought of the orderly, collecting Denis's belongings from his room flashed through his mind.

-

Suddenly George's subconscious floated upward and drifted along the old roof beams. He looked down at himself, confused and alone on the pew. He felt calm and peaceful as he floated over the rows of pews and round the candlelit altar.

-

George panicked wondering what was happening and he stood up. He looked up at the beamed roof of the church, and over towards the altar, but there was nothing there. Bewildered he sat down. The warm sensation faded and the floating feeling disappeared. He took a deep breath and wondered what had happened. Morning sun began to shine through the stained-glass windows above the altar, reflecting rays of coloured light beams into the church. His stomach rumbled and he thought of breakfast. He remembered the commitment he had made during last night's operations sortie, to be Henry's best man. He smiled to himself, happy that he had posted his love letter to Jean. George closed the church door behind him and marched briskly to the NAAFI for his breakfast.

He joined Blue Hornet's crew, still drinking tea and chatting when Charles arrived with an attractive guest.

"Look who I found!" said Charles, drawing attention to himself and his guest as he approached the long canteen table.

"Hey, make way for the lady," said 'W', the first crewmember to recognise and respond to Frances' being the surprise guest. "Henry, you are wanted in the maps room urgently," 'W' jokingly added.

"Hello everyone, nice to see you are all busy," laughed Frances, walking around the table to greet Henry with hugs and kisses to rounds of applause and greetings. "How is everyone?"

James stood up from his chair, offering his place next to Henry. "You can sit here if you like," he said politely, accompanied by suggestive comments from the crew.

"Thank you, James, take no notice of them, they are only jealous," Frances remarked, smiling and sitting in James' seat. "How are you, Captain Finch?"

"Much better now, thank you, it's good to see you again. How long are you here for this time?" replied George.

"As it is Easter, I don't have to be back until Monday morning, so just one night really. What about all of you, are you flying?" said Frances, hopefully.

"Unfortunately, yes, but I am sure Henry will make plenty of time for you, and congratulations to you both on your engagement," George replied with a smile, then holding his mug of tea aloft. "Here's to the two of you."

The crew responded likewise with raised tea mugs. "To Henry and Frances," they all chorused.

"Thank you, thank you, everyone," Frances responded, smiling excitedly, holding Henry's hand, and giving it an affectionate squeeze.

"I hear we can look forward to a May Day wedding?" stated Charles.

"Yes, we hope so," replied Frances. "We are still trying to arrange that. We just hope we can fit it into your flying schedule."

"Well, if you will excuse me, I have some business to take care of; I will see you in the morning hopefully, at breakfast. Henry, James, I'll see you at the briefing, fourteen-hundred," said George, by way of a reminder as he stepped away from the breakfast table, leaving the crew to chat with the engaged couple.

Together, Henry and James attended the navigator and bomb aimers briefing, followed by joining George at the main ops briefing. From there all crews assembled for transportation to the communal site, for evening tea, before transportation returned them to the technical site, to kit out in flying suites. Finally, crews were transported to their aircraft and thirty minutes later, they were roaring down the runway on another operational sortie.

"Where are we tonight Skip?" asked Charles.

"Dusseldorf, Happy Valley," replied George.

"What's the missis doing, all alone, Henry?" asked 'W'.

"Going to the cinema, to see some B-Bogart film about the Sahara," replied Henry.

"Sounds like a real romantic tear-jerker that one," joked 'W'.

"It's on at the Savoy in Grimsby; she's going with someone from her accommodation building. She said they can w-walk there," said Henry, laughing. "I told her it will be more like a hike than a w-walk."

"Yeah, that's a long walk Henry, I reckon we'll be back home before she is," 'W' agreed, before announcing. "There's lots of radio traffic Skip, it could be a busy night for someone."

"Roger that 'W', did you hear that boys? keep a lookout," announced George.

Despite 'W's warning, the route to Dusseldorf was trouble free with regards to Luftwaffe presence. However, anti-aircraft defences were very prominent, making for another nerve-wracking flight to and from the target.

James was as accurate as ever with his release of bombs and was beginning to cost 'W' quite a few beers.

"I'm not playing anymore James, if this is another bullseye tonight I'm quitting, no more free beer at my expense," 'W' announced over the intercom.

"Does that mean I have to buy my own beer too?" asked Charles.

"Afraid so Charles, I know when I'm beat," responded 'W'.

Approaching Waltham's runway 18/36, Charles noticed the glow of fire spread across the Grimsby horizon as he put the bomber's landing wheels down

"That doesn't look good Skip, that's a lot of fires over Grimsby," said Charles, over the intercom.

"Fire, where?" asked Henry, sounding concerned.

"Grimsby," replied Charles, "It looks like it's been hit by a significant raid."

Alarmed, Henry stood up and looked out of his observation canopy.

"She'll be alright Henry," said 'W', sympathetically, looking up at Henry, knowing what he was looking at and thinking.

"Let's hope so," Henry answered quietly, as George landed Blue Hornet along the narrow concrete runway that pointed towards Grimsby.

George sat in the locker room and relaxed in his flying suit before changing to his blue uniform.

"That's fourteen ops completed Charles," said George. "And we haven't fired a single cannon in anger yet. I don't want to tempt fate, but I'm beginning to wonder if there is any Luftwaffe up there."

"Let's just keep it that way Skipper," replied Charles. "I prefer it if they can't see us, it makes our job a whole lot easier. And besides, James is causing plenty of damage for all of us; he's not missed a target yet."

"Yes, I heard 'W' say he was quitting on their beer betting," said George.

"It will mean I lose my free beer too," sighed Charles. "Just as I was getting to enjoy a free pint,"

George and Charles finished changing and made their way to the NAAFI for an early breakfast.

"Frances not up yet Henry?" asked Charles, sitting at the table with his breakfast tray, together with George.

"It's still early m-morning, give her chance," replied Henry.

"She's probably still walking back from the cinema," 'W' commented.

"Not with all the raging fires I've just been looking at," said Charles.

"Yes, I think I'll finish my breakfast and go find her, just to be on the safe side," said Henry, growing anxious.

"Can you find your way or should I come with you and hold your hand?" laughed 'W'.

"Haha," replied Henry. "Sometimes 'W'..."

"Hey go steady 'W', that's his fiancé he's worried about," said Mr President, cutting over Henry's response to 'W'. "He'll have someone to hold his hand coming back sure enough,"

"Aye, sorry, your right there Mr President," 'W' responded. "Sorry about that Henry, me and my big Welsh mouth."

"It's alright, you can't help being W-Welsh," said Henry, leaving the table.

"While you're away Henry, I'll get de-briefing out of the way and see you guys later in the Crew's Mess," George announced as he too left the table.

As de-briefing concluded, George was called into the Squadron Admin Office. Devastated by the news he received; he quickly made his way to the Crew's Mess to meet with his crew.

"Frances is m-missing apparently," announced Henry, greeting George with a concerned and worried look on his face. "She hasn't returned from the cinema yet,"

"I'm afraid it's worse than that Henry," replied George, with a sombre voice, drawing solemn silent attention from each of his crew. "I'm sorry to say this but, Frances was killed last night during an air raid over Grimsby."

Blue Hornet's crew sat in disbelief silence, each looking from one to the other, from George to Henry and back again.

"How, how do you know Skip?" asked Collins.

"I was called into the office. Apparently, some new types of anti-personnel bombs were dropped over Grimsby last night.

The town is in a bit of a mess at the moment," George responded. "Some sort of butterfly type bomb I'm told."

"That's what all the fires were as we landed then," said Charles.

"Yes, it's pretty bad," replied George. "I'm deeply sorry for you Henry, all the things you have planned together, getting married and such, you don't deserve this Henry."

"If you'll excuse me, I'll be in m-my room Skip," said Henry, holding himself together and getting up from the table. "See you all later for briefing."

"I'll come with you Henry," 'W' offered.

"It's alright, I just w-want some time alone at the m-moment thanks," said Henry, placing a friendly hand momentarily on 'W''s shoulder as he passed.

Course Two-Eight-Zero

Later in the afternoon, George met Henry and James in the Ops Briefing Room for the coming night's sortie.

"You alright Henry?" asks George.

"I'm better now I have something to take my m-mind off Frances," Henry replied.

As the meeting concluded and aircrews were leaving the room, James pulled George to one side.

"I don't think Henry is totally with it Skip," James said softly while turning his face away from Henry.

"What do you mean James?"

"At the navigation briefing, he's usually on the ball, almost leading the meeting. I know it's not nice about Frances Skip, but he just sat back at today's briefing, never said a thing."

"Thanks for that James; I'll keep a check on him. We're back over Dusseldorf, so he should have routes there and back already done, I hope."

Ground preparations for the sortie concluded and the flight to Dusseldorf and the target went according to plan, with James once again hitting the bullseye.

"Bombs away Skip," said James.

George stayed on course allowing time for the photograph to be taken when ack-ack shrapnel suddenly peppered Blue Hornet's fuselage.

"What the hell was that?" called 'W' through the intercom.

"Everyone alright?" quizzed Mr President.

"What course Henry?" asked George, concerned how long he had been flying in a straight line.

"One m-minute," replied Henry.

"Goddamit Henry," shouted George, turning to starboard as a loud crack shook Blue Hornet.

"Bomb doors are stuck Skip, whatever it was that hit us has damaged the doors Skip."

"Give me a..."

"Two-eight-zero Skipper, s-steer two-eight-zero," Henry said, panicking and overriding George's voice. "Sorry Skip, lost m-my m-maps for a m-moment."

"Not acceptable Henry, not acceptable," replied George, turning to course two-eight-zero. "Can you do anything with the doors, Charlie?"

"The framework is damaged Skip, nothing I can do."

"You're lucky it's only the doors Henry when I want a direction I expect one, that delay could have cost us," said George angrily.

"That's life number five Skip," said Mr President.

Henry did not reply and his silence spread through the crew as Blue Hornet flew quietly home with her bomb doors wide open. The crew were cold and relieved when George safely landed the damaged Lancaster on runway 18/36 and taxied to the dispersal pan, though no one rushed to get off.

"Sorry about that Skipper, I let other things distract m-me there, sorry boys," said Henry quietly and remorsefully.

"Forget about it Henry, put it down as experience and a near miss, not to be repeated. Charlie, make sure the Erk's know about the doors, I didn't like it with them open all the way back," said George. "Let's go get breakfast shall we, this one has been a tough one."

Blue Hornet was grounded for the following night's operation, as it would take time to repair the damage to the bomb doors. George suggested that they, as a crew, should attend church that evening in respect for Frances and Denis, and he would try to get the vicar to say some words and prayer.

Early that evening, Blue Hornet's crew were standing outside All Saints Church waiting for 'W' and Henry to arrive before they entered the church. 'W' appeared and walked up the church pathway.

"Where's Henry?" called George.

"He's not coming," replied 'W'.

"What do you mean he's not coming?" asked George. "It's his fiancé for heaven's sake!"

"That's what I said Skip, but he said he doesn't believe in the church, he'll remember her his own way," said 'W', a little out of breath as he arrived at the church door. "Phew, I thought I was going to be late arguing with him."

George looked at the time and suggested they go inside or the vicar would be waiting and starting without them. The crew took their seats, three on two rows of pews, one behind the other. Once seated comfortably, the patient vicar commenced with his service. Curiously, George looked up at the roof beams remembering the last time he was in the church and wondered if he was about to leave his body. The organ began playing and sadly drowned the crew's soft whispered voices as they sang along to the tune of the hymn. George remembered Frances's sweet strong choir voice, and he looked up at the roof beams wondering if she was there looking down on them. Though he suddenly thought, she would be sadly disappointed not to see Henry standing amongst the crew.

Following the short remembrance service, George suggested that as they were not flying they should visit The King's Head for a quick refreshing beer as they would surely resume flying operations the following night. He was not wrong and operation preparations resumed immediately after lunch the next afternoon as Blue Hornet had been successfully repaired and ready to fly.

As George left the briefing room, he was handed a small white envelope. He looked at the neat flowing handwritten address, FLT LT G. Finch; he turned the letter over and read SWALK. George recognised the smell of perfume, smiled and carefully placed the letter in his locker for when he returned.

Transport to Blue Hornet commenced, followed by the embarkation ritual of placing kisses on her fuselage. George announced the target was Berlin, a more distant and heavily defended objective. Fuel and bombs were loaded to the maximum, making Blue Hornet extra heavy to lift off the runway and up into the air.

"Give it all she's got tonight Charles, this is one heavy bird to get airborne," said George, waiting at the end of runway 18/36 for control tower clearance.

Charles gave the Erk's standing at the end of the runway a wave as Blue Hornet began her run down the long concrete strip. Slowly the wheels lifted and the heavily laden Lancaster steadily climbed into the night sky.

"Course zero-eight-five Skipper," Henry announced through the intercom.

"Roger," replied George. "You alright at the back Collins? It's a long night tonight I'm afraid."

"Let's just get it over with Skipper, and I can get back to my bed," laughed Collins.

"You're always in your bed Collins," said Mr President.

"He needs his beauty sleep," added 'W'.

"Well, it works for him I guess," replied Mr President.

Blue Hornet skimmed above the North Sea waves before climbing to eighteen thousand feet to fly over Germany towards Berlin, part of a one hundred and twenty plane assault force. On this occasion, the number of Lancaster Bomber's exploding and falling out of the sky demonstrated the presence of the Luftwaffe. Anti-aircraft artillery pounded the sky supported by roaming searchlights.

"Steer one-seven-zero to target," said Henry, breaking the unusual silence of the crew. "Target ten minutes ahead."

"Roger that," replied George. "One-seven-zero coming up. Can you see the target flares, James?"

"Roger that, bright and clear Skipper," James confirmed.

"It's all yours James, here we go Charles," said George concentrating on his compass and instrument.

"Dead ahead Skipper," commenced James.

Suddenly a bright white searchlight locked onto the cockpit of Blue Hornet, blinding George's vision.

The First Parallel

Tao

Is

Constant And Everlasting

You Are Tao

Therefore

There Is No Death

Just

An Ever-Changing Consciousness

Within

A Universe

Of

Constant Change

The First Parallel

Time slowed, George left his body and watched his plane plummet earthwards in slow motion. He no longer felt the pain of his torn and shattered body. Floating effortlessly in the dark night air he prayed for his crew trapped and burning, spiralling downwards. He could hear himself screaming as he watched himself desperately trying to escape the cockpit of his burning, falling bomber.

-

Momentarily, before his plane hit the ground far below and exploded violently into a bright orange ball of flames, time accelerated George across the parallel.

Instantly George was warm, surrounded in bright white light. He felt he was travelling at supersonic speed, but slowly and gently. He felt secure. There was no futuristic spacecraft, no machines, nothing physical, no body, not even his own. Yet George felt peaceful and protected in the light. He was the light; he was his thoughts.

There seemed to be nothing more and yet George did not feel alone, he sensed and felt the presence of others, friends, family, crew, acquaintances from time immemorial. This place gave him a sense of belonging, of time everlasting, and of the moment, all at the same time.

Slowly the light started to change. As white began to fade and the comfort of purity and neutrality gave way to a spiritual feeling of compassion and self-awareness that began washing over him as pastel shades of violet merged with and into the warm surrounding light. George became sensitive and he began reflecting on his life, on all of his lives, past, present and future. Visions of his life passed before him, good times, bad times, people, faces, places, darkness, light. Faster and faster the images flowed, each one clear and meaningful. As the shades of violet strengthened and intensified so each reflection deepened and stirred his thoughts.

George tried to focus, the colours rippled and swirled, a hue of blue flooded in, protracting images, stretching time to slow motion.

"Turn to one-seven-zero Skip, target dead ahead." A brilliant bright light drowned the cockpit as the searchlight locked onto the bomb-laden Lancaster. "Hold her steady... steady Skip." The blue hue merged with soft shades of indigo. Anti-aircraft shells ripped into the bomber's fuselage and starboard wing, crippling both the engines and setting them ablaze. "Bombs away Skip, let's go home." A flak shell exploded the Lancaster's cockpit into flame, shredding George's right leg and arm; he felt nothing and let the thought go as bright white light overwhelmed, comforted and transported him.

The light ebbed and flooded, light and dark, green, yellow, red, black. George felt a growing simplicity amongst the changing colours. And, as the colours flowed, slowed and accelerated time and thoughts, so did George. He was the light, he was thought, he was everywhere, and everywhere surrounded him. Here in this place, he felt whole, masculine, feminine, complete. Love engulfed him. Pure love saturated every moment and comforted him, guided him, and filled his presence.

Time slowed...

The sun was shining; George and his crew were laughing and joking outside their mess hut. Having just assembled as Lancaster crewmembers they were discovering facts about each other and learned it was the Skipper's birthday. A spontaneous chorus of Happy Birthday erupted. "How old are you Skip?" called one of the crew.

"I'm as old as my tongue and a little older than my teeth," ...time accelerated away.

A pink hue flooded with femininity and tranquillity dominated youthful, safe thoughts. George floated in the endless, perpetual flow of light, thought, and colour. How long had he been here, forever, a few moments? Here time has no relevance. He was in the parallel of everlasting universal space-time conscious, that Wuji moment of stillness and emptiness, when time stands still before Taiji disturbs the balance and creates Yin and Yang. Where love and Chi are one Tao, where angels live for eternity and only conscious thought exists, here he is at peace, he belongs here, he is this place.

George stopped playing with his stick and watched as three monks walked into the courtyard of his home. He knew of the coming of these men, passing time, waiting for them to present themselves and transform his life.

George drifted with the speed and flow of colour, influencing his conscious thoughts.

He watched as the tied and bound body lowered into the cold flowing water of the Ise River, wriggling and gasping for breath like a fish out of water, he watched as he exhaled his last breath in the dark confines of Rushton Hall's escape tunnel, and he rubbed his neck as the sword severed his head from his body.

George remembered the moon seat and the view of the universe. "You will learn and understand more when you implement that which you have learned."

A golden light filtered into his conscious, and time slowed to slow, slow motion. He felt a new, higher enlightened presence surround him, a higher vibrating conscious that held him and guided him. Here in this light, this golden glow, angels, and demons exist along with the balancing energy of yin-yang. Here angels reside and prepare your future, and demons stalk the present and terrorise your afterlife. Where spirit and all creation, influenced with positive and negative charges of energy releases into the universe of consciousness.

Beyond this golden light, life's energy force of Chi animates all creations of the universe, from the speed of light to the stable force of matter, governed by Tao, the creator of space-time and the natural order to the cosmos.

Here in the presence of angels and demons, held in a future space-time conscious, the balancing yin-yang visions of his future flowed and filtered into his conscious, into his subconscious. The teachings of success, failure, anger, love, femininity, masculinity, life, death, sadness, happiness, loneliness, friendship flooded into the consciousness of his existence. Visions of a new re-birth with the knowledge and experience to live it and patiently learn the wisdom presented from participating in it.

-

Time began to accelerate, and George began to slowly spiral. The bright warm light faded, colours ebbed and flowed, mixing merging, flashing, spiralling faster and faster, darker and darker, until a heavy darkness surrounded and engulfed him as he crossed the parallel.

Parallel Eleven

Life Exists

Only

In That Finite Moment

Of The Present

Between

What Is To Become

Your Future

And

What Has Become

Your Past

Measured

Only By Your

Memory

Somewhere
2143

The ornamental ambience and ancient majesty of the cathedral was breath-taking. Colourful and decorated historical flags and regalia floated between the congregation and the high vaulted ceiling. Candles flickered along the aisle and adorned the altar. Grand festoons and bouquets of flowers filled the atmosphere of the church with the heavy scent of a summer meadow.

Henry stood in front of the altar, his fine red tailored suit and brightly coloured dicky-bow; so fitting for such an extravagant occasion. Francis stood at the end of the aisle by the first row of pews, looking nervously at Henry. The grand organ played the first notes of the wedding march as the bride appeared at the entrance to the cathedral.

-

Georgina crossed into the parallel as a long déjà vu moment caused her to stop and reflect on where she had been for a moment. The roar of Merlin's echoed round Master Fu's smoky hall, and galloping hooves clattered with the sound of Roundhead armour.

A cold shiver ran up her back as she visualised a skeleton slumped in a dark lonely tunnel and she rubbed the sharp tingling sensation in her neck.

-

Georgina looked down the aisle at the rows of tightly packed pews of excited onlookers.

The colourful regalia above their heads shadowed by the opulent display of the congregation garbed in fancy dress partygoer's costumes, gay pride exhibitionists, pantomime frocks and elaborate steampunk costumes, all taking selfies and hiding behind ornate face make-up that negated generations of parent, offspring, and gender.

A wave of sadness passed over Georgina as she observed the congregation gathered in this magnificent empty shell of what had once been a holy sanctuary for prayer and reverence. Gone was the abundant energy of Chi. Gone were the mystic ways of the Tao, and the balance of yin-yang lay positively in the negative. She recognised the moment like a mirage from long long ago, only now, for her, something had gone, its meaning was missing, and she reflected on how time had changed.

Georgina composed herself and walked down the aisle on the arm of her father, followed by five beautiful bridesmaids holding her long trailing train. Her white silk dress fitted perfectly over her large round stomach. She stood next to Francis and gave him a warm loving smile before handing her bouquet of flowers back to her bridesmaid.

"Ladies and Gentlemen, we are gathered here today to join together this man and this w-woman," began Henry.

Georgina stood attentively, patiently twiddling her fingers behind her back.

"Do you Francis take this woman to be your lawful w-wedded wife?"

"I do," answered Francis.

"Do you Georgina take this man to be your lawful w-wedded Husband?"

"I do," answered Georgina.

"I now pronounce you Husband and W-wife," concluded Henry.

To the glorious rousing sound of the cathedral's pealing wedding bells, Georgina and Francis stepped out of the church into the bright sunshine of a new life, a new rebirth, and a new parallel.

The end... and the beginning

Across The Parallel

If you doubt what you have read and experienced through this book and believe that death is the final chapter, then wouldn't that be a tremendous waste of a lifetime, accumulating such experiences and wisdom?

And

If That Is The Case

How do we explain Death as the one cycle of exception that flies in the face of what we know about reality?